THE VOYAGE OF
JULIUS PINGOUIN

Borgo Press Books by FRÉDÉRIC BOUTET

The Antisocial Man and Other Strange Stories
Claude Mercoeur's Reflection and Other Strange Stories
The Voyage of Julius Pingouin and Other Strange Stories

THE VOYAGE OF JULIUS PINGOUIN

AND OTHER STRANGE STORIES

FRÉDÉRIC BOUTET

Translated by Brian Stableford

THE BORGO PRESS

MMXIII

CLASSICS OF
FANTASTIC LITERATURE
NUMBER ELEVEN

THE VOYAGE OF JULIUS PINGOUIN

FIRST EDITION

Published by Wildside Press LLC

www.wildsidebooks.com

THE VOYAGE OF
JULIUS PINGOUIN

CONTENTS

INTRODUCTION

This volume is the second of a set of three showcasing the work of Frédéric Boutet, the other two volumes being *The Antisocial Man and Other Strange Stories* and *Claude Mercoeur's Reflection and Other Strange Stories*. Viewed as an ensemble, the collections illustrate the range and development of Boutet's early work, and provide a few representative samples of its later evolution. Although several stories by Boutet were translated into English in the 1920s, especially in America, they were selected from his later works, when he was mostly writing sentimental stories and crime fiction for popular magazines; no examples of his early work, most of which consisted of offbeat supernatural fiction, have previously been rendered into English (although his work of that sort became quite popular in German translation, where it retains a higher reputation than it does even in France). This set of three volumes will hopefully serve to introduce the work of a highly distinctive writer of weird and baroque fiction to a new audience.

A brief account of Boutet's life and the overall shape of his career can be found in the first volume of the set, which contains translations of the contents of the 1903 collection *Contes dans le nuit* [Tales in the Night], featuring stories originally published in 1898-99, plus the novella "L'Homme sauvage du Quai Bois L'Encre" (tr. as "The Antisocial Man of the Quai Bois-l'Encre"), written in 1901 and first published in *l'Homme sauvage et Julius Pingouin: Deux petits roman fantaisistes* (1902). The present volume leads with the second novella from that collection, "Le

Voyage de Julius Pingouin," translated as "The Voyage of Julius Pingouin."

The next three items are taken from the 1899 collection *Drames baroques et mélancoliques*. Three items from that collection had been reprinted in the 1903 *Contes dans le nuit*, but the three translated here were not included. "Des Choses passent près des potences," here translated as "Events Occurring in the Vicinity of Scaffolds," might have been excluded from the 1903 collection because of its lurid nature, but was more probably omitted because of slight similarities to a more earnest story featuring a scaffold and its unexpectedly loquacious occupant. "Conversation entre un poète, deux croque-morts et une prostituée," here translated as "Conversation between a Poet, two Undertakers and a Prostitute," also repeats a motif contained in one of the stories included in the 1903 collection, and tends even more obviously toward black comedy. "Scènes dans une taverne," translated as "Scenes in a Tavern" is a very different kind of narrative, included for comparative purposes, which is illustrative of a later direction in Boutet's work, when he began to produce accounts of the tribulations of the social underclass, but which also exemplifies the continuity between that concern and the concerns of his early supernatural fiction.

The remaining items in the present volume were originally published in the evening newspaper *Le Français* in 1903 and reprinted in the 1908 collection *Histoires vraisemblables* [Plausible Stories]. They illustrate the commercial work that Boutet began to turn out in considerable quantities in 1903. His short fiction eventually filled some thirty volumes, and not all of his work for periodicals was reprinted. As might be expected, his work in that vein eventually became routinized, but as the items reprinted here illustrate, it retained an idiosyncratic buoyancy and wit as well as a good deal of variety and a slick dexterity.

The translation of "Le Voyage de Julius Pingouin" was made

from a copy of the 1922 edition of *L'Homme sauvage et Julius Pingouin: Deux petits roman fantaisistes*. The translations of the three items from *Drames baroques et mélancoliques* were taken from the electronic version of the 1899 Chamuel edition made available on-line by the University of Toronto, accessible via *archive.org*. The translations of the stories from *Histoires vraisemblables* were made from a copy of the 2004 reprint edition published in Rennes by Éditions Terre de Brume.

THE VOYAGE OF JULIUS PINGOUIN

Everyone knows how immensely excited the entire world was by the announcement that a new Golden Fleece, the only one since Jason, had been identified, and that the phenomenon was available for conquest. All the newspapers devoted their front pages to it, and a part of the second. All governments organized expeditions, and a furious delirium took possession of all the adventurers scattered across the globe, who, intoxicated by the desire to appropriate the advantageous marvel, sacrificed all of their energy and much of their lives in the course of innumerable attempts, solo or collective.

Everyone also knows what a dearth of precise indications there was, and how contradictory opinions were, regarding the location of the prodigy. No one ever found out when, or by whom, its miraculous existence was first determined, but the entire world was absolutely convinced of its real existence, and there was a dementia in the human soul.

The best laid plans and the most tenacious efforts were, however, in vain.

Pitiful and empty-handed, the official expeditions returned, simultaneously or successively, to present fallacious and desperate reports and accept criticism. The adventurers came back, discouraged. Solicitously, the newspapers abandoned to silence the question from which they had obtained so much copy for such a long time, and the opportunity for such large print-runs. Then, a few people began to insinuate the possibility of a hoax sprung from the bosom of free America, and there were more disputes.

Time passed.

Now, the fact is that the Golden Fleece really did exist, and one man—one of our compatriots, the *bateau-mouche*[1] captain Julius Pingouin—found it. The following narrative of his astonishing voyage was communicated to us by—as the author says himself in his title—"one of two men who made the entire voyage with him and took part in the discovery."

That "one of two men" has recently returned among us, doubtless to die here of his superhuman ordeals. We are delivering his story to the public; some will believe it to be a lie; others will judge it to be considerably embellished; few will believe it completely. For ourselves, we have seen the man and we are sure that he is telling the truth.

> *Veridical relation of the voyage of Julius Pingouin, captain of the* bateau-mouche Argonaut, *in search of the Golden Fleece, recounted by one of two men who made the entire voyage with him and took part in the discovery.*

My name is…I shall say no more, and no one needs to know. My nickname is le Homard,[2] because the good God, or someone else, has put a strength into my arms and hands capable of giving a thrashing to any of my contemporaries. I once had a good family, money, education and better days, but they were erased long ago and their definitive disappearance drove me mad. My personality is, in any case, of no interest in itself. I only exist in my relationship with the immense Julius Pingouin, a prodigious and misunderstood man, stifled by evil destiny and the blind jealousy of a society stupid enough, first to have

---

1. A *bateau-mouche* (the term is a registered trademark) is one of the excursion boats that take visitors to Paris on trips up and down the Seine.

2. *i.e.* "the Lobster." *Pingouin*, of course, is French for Penguin.

left him without employment, and then to have pusillanimously combated the strength inclusive in a genius of that amplitude.

Before Julius Pingouin, I forget the mockery, indifference and disgust that a rather stormy life has permitted me to adopt toward all men, including myself; before Julius Pingouin I kneel in veneration. Let no one tell me any more apocryphal stories about the august and disinterested makers of laws whose application varies according to the power of those they judge; let no one bend my ears any longer with the bloody exploits attributed to famous captains and accomplished by their soldiers, who remain obscure; let people cease to bore me with relations of the great discoveries made by intrepid navigators whom their governments crammed in advance with all kinds of support and afterwards with all sorts of honors—all that is, if I might put it thus, affectation. I have someone stronger, cleverer, and more sublime: I have Julius Pingouin—and Lycurgus, Magellan and Bonaparte were very little by comparison with that god among men.

So, I've partied hard, in my youth. I've been a soldier, I've been a monk, I've been a thief, I've been a professor, I've been good, I've been wicked, I've been cowardly, I've been brave. I've been everything one can be. I've lived. But—and this is my most cherished and most radiant glory—I've known Julius Pingouin, and I believed in him right from the start, and he was generous enough, in accepting me among his apostles, to open up his great soul to me, full of audacity, full of sagacity, full of power, full of dreams....

O Julius Pingouin, giant astray among pygmies, lion silently shaking the bars of his cage, sublime adventurer passing like a devouring lightning-flash over the vile dung-heap of humanity, permit your unworthy disciple to weep in saluting you! People have been unjust, vapid, lax and oppressive toward you, heroic heart! Your superhuman progress has been impeded by the worst means. Not only have you been left alone, but you have been fought, and treason has sprung up all around you, and your motherland has been a wicked stepmother!

Nevertheless, invincible fighter, you were able to perse-vere. Now that I am telling your story, I know that people will conspire to drown the memory of such noble deeds in hollow silence and forgetfulness, but I shall speak, I shall howl, I shall scream! I shall write with ink, with my tears, with my blood, and never fall silent until the furious wind of universal glory will cause your name to resound in the four corners of the round Earth—for you, O master, have found the Golden Fleece!

And now, the story.

On the sixteenth of October last year, when I was dying of hunger and no longer knew what to do, I got a job on the Bateaux-Mouches. I embarked on number 318 as conductor. Julius Pingouin was the captain. I saw him, I heard him, and at a stroke, I was his disciple, his admirer, his instrument. In an instant, I was his. My eternal glory will be that he chose me as his first mate.

One day, he said to me: "Homard, old chap, I know where the Golden Fleece is. I've found a bottle thrown out of a doomed balloon. Inside, there was a map indicating the location. I'm going to go there. I've had enough of rotting away like this. You're going to come with me."

That was on the thirteenth of November.

He also said: "Listen—we're leaving tonight. Instead of landing at the last stop, we'll put on full steam and forward ho! I'm sure of the pilot and the men down below. With us two, the rope-man and two old friends I'm bringing, that'll be eight. The boat's sound, it's all that we need. The stoker will take care of the coal, the pilot the instruments. You'll buy a barrel of sea-biscuits, two more barrels for water, a cask of salted beef, seventy tins of sardines, rum, coffee and quinine. You'll have everything embarked at six o'clock while we're having dinner. Don't forget your knife. I'll take care of the flag and the revolvers. We'll be at sea tomorrow morning. There, we'll find everything we need. I have my map."

I said: "Good."

I would have gone to Hell—if there was one—with him.

Thus the expedition was decided and prepared.

Now, I'll copy out the boat's log, which I kept carefully from that moment on.

Log of the Argonaut
(Former Bateau-Mouche *no. 318)*
Captain: Julius Pingouin.

On 13 November, at eight forty-five p.m., the members of the crew of *Bateau-Mouche* number 318, commanded by Captain Julius Pingouin, resolved to abandon the service *en masse* and consecrate themselves exclusively, body and soul, to the expedition that the aforesaid Captain Pingouin has decided to undertake with the objective of finding the Golden Fleece. The crew having gathered on the deck, conjointly with two volunteers, Captain Pingouin's personal flag—an emblem representing the bird in question in white on a black background—was hoisted in place of the Company's dirty duster, which was thrown overboard. That deployment of the expedition's flag was accompanied by seventeen revolver shots. The boat was then solemnly baptized the *Argonaut*; a strip of cloth bearing that name was nailed to the bow.

Finally, the crew, consisting of:

The Homard, lieutenant;
Bouture, pilot-steersman;
Bayados, engineer;
Cristallin, stoker;
Constant Magloire, crewman;
plus, as volunteers:
Dr. Saturnin Plair, physician;
Joseph, mathematician and geographer;

swore fidelity until death in the hands of Captain Pingouin, and supported that oath with seven loud cheers and the absorption of a glass of rum mixed with gunpowder. Messieurs Bouture and

Magloire were unable to keep the mixture down and returned it immediately to the muddy waves.

I, le Homard, was entrusted with the keeping of the present log.

At that moment, we were already a hundred meters past the lights of the pontoon on the terminal station. Then, the travelers who had not disembarked at previous stops and were desirous of doing so at that ultimate point manifested their existence by a tumultuous exit from the cabin, where they had taken refuge because of the cold fog. The group—there were seven or eight—irrupted on to the deck. At their head was a short fat man.

"Monsieur," he roared, addressing himself to me, le Homard, "Why aren't you stopping?"

Julius Pingouin advanced. Constant Magloire and I were at his sides with our revolvers. He was calm, and spoke.

"We're never going to stop again. This is how it is: I want the Golden Fleece. I'm going to look for it. Let those who aren't mollusks and have had enough of going moldy here come with me. The good God has sent them to me, and I'm disposed to keep them. We might die, but we might gain everything that's good in the world."

"What does that mean?" howled the short fat man. "Are you making fun of us? My name...."

"What? What?" interrupted a hoarse voice. "Have you finished annoying us, you rotten pudding? Le Rempart du Quartier Rouge is *my* name, and as for rubber stamps, I don't fear six together, and the man who'll sort me out isn't yet born. I'm going with the captain. I like him. He's a man, he is, and straight up! I know that. Do you want to have it out with me, M'sieu? I'm ready."

And a Herculean ruffian in a cap and scarf came strutting forward.

Julius Pingouin shook his hand. "I'll make you my second mate," he said.

"Me, good negro, you, good master. Me want to go." And a

sort of baboon, a gaudily-clad nougat-salesman, came prancing toward us.

The other passengers, however, formed an agitated and inter-rogative group.

"What's going to be done with those who don't want to go?"

"And the profits? How will they be divided?"

"Oh, of course, I'll be able to spread the word of the Good Lord!"

"Will there be enough to eat?"

"Nevertheless, I have to get back to my duty."

"Monsieur, my masters are expecting me."

And above all, the short fat man vociferated: "I don't want to! I protest! The rights of man, damn it!"

"Would you like me to punch you on the nose?" proposed le Rempart. "The rights of man are squashed from above."

Julius Pingouin imposed silence with a gesture, however, and spoke again. "Those who don't want to come will be free to disembark."

"Where?" a voice asked.

"Into the water, naturally. We're not going to compromise the safety of the expedition for the personal affairs of people we don't know. The profits will be shared between the survi-vors, in accordance with my personal appraisal and the services rendered, without the families of the deceased having any right to them. Naturally, there'll be enough raised for the smallest share to be capable of buying half the world, if that gives you pleasure, and still to have a nice income, not to mention the glory, the power and all the rest. As for food and drink, it won't be sumptuous, but we'll make up for it later. Now, you've got five minutes to make up your minds. I advise you to reflect. It's an opportunity to be men for once, and that can't happen to you often. What I said just now is for your benefit. Personally, I'd just as soon go alone. Go back into the cabin."

They went back. Three minutes later, we learned that they were all joining us except for one.

There were five, to wit: the short fat man; an enormous

Swiss, stupid and feeble-minded; a tall blond Norwegian, whom we subsequently discovered to be a pastor, and whom, similarly later, bored us in an uncommon fashion by singing hymns furiously, or playing them on a collapsible clarinet, independently of him drinking all the rum; a female basket-seller; a maid-of-all-work; and a fireman, who doubtless stayed because of the maid.[3]

The passenger who refused to go with us was a uniformed officer in the city constabulary. "I have orders; I have to go back," he repeated. "I'd very much like to stay, but it's nevertheless necessary for me to go."

And he went, after having sworn not to reveal anything about us or about the goal of our expedition.

"We're well rid of him," le Rempart said to me.

I went with him to explore the cabin. To my amazement, I found another two passengers. First, there was a thin man clad in a long yellow-tinted garment who was smoking his pipe impassively and silently. He had not shared his companions' excitement. He only replied to my questions, and my proposal that he join us, with movements of his head. I thought I understood that he accepted, and, in fact, he came. I also found, under a banquette, an undertaker's employee who was asleep, dead drunk. Woken up—not without difficulty—he declared that he wanted to die if anyone moved him; however, he agreed to live and to go with us when he learned that we had rum aboard.

Everyone gathered on the deck and I entered the following travelers in the list of the crew as follows:

Passengers embarked on the former bateau-mouche 318, now the Argonaut, were invited to enroll in the expedition. Accepting:

Hippolyte, alias Le Rempart du Quartier Rouge, ex-coal-heaver, *second mate of Captain Julius Pingouin*:

---

3. This makes six rather than five, although—as will shortly become evident—only five of them actually remain on board, plus the two who have already volunteered and the two subsequently discovered.

Coco, negro, former nougat-salesman, *able seaman*;

Gustave J. K. S. Heysbergch Tantsticktor, former Norwegian pastor, *piper*;

Claudius Zafolin, foreman, *functions reserved*;

Flaum, ex-courier of fake diamonds, *cook*;

....I searched in vain for the short fat man. "Where is he?" I asked le Rempart, to whom I appealed.

"He's gone," he told me, sniggering. "He was already speaking ill of M'sieu Pingouin behind his back, so I helped him to leave, He won't be coming back."

I didn't persist and continued with my list:

Ezéchiel Binaire, undertaker's employee, *functions reserved*;

X..., unknown, *functions reserved* (he was the man in yellow, whose calm mutism and serene indifference defied all efforts);

Honorine Dupont, maid-of-all-work, *functions reserved*;

Zoé Nèfle, former seller of vegetables from a basket, *nurse and laundress.*

All these travelers swore fidelity to Captain Pingouin and recognized him as the sovereign master of the vessel, before God, with the right of life or death.

It remained understood that, in the event of war, every sound man would take up arms for the defense of the expedition. Dispensed from this obligation were: Dr. Saturnin Plair, facultatively, in view of his functions; Pastor Tantsticktor, in view of his humanitarian convictions and his employment as piper, necessary in battle; the cook Flaum, in view of his abnormal fatness and a natural cowardice of which he was aware. The two women would help Dr. Plair in tending to the wounded.

Monsieur Clodoald Résistant, corporal in the city constabulary, who was among the passengers, having declared that his duty called him elsewhere, was disembarked into the river according to his wishes, under oath not to reveal to anyone what he had learned concerning the expedition.[4]

Disappeared without giving his name: one short fat man, bald and bad-tempered, who was believed to be an employee of the Mairie or the post office.[5]

The expedition thus constituted is going forward.

14 November, 5 a.m. The night is still dark. I am writing by the light of a combat beacon. We are about to reach the mouth of the river and the captain thinks that the filthy institution knows as the customs will torment us in passing with the humiliating rods that civilized societies have in reserve for freewheeling men of heart. Julius Pingouin hopes that we will get by without incident, but in order to be prepared for any eventuality, he has ordered us to take up battle stations. Every man has been equipped with a revolver and one other weapon, trenchant or blunt. The women have been locked in the cabin. Dr. Saturnin, invited to go with them, has refused to do so, preferring to remain in order to keep a lookout, Pastor Tantsticktor, given that he is unaccustomed to battle, has been authorized to take cover in the engine-room, under the express condition that he will play martial hymns on his pipe throughout the battle, with all his might and without stopping. The pilot Bouture will natu-

---

4. The author inserts a footnote here: "The worthy Clodoald Résistant, corporal in the city constabulary, was recovered thanks to our cares, but, immutably faithful to his word, he has never said a word about what he might or might not have seen. The efforts of everyone, from his immediate superior to the Head of State, were in vain, and his mutism remained absolute. To have something in such conditions is as good as not having it. [Editor's Note.]"

5. The author inserts a footnote here: "No one ever discovered the identity of the unfortunate short fat bald man with the bad temper, nor exactly what became of him. It is true that the vagueness of the description, which could apply generally to all public functionaries, especially those employed in the Mairie or the post office, has impeded research. A reward of ten thousand francs is promised to the short, fat, bald, bad-tempered man if he cares to make himself known, in the probable case that he is still alive. [Editor's Note.]"

rally remain on his bench, and the men down below, Bayados the engineer and Cristallin the stoker, will remain at their interior posts. The disposable men have orders to be ready for any eventuality. Everyone must adopt an inoffensive and indifferent pose, until the captain gives the order. Everyone has received a little white calico penguin and has pinned it to his breast, as a sign of solidarity and military badge.

I will note that the Man in Yellow has refused, silently but formally, to arm himself in any fashion whatsoever. Nor did he want to put on a penguin. He has been content to stuff his pipe and go sit down in the bow.

Now we're awaiting the battle. We still hope that it won't take place, but the threat of action has affected my companions variously. The fireman seems pale and resolute. The young maid-of-all-work is weeping copiously. Coco, the negro, has taken off the clothes he usually wears, in order, he says, not to get them dirty; he is as naked as a worm and is capering around after having rubbed himself with an evil-smelling grease. Pastor Tantsticktor is playing his pipe with chattering teeth. The fat cook Flaum has been obliged to take shelter in the cabin with the women, in a sobbing and fearful condition that provokes pity and disgust. He offered the sum of two francs fifty to the vegetable-seller Zoé Nèfle if she would consent to lend him her clothes so that he can hide better. The stout woman, who is making lint with the fragment of her chemise, which she has taken off and cut into pieces for that purpose, refused indignantly and reproached him for his cowardice. Ezéchiel Binaire, the undertaker's mute, completely drunk, is writing his will and extracting a supplement of intrepidity from a bottle of rum. The remaining crew members are fine. Le Rempart is manifesting a particular joy and juggling with a steel bar, a former piston-rod from the engine, weighing forty-five pounds.

"Thumping those Chinamen on the noggin," he said to me, "will be more fun than knocking down ordinary folk, and the man who can sort me out hasn't been born yet."[6]

Dawn is breaking; we're now at the mouth of the river. The sea appears. Directly in front of us, barring the way to liberty, fortune and space, are the customs coastguards. It's time for action.

"Forward ho!" commands Julius Pingouin.

Same day, noon. We're in the open sea. We are victorious.

We had to fight. As we were passing by, the coastguards gave us an order to halt. Pingouin obeyed. Then two large launches came toward us, manned by twenty men and commanded by a customs officer.

The latter came aboard with his soldiers. There was grumbling and mockery.

"Well, well!" he said to our captain. "It's like this that we're going away, is it? And the exit permits, have we forgotten them?"

"Monsieur Customs Officer," said Julius Pingouin, "I have no merchandise. We're going for a little sea-trip and I have nothing to pay."

"We'll see about that," said the officer. "Where are your papers, first? Then again, no one takes trips at this hour. It's shady."

Coco, the negro, seeing that things were going badly, attempted to create a diversion. It was unsuccessful.

"Me good negro," he said. "You not want nougat? Good stuff, Massa." And he presented his tray.

"Do you take me for a fool, you dirty monkey?" howled the officer, hitting the tray with his fist. "Wait a minute! I'll start by searching you."

"Me good negro," said Coco. "Me all naked. You not search."

---

6. It ought to be noted that le Rempart's speech is rendered in the original in an eye-dialect supposedly representative of lower-class Parisian parlance, which is untranslatable, and there does not seem to be any point in mangling the English translation randomly. The same applies to the cook Flaum, whose speech is dressed up in a tortuous eye-dialect supposedly representative of a native German-Swiss speaking French incompetently.

He took two steps backwards as if to run away, and then bounded forward. His head rammed into the officer's midriff and launched him over the side.

"Play, piper!" commanded Pingouin. "Forward, the rest of you!"

"Crunch!" roared le Rempart. "Good for you, Coco!" And he rushed forward, wielding his piston-rod.

We rushed them. Our revolvers came into play. The customs men charged, sabers in hand. The skirmish was soon general. Le Rempart struck out like a man possessed, and anyone touched by his bar didn't get up again. The negro butted his enemies one after another. He was wounded in the face. Meanwhile, Joseph, Magloire and the fireman were destroying the customs men to my right, Julius Pingouin and le Rempart, to my left, had already run out of adversaries. In the center, aided by the jovial under-taker's boy, who had rolled his sleeves up and was flailing with his fists, I cleared the deck in no time. The pastor's shrill piping drowned out the groans and blasphemies. From the cabin, the fat Flaum was bellowing with fear so loudly that he could be heard in spite of everything. Young Honorine, the maid-of-all-work, was mewling as loudly as she could. Dr. Saturnin was already bandaging the brave Coco. As for the Man in Yellow, serene and immobile, he was smoking his pipe on a banquette, paying no attention to anything. A customs man had hurled himself upon him at the beginning of the action, but he had killed him with his foot without disturbing himself overmuch.

Of our enemies, none remained

"Forward ho!" commanded Julius Pingouin. "Attack the coastguards! Prepare to board!"

The *Argonaut* was going at top speed. In the blink of an eye, we fell upon the customs boat. There was further carnage, rapidly concluded. Unfortunately, the brave Magloire, the former rope-man, was killed in the battle, by a bullet in the head.

We didn't leave a living soul aboard the boat, and, on the orders of our captain, we transported everything aboard, with our possessions, for it was more comfortable than the *Argonaut*, whose name we immediately gave it.

We then emptied three barrels of tar on the Compagnie des Bateaux-Mouches' former number 318, set fire to it, and made off. Behind us, it burned very nicely, a fuliginous torch in the mist, and through our binoculars we saw a crowd of people on the quays watching the spectacle.

By the time it blew up, we were already far away.

Tearfully, we gave Constant Magloire the solemn funeral due to brave men who die on the field of honor. The pastor, whom he had begged to interrupt his piping, in which he persisted with a kind of intoxication, and who seemed quite bewildered, nervously recited prayers in a foreign language over the body, which was immersed. Then we cleared the deck of the uniformed cadavers littering it. There were no wounded except for one man, who had been hit by le Rempart and who died before long.

"Good Lord," said Ezéchiel, who seemed to be in his element, as he bundled the body of a brigadier into the waves, "that's good work gone to waste."

When everything was tidy, we ate breakfast. The women had done the cooking, the cook Flaum still being almost dead of fright.

"It's curious," the doctor remarked, cheerfully, "that battles are no worse than surgery. I prefer a battlefield to an operating theater. It seems less cruel to kill than to cure."

"Oh!" said the pastor, with his accent. "So many have died who would have lived for a long time! And the screams! And the blood!"

He shivered and drained a full glass of rum.

"Me great famine, Massa!" moaned the wounded Coco, who was on a starvation diet. "Me good negro, nothing in teeth."

"He's like me, the negro," observed le Rempart. "Excitement makes him hungry." And he took a slice of lard.

"That's life, old chap," said Ezéchiel Binaire.

Such was the glorious beginning of our quest.

15 November. Nothing particular to report. The sea is calm, our new boat is performing well. It's making about twelve knots and can reach fifteen or sixteen. Presently, le Rempart is keeping watch on deck. The impassive Man in Yellow is chewing a plug of tobacco, and spitting over the side—which is six meters away from him—with an incredible precision and force. He's agreed to abandon his pipe, in response to my observation that one doesn't smoke aboard warships. Ezéchiel Binaire has followed his example in that respect. The undertaker's boy is presently painting the name of the ship, *Argonaut*, on the stern, in white on a black background. He's adding decorative embellishments, representing skulls and crossbones. He's singing a sentimental ballad that I can hear. The fat Flaum is sweeping, under the direction of Zoé Nèfle. The fireman is in the hold. The maid-of-all-work isn't doing anything, and Pastor Tantsticktor is pronouncing an incomprehensible homily, for the personal benefit of the negro Coco, who's howling and sobbing, his soul refractory to any other sentiment than hunger, because his diet won't end until this evening, in accordance with Dr. Saturnin's orders.

Captain Pingouin is shut up in his cabin, making calculations with the doctor and Monsieur Joseph. I ought to say something about the latter. He's a distinguished man, one can see that right away, and very fit, and not clumsy. He doesn't talk much, but he's likeable anyway and one senses that he can be trusted. Julius Pinguoin had a word with me about him this morning.

"Lieutenant Homard, old chap," he said to me, "you see that man there—well, he's an aristocrat, a true one, and not a mollusk, as they often are, but intelligent and knowing everything one can know. And he has all that he needs and could have become famous—more famous than anyone—if he had wanted to. Well, it's for a woman that he's broken with his life, which was all set and happy.

"It bowls you over, doesn't it, that a man like that, who has everything needed to be loved, should suffer in that way? That's how it is, though. Our success doesn't interest him—it's all the same to him. He wants to forget, and if he can't, you see, he'll get himself killed....for a woman. I can't say any more...but it's a real shame, damn it!"

Le Rempart has just interrupted the course of my reflections by coming over to me.

"Lieutenant Le Homard," he said to me, in an embarrassed fashion, "I need to tell you something. Me, you see, I'm a straight-up type. I've never flinched, and the man who can get the better of me hasn't been born yet...that's why I've come to you, who are all attack and good faith. And Monsieur Pingouin, I like him as if he were my father, since I've had enough of knocking fellows over and dragging my old lady outside and correcting her with a few kicks, even though she's in the hospital because I kicked too hard.... Anyway, one can't remake oneself and me, I'm lively...and M'sieu Pingouin has got me out of that, without knowing me, without knowing whether it's luck or Providence. And anyway, I don't know, it's for himself.... They get to you, that type; I'm totally devoted to him, and for me, there's only him in the world. And then, I'm telling you this, since you're a brother and I like you too...well, here it is: the pilot, Bouture, is a spy for the Jews."

"What?" I said.

"For sure," he went on. "That cuts you, me too, but that's the way it is. You see, yesterday, in the night, before we gave those filthy aquatic cops a thump on the head, he lit his pipe with a match that wasn't quite regulation, and had the air of a signal. One knows what one knows...."

"I don't understand," I said.

"Yes. And the fat cook might be up to something, however stupid he is. For the other, there's no mistake. You think it's quite natural, do you, that they'd have sent twenty customs men at one go if they hadn't known something? Anyway, there's no mistake, I tell you, with our filthy government....he's a Jewish spy!"

"If he's a spy, he's a Jesuit spy, and that doesn't astonish me," said a voice beside us. I recognized the engineer Bayados. He went on: "It's only the Jesuits that pull dirty tricks like that. You find their hand everywhere. Clericalism, that's the enemy."

"Me, I've got religion, I say it's the Jews," growled le Rempart.

I interrupted. "Whether it's the Jews or the Jesuits, it makes no difference."

"It makes a lot, from the social point of view," said Bayados.

"The social point of view," I went on, "has to be set aside. What interests us is knowing whether one of us is a traitor. Personally, I don't think so. In any case, it's better not to say anything. There's no need to mention this to the captain, nor to talk about the affair, especially as we don't know anything. You have no proof, have you? We mustn't be unjust. Keep an eye on Bouture with me; if he's already communicated with lights or by any other means, he'll do it again, and we'll pinch him."

"All right," they said. "We'll keep quiet, that's agreed—but we'll keep our eyes open."

They both went away, and went off to have a political discussion somewhere in the nether regions of the *Argonaut*, which, I fear, might never end.

Now I'm meditating on that singular phenomenon. I'm trying to remember the actions of the aforesaid Bouture. The man had never inspired me with complete confidence, I confess. Fat and clean-shaven, dressed in blue, he plies his tiller placidly. He's an intelligent man, well above his position, Pingouin's told me. I find him sly. Has he, then, been placed among us in order to steal the providential map, fallen from a balloon, from the captain? How does anyone know that Pingouin has it? Of whom, in reality, is Bouture the instrument? What will he try against us?

Anyway, we'll see. We need to be squarely on our guard, and trust in destiny.

Same day, 10 p.m. We've just had a punch in honor of yesterday's victory. The captain gathered us all together in the big cabin. He made a speech and I'm sure that now every one of us is ready to let himself be cooked over a slow fire to give him pleasure. I would never have believed that a man could take hold of others to that extent with nothing but words. It's true that the man in question is Julius Pingouin.

His speech has made us crazy. I'll reproduce it.

Speech made by Captain Julius Pingouin
aboard the Argonaut, *14 November.*

"I have to tell you that I'm content with you, and that you have my esteem. I know now what you can do. Everyone has done well, on the whole. The exceptions, if there are a few minor ones, will get used to it or render other services. We mustn't be scornful of anyone. Not everyone can be a hero, and no one can be sure that he can be one every day. We've won. That's good. I don't want to name anyone among the living, however noble the deeds that they accomplished were...."

Here the captain launched a glance of congratulation toward le Rempart and Coco, the negro, who swelled up with expressions of false modesty.

"I'll only talk about the man who died. Honor to Constant Magloire! He's the first to fall for the sake of all of us. Let the memory of that brave man be venerated. Many among us will go the same way as him, that's certain, but it's of no consequence. It's necessary to have no fear of death. No one knows what it is. When we get there, we'll learn, but so long as one is alive, it's necessary to live, and not go moldy without looking at anything but the end of one's nose in one's comfortable little routine.

"We've had enough of cowardice, of principles, of politics, of poverty and the sewer in which we were always turning round without ever being able to see clearly or breathe. When you have a heart in your belly, it's necessary to stand up, and to send anyone who tries to prevent you from being a man to sleep. If society is so disgusting from top to bottom, not to mention those who are alongside, it's because people talk too much and don't act enough.

"Humanity, nowadays, has a soul in felt, like the plugs they put in beer-bottles in cafes. No one can march if there isn't someone to initiate the movement with kicks up the backside. No one dares murder overmuch, but everyone steals, and everyone has dirty little vices that rot you from the inside, and would like to render everyone the same. It's enough to make one vomit woodlice!

"We're acting! Very good! When one wants to go somewhere, it's necessary to go there, and not elsewhere, like a booby, because your neighbor tells you to. It's necessary to live for oneself and not for the opinion of others. It's necessary to know how to laugh, weep, hope, want, suffer, love, hate, live and die. And to hell with the rest!

"Look at yourselves now—aren't you more content for having done what we've done, instead of staying quiet, like pot-plants? Haven't you lived more, in the last two days, than in all your stupid lives before, when you knew that the next day would be just like the day before? Everyone puts up with it, though. You'll tell me that they need the opportunity. Agreed—but when one has blood in one's veins, one makes the opportunity; one seizes whatever's passing. Something's always passing, and one thing leads to another; one gets into the habit of moving.

"And then again, now that you've found the opportunity, it's a matter of not messing it up. It's necessary to succeed—and that won't happen of its own accord, you can count on that. They've already tried to stop us; they'll try again. It will make no difference—we'll go anyway. Let's be united, that's all— one for all. If there are disagreements, we'll settle them later. For the moment, we need to act as one man, if we want to get through to the end, where we'll find independence.

"Some will fall along the way. That's unfortunate. Let's go on anyway. No jealousy, no treason"—here le Rempart cast a glance of menacing suspicion at the pilot Bouture—"no cowardice, no hesitation, no egotism, but strength, devotion, concord, determination, decision, and the world is ours! Have confidence in me, damn it! I'll take you to the end, even if the

Devil's there!"

16 November. Sea a trifle choppy because of a fresh south-west-erly breeze. The maid-of-all-work, who's sniveling, the fireman and the undertaker's mute are sea-sick. For myself, I've had nightmares all night, thanks to the speech the captain made yesterday. All the same, what a man! I'd give my life to please him.

18, 19 & 20 November. Nothing to report. We're progressively getting used to one another's society; everyone's doing what he has to do. The maid-of-all-work seems fatigued already. The Man in Yellow doesn't do anything and no one's got used to him. One can't get used to a void, and for us it's as if he didn't exist.

21 November. We're now outside the regular shipping lanes. Since midday we've been adrift, the engine no longer working in consequence of a small breakdown that requires a few hours to be repaired. We've been carried far enough to be within sight of a mass of smoky yellow fog, excessively dense and clearly limited by the exterior atmosphere, without having any overlap with it. It looks like a misty wall, the summit of which is lost in the clouds, and which follows an immense curve to the right and the left.

Dr. Saturnin Plair tells us that it's the Livid Isle, enveloped in the fog that is characteristic of it. The doctor tells us that he once dropped anchor near to its shores.

"There," he said, "a furious pale yellow fog always reigns. It's so thick that objects are scarcely visible through its lividity and appear vague and astonishing. The fog trails over the skin like a viscous liquid, its perfume is exhausting and intoxicates all those who breathe it.

"If a man lands on the island and eats its unusual vegetation, and advances into that deadly phenomenon, his double—another self—comes to met him, takes him by the hand affectionately and makes him stand in front of him. Then, face to face, they exchange words regarding life and death, and unknown confidences. And very few are those who, having had that adventure, want to return to their previous existence, and to their ship, which they can no longer find. And there are ships that have never emerged from that poisonous shadow.

"I believe that it's the land of forgetfulness, the land of the Lotus-Eaters, of which Homer and Tennyson speak. I believe so—but I'm not sure.

"When the ship on which I was the doctor was obliged, to avoid an ill wind, to take refuge in the perilous and immutable calm of the fog that you can see out there, the captain, who had experience of these things, absolutely forbade us to go ashore. In spite of that, five men, including three passengers, disembarked covertly.

"Only one of them came back, and his face, and his eyes, and his entire person, had taken on the troubled pallor of that mortal fog. He never told us what he had seen on that island, nor what he knew about his companions. He seemed drunk with sloth and indifference. Shortly afterwards, he died...."

As we listened to all that, we contemplated the Livid Isle— or, rather, the sovereign fog that enclosed it in its glaucous mass. Night fell then, and we were very close to that mysterious zone. We were only able to get moving again three hours later.

Same day, 11 p.m. Monsieur Joseph is no longer with us. That was discovered at the evening roll-call. He left a letter with the captain. I'll copy it:

> *Forgive me, Julius Pingouin. I'm leaving you. I hold you in high esteem and love you as the greatest man I have ever known. I desire, with all my heart, that you should succeed; but I've had enough, myself, and since the opportunity is tempting me, I'm going to try to get what is, for me, the Golden Fleece.*

"Damn it!" said Pingouin. "He's gone to the Livid Isle in search of forgetfulness. As if a month of the voyage wouldn't have given him that! Go look for him? We'd all stay here! I don't have the right. And after all, if that's what he wants....

"The rest of you, forward ho!

"For a woman…a man like that…it's enough to make one vomit...."

And I saw that he was weeping.

22 November. Nothing.

23 November. This morning, we fished up a singular creature that was swimming in our wake and waving to us. Having lifted him on to the deck we recognized him as a man, but in what a state, dear God! Long hair mingled with algae and seashells, skin all red and scaly, and fingers and toes connected by a kind of membrane.

He started jabbering in an unknown language, into which he inserted words from all countries. By putting them all together, we were gradually able to understand him. This is what he said:

"I'm a great hero. I seek the Truth. Do you happen to have it in our cargo, by any chance? No—I can see that you don't. What a pity!"

He sobbed.

"It's been a long time, since my youth. I've searched everywhere, without being able to find it anywhere.

"I've studied with the most intelligent men, however, and also with the most idiotic—with everyone....

"I've been everywhere, from the highest to the lowest, from right to left, forwards and backwards, shouting to everyone; 'Give it to me!' But no one has given it to me. Perhaps they didn't have it, or perhaps they were keeping it to themselves.

"When I became convinced that I wouldn't be able to find the Truth on land, I resolved to try to catch it in the sea. Then I learned to live in salt water. When I'd become thoroughly accustomed to it, I went straight ahead, facing the sun, led by the tide. I'm always swimming, I eat raw fish, I dive very well and my hands have become webbed."

He raised his right hand.

"A superb example of transformism," said the doctor, admiringly. "It reminds me of refrigerator rats."[7]

"Yes," said the Marine Man. "Yes, I too know the great Darwin and his theories; I'd like to believe that I'm an ape, but I rather think that I'm a fish, and doubt torments me. It's many years since I last cut my hair, because I've lost my pen-knife. It's frightful."

He paused, and then continued: "It's also a long time that I've been floating, rolled by the waves of the powerful sea and exploring all the way to its abyssal depths, in every direction. My heart is all but broken by despair, and my mind's coming apart by virtue of having thought so much, but I don't have the truth. I haven't found it on any ship, either at the tops of masts, or in the depths of holds, or in the souls of passengers. The stars don't tell it to me, at night when I put my duck's hands together for them; the sun has dazzled my imploring eyes, cruelly, but hasn't taught me anything; and the swell has sung that it doesn't know; and the flying fish fly away without making any reply... Oh, my God!"

He stopped again, and resumed: "Can someone give me a plug of tobacco? Good."

He started chewing it.

"I had an adventure a few days ago, though. I shouted at a large ship in order to be picked up, thinking that I might find the Truth in one of its cannons, but a fat man wearing braid put his detestable face over the stern and asked me what I thought about

---

7. When refrigerated meat began to be transported from New Zealand in the 1880s, the rumor rapidly spread that the rats that lived aboard the ships had adapted to the low temperatures within a few generations to spawn a new race of "refrigerator rats" or "freezer rats," and the circumstance was often quoted as anecdotal evidence for the inheritance of acquired characteristics. The notion of freezer rats persists today, although it is dubious that any hereditary adaptation has actually taken place.

the Dreyfus Affair. I wasn't able to reply, because I don't know anything about the Dreyfus Affair, and I don't know whether there's any truth in it. Then the fat man, malevolently, refused to pick me up, and took his face away."

The human fish paused for breath. We all looked at him fearfully. He continued, curtly: "So, there it is. Now, I wanted to come aboard to ask you: What's the Dreyfus Affair?"

"Go away!" howled Pingouin, hoarsely. "Get out, murderer! Not another word! Over the side, and don't let me see you again!"

We all leapt on the wretch and, without further ado, threw him over the side, in order that he would not contaminate the *Argonaut* any longer with his terrible presence.

"May he die of it!" cried Pingouin. "And thus will all those who act thus die, damn it!" And he wiped away the sweat that emotion was causing to run down his face.

"That was the greatest danger that we have ever run, and that we ever will run," he told me, afterwards, when we were alone.

23 November. I really do believe that the pilot Bouture is involved in shady dealings. Last night, as I was asleep in my hammock, le Rempart, who was on watch on the deck, came to look for me in great mystery. Once up top, I noted the existence, toward the East, of an unknown blue-tinted star shining in the vicinity of Vega, which was suddenly extinguished.

"A moment ago it was red," le Rempart told me, "and the autocamel's[8] taking notes."

Indeed, Bouture was observing with a pair of binoculars and writing figures in a notebook. When he saw us he calmly put his notebook in his pocket.

I'm perplexed. Should I warn the captain? I'll think about it tonight.

---

8. In nineteenth-century French literature, vehicle-drivers of all sorts were often referred to, mock-poetically, as "*Automedons*," after the driver of Achilles' chariot. Le Rempart's "*aut'chameau*" [autocamel] is probably mangling it at hazard, but might conceivably be confusing the second part of the word, somehow, with the second part of "*dromadaire*" [dromedary].

24 November. I've talked to Julius Pingouin. He stopped me at the first words and told me that he was sure of the pilot and that, moreover, he was the one who had ordered him to observe the stars.

"But what about the blue star?" I said.

"Bah! A bolide," our captain replied. "I repeat, my old Homard, Bouture is a reliable man. I've saved his life. He's as devoted to me as...you, for instance."

"Thanks very much," I replied, vexed. Anyway, we'll see.

25 November. All well. The same for *26, 27 and 28 of the same month.*

29 November. Festival of St. Saturnin. We wish the doctor well. Dancing, singing, drinking, all-out party. The dear man, very emotional, embraced us effusively, except for the Man in Yellow, who did not lend himself to it. Coco, having eaten too much after a furious bamboula, has had to remain in bed, motionless, for fourteen hours, in order to digest like a boa constrictor. Pastor Tantsticktor, having drunk two bottles of rum, played hymns on his clarinet all night.

30 November. Sad event. The young maid-of-all-work died today of overwork. She leaves a great void behind her, and the regrets are unanimous.

1 December. Nothing. General sadness.

2 December. A furious tempest. We are within an inch of doom. The wind is blowing with rage, and has been all day. It eases a little after sunset, but such a frightful swell succeeds it that it's a miracle that we aren't swallowed up at every instant.

Everyone is afraid except Pingouin. The cowardice of the big Swiss is repugnant. The brave Zoé Nèfle, although very frightened herself, boxed his ears to put some backbone in him.

Midnight. There's just been a renewal of the wind, brief but so furious that we all thought our last hour had come. The ship shook and creaked lugubriously, one of our launches was smashed, the abyss opened up to receive us and the tempest, ever more violent, drove us before it with a deafening racket into the pitch darkness, where liquid mountains rose up and collapsed as if to bury us. Then Pastor Tantsticktor appeared on the deck. Bare-headed, his hair lifted up by the wind, he stood before the feeble glow of the lights like an apparition. He held out his long arms toward the black sky, and, in the midst of the terror, the din and death, he shouted:

"Venerably, I commend myself to three, Lord God; I utter my cries to you! Men will die on the sea if you do not look after them. In the perils, take pity on them and know what sinners they are. Give them time to repent!"

He knelt down and prayed in a loud voice, in a language I don't understand, beneath the waves that broke over him. Then...I think we did likewise, all of us, or almost all. It was so dark that I couldn't see. Then, believe me, we felt death beside us, and did not look that way.

3 December. At daybreak, the swell had calmed somewhat. The ship has suffered quite a bit, but not as much as we could have believed.

The wind, which was driving us in the right direction, has enabled us to make a lot of progress, although we've deviated eastwards.

"We've come a long way," observed the pilot Bouture. "It's curious; the region we're in is ordinarily calm."

"It's necessary to believe that it's changed character," grumbled le Rempart. In my ear, he whispered confidentially: "It's more likely his fault, the Chinaman...."

It's now half past eight. Coco is on watch on a mast.

"Good Massa!" he cries, all of a sudden. "Me see package, which is land."

Pingouin consults his map.

"It must be a desert island. We can land briefly, and take a rest."

It is, indeed, a large island, which seems verdant and beautiful.

We disembark with the launch. There are eight of us, well-armed, to wit: Julius Pingouin; the doctor; me, le Homard; le Rempart; the foreman Zafolin; the pilot Bouture; Ezéchiel Binaire; and the negro Coco, the ship being left in the guard of the brave Bayados and the others.

Same date, evening. For a start, the island isn't deserted. There are sixty people on it, men and women.

When we arrived, they were in a big field, busy digging up potatoes. They were working sitting on the ground, without talking, all watching one another—one potato dug up, one glance at the next person to be sure that he's also dug up his own—another potato, another glance. They went on like that.

Suddenly, at a frightful blast from a hunting horn, which came from some kind of big building that could be seen in the distance, they all stopped and lay down.

After a few minutes, another blast. They resumed work—one potato, one glance at the neighbor—another potato, another glance—and so on....

"That's a curious sight," observed the doctor.

"It must be an asylum for tranquil lunatics," Pingouin replied.

"Tranquil?" said the doctor, anxiously. "I'm not so sure of that."

Not fearful of showing ourselves, however, we advanced into the woods toward the building I mentioned. The trees were rather nice, but Coco seemed disgusted by them.

"No match for the coconuts back home," he remarked, sadly.

Soon we arrived at the houses. There were five of them. They were immense, caked with mud and rather sinister in appearance. Each of them had a word engraved over the door: *Refectory; Dormitory; Workshop; Reproduction.* The largest one, which was also the most abominable, because it had ornaments in the form of dripping-pans, was entitled: *Communal House*. In front of it, between two very tall masts, a strip of dirty canvas was stretched, on which was written:

ALL MEN ARE BORN AND REMAIN EQUAL

And there was no one anywhere.

We were rather nonplussed. Noses in the air, we looked at the inscription and everything else, without understanding any of it.

"Aha! You're admiring our declaration of principles, Citizen?"

That was said to the doctor by a thin man dressed in clothes that were too big, who came out of the big house in the middle.

"I'm admiring it without admiration," replied the doctor. "You declaration lacks something."

"It lacks nothing," said the man, proudly. "It's the criterion of human dignity."

The doctor looked at him with astonished eyes. "It's the... what did you say? The criterion of...very good, truly very good! But that doesn't prevent it from lacking something. It ought to say: equal before the law. Without that, it's meaningless."

"There are no laws any longer," said the other. "We're free of all the odious bonds that tyranny has invented to set its yoke and oppress nascent liberty."

"Extraordinary literature," said the doctor. "Is it from a book that you learned to talk like that? Perhaps one can procure it somewhere?"

"I will add, Citizen," the man went on, "that you astonish me in wanting to insinuate that all men are not equal."

"Did I appear to insinuate that?" said the doctor.

"Yes. Now, I proclaim it loudly, and no mandatory of a free society can contradict me: all men are equal in every way...."

"Fool," le Rempart interrupted. "If you gave me a slap, it would be like a fly; if I gave you one, it would kill you. So you're not my equal."

The islander, however, without paying any heed, continued

fervently: "All men are equal. No more laws, no more trades, no more masters, no more capital, no more bosses, no more humiliating wages, no more despotism, no more vicious aristocracy and avaricious tyranny! There's nothing any longer but free, equal men, enfranchised and conscious of their human dignity."

"Very, very curious," said the doctor. "From what I can see, you constitute a colony, yes?"

"Exactly, Citizen—you've said it, and I think highly of you for it. All men are brothers. Each for everyone, all for all. The great dawn of liberation and enfranchisement has risen for us and we have been liberated from social slavery."

"Very good," said the doctor. "I understand and I admire— but this is a foreign prince"—he pointed at Pingouin—"who might not understand entirely. It would be desirable if you were to explain it to him in detail. Take these hundred sous for your trouble."

"I'm at the prince's orders, and you're a worthy citizen," said the other, taking off his hat and putting the hundred sous in his pocket. "All men are good, worthy and virtuous when civilization has not corrupted them. Humanity is essentially admirable."

"Damn!" said Pingouin.

"First of all," said the doctor, "what's your name?"

"I don't have a name. There are no more names. I'm number 29. In a more or less beautiful name, one can take pride, like those infamous aristoc…hmm! A number is an anonymous leveler."

"Superb," said the doctor. "Well, Number 29, tell me why you aren't doing anything, while your brothers are working."

"Because it's my turn. We each take turns to be the public man—which is to say, to represent the executive power."

"What does he execute?" asked the doctor.

Meanwhile, the undertaker's mute Ezéchiel Binaure, who was slightly drunk, interrupted and interrogated number 29. "Tell me, old chap, do the others all talk like you?"

"Not as well, no," replied the man, flattered. "I'm much the best...."

"That's not true, since you're all equal," reflected le Rempart.

The other continued: "You've had good luck in running into me—there are some who can't say anything at all. All the same, there are a good twenty with whom one can chat."

"Damn!" muttered Binaire. "It must be fun if they all let go at once."

"But the executive power," the doctor persisted, "what does he execute?"

"He represents his brothers," said the other, majestically, "and ensures obedience to the decisions of the parliamentary Assembly."

"There's a parliament!" said the doctor, with horror. "Who composes it?"

"Everyone. There's no reason for some to direct all the others. We're all our government. Naturally, the women sit too; they're our equals. The Parliament Hall is the most beautiful in the Communal House. There's a session every evening. Everyone speaks in it for the same number of minutes and possesses the same authority. Everyone here is the equal of every other. Everyone works in the same fashion and does the same work at the same time, in accordance with the decision made by the government. Everyone eats the same thing at the same time in the same quantity in the communal refectory. Everyone sleeps in the communal dormitory for the same number of hours as his neighbor, in a similar bed. Everyone amuses himself in the same fashion, at the same time.

"Everything is regulated. There is no longer any personal will. There is no longer any superiority of any sort. There are no more weak, condemned to iniquitous oppression. There is now only an equalized median. There's now only justice, life for all, the total and complete unification of the conditions of existence. The tyranny of the strong, the rich and the powerful has ceased, since there are no longer any strong, and rich or powerful. The individual no longer acts for himself and by himself; the mass acts for the mass. The individual has disappeared. Collective society is everything."

"Damn!" said Pingouin.

"There is no more God," said the other. "There are no longer any prejudices, by means of which the greater number were too long maintained in irons for the benefit of a vicious, cruel, despicable and oppressive minority."

"And what abut liberty?" asked the doctor.

"Liberty is integral, since everyone does what everyone has decided to do. We have thus leveled unjust superiorities and established the primordial and imprescriptible right to life that every being acquires in coming into the world."

"Very good," said the doctor. "There's perfect agreement in your Parliament, then?"

"No, there's an opposition. It's composed of twelve members, periodically renewed. The have the mission of combating the decrees adopted and refusing their confidence in the rest of the members, who are required to agree."

"Impressive," remarked the doctor. "You form a very interesting nation."

"A nation!" said Twenty-Nine, indignantly. "What blasphemy! We open our bosom indiscriminately to all the citizens of the entire world who want to experience the joy of being free and equal,"

"And outside of the...how shall I put it?...governmental opposition," said the doctor, "there's never any grave dissent?"

"Oh, yes—then we argue. The majority always want to reduce the number of hours of work and the opposition doesn't oppose it sufficiently. Some time ago, it was reduced to twenty minutes a day. That wasn't sufficient. We were dying of starvation. There was a violent movement and the work time was increased to four and a half hours. There was a furious battle in Parliament. Fortunately the public man in service had been a wine-merchant and the manager of a hall of electoral meetings. He was used to it and extinguished the lights. In the dark, things calmed down, and the deliberations were continued the next day."

"Very, very curious," said the doctor. "This Babouvist[9] system has my complete approval. But what about invalids? What do you do with them?"

"Everyone has the right to one and a half days of illness per month. That's the mean supplied by our statistics. On that day, he does nothing and is cared for. One also has the right to get drunk once a week. There's a coupon for that."

"What about marriages?"

"No one marries any longer. That question astonishes me, Citizen. There's no reason for equal men and women to have different conjuncts. Then again, to have a conjunct is to have property. Now, property is theft. The same reasoning applied to everything else."

"We'll come to that," said the doctor. "Let's settle the question of marriage first. What do you do? Free union?"

"Certainly not! What mores! A pox on that! What about equality? No, no, no more personal choice! No more unjust and egotistical inclinations, no more jealousy, adultery, vice, immorality and depravity. We've got rid of all that. Every man or woman receives one reproduction coupon per week, bearing a number determined by lot. There are two draws, producing two parallel series of numbers. With that coupon, everyone has the right, for one designated night, similarly determined by lot, to the person bearing the corresponding number.

"Thus is accomplished, anonymously, the great work of conservation of the species, which is the one thing that can excuse those practices. I have no need to tell you, Citizen, that there is one series of male numbers and one of female numbers."

"Yes, confusions could lead to awkward results," said the doctor.

"So," the other continued, "everything is for the best. The thing takes place in the house of reproduction, which you can see there on the right. The two corresponding numbers evidently go

9. *Babouvistes* were followers of François-Emile Babeuf (1760-1797), a radical communist Revolutionary condemned to death for conspiring against the Directoire.

to different individuals every time. The women go more often than the men because there are fewer of them. We haven't been able to remedy that small inequality between the sexes, but it's slight. Naturally, it's forbidden to surrender or exchange one's number. Thus, a rotation is established....."

"Oh!" said the prudish fireman, blushing.

"Admirable," said the doctor. "And the children?"

"The children? Obviously, they're liberated from abusive parental authority. The children are all brought up together without knowing their parents, who don't know them. They only know their civic duty. They're the offspring of society. All the women take turns to look after them. That way, the unfortunate tendency to individualism to which the family gives birth is avoided. The ignoble sentiment that encourages an individual to deprive one's neighbor in order to enrich one's own child is also cut off at the root. One's child! Property again!"

"Oh yes," said the doctor. "To whom, then, do the land, the crops, the tools, the provisions and everything else belong, then?"

"To everyone, naturally," Twenty-Nine replied, proudly.

"And of what can each individual dispose?"

"Of nothing, since everything belongs to everyone."

"Precious for everyone...and who among you was the architect of these...interesting monuments?" The doctor pointed to the mud houses.

"You're attempting mockery, Citizen," replied 29, with dignity and scorn. "I see that you still have the vain prejudices of luxury and decoration. These houses are made to shelter us from cold and rain; they fulfill that function sufficiently; one cannot ask for more. Quests for elegance are the actions of societies spoiled by capitalism and rolling down the slope of decadence. We form a new world, denuded of prejudices, denuded of weaknesses and denuded of refinements. Art and luxury are useless, and unjust, since not everyone possesses them to the same degree—superiority for some, since the unequal beauty is exalted that we have succeeded in abolishing by means of a perfect community of life and a continual admixture of individuals for reproduction. We want nothing more than to repeal tyranny and despotism, the odious past of suffering, misery and oppression. Before us, there was nothing. Such is our will. We refuse to collect the vestiges of ages disappeared into their mire.

"After a shipwreck, a crate of paintings ran aground on our shore. They were ignobly magnificent. Can one nourish oneself on a painting? So the colony, gathered in solemn parliamentary Assembly, decided to consecrate those odious products of corrupt civilizations to the proclamation of Truth and Justice. Those paintings, sown together—here they are—make up the strip on which our declaration of principle covers up the immoral subjects that detestable inutility had spent years perfecting, instead of working for its peers."

"Damn!" said Pingouin.

"The frames were burned," Man 29 continued, talking to the doctor. "That explains the virtuous simplicity of these constructions that you mocked. They are more beautiful because they are useful."

"Personally, I don't think they're that bad," murmured the naïve Zafolin. "They resemble barracks."

The islander heard and jumped. "Barracks! Barracks! Wretch, are you a vile partisan of praetorian tyranny? Barracks! But that implies an army! An army, do you understand? An army! For educated men to kill their fellows—the abomination of barbarity!"

"Well, yes," murmured Zafolin, intimidated. "All the same, if you have a war...."

"War!" Man 29 laughed uproariously. "War, here? It would be quite impossible, since we have no army, since we will never have one...." He was triumphant.

The fireman, bewildered by this bilateral reasoning, withdrew from the conversation, but he murmured: "All the same, he has funny ideas, this chap. Even if one got rid of firemen, that wouldn't prevent fires...."

Meanwhile, the doctor asked: "And you've never had any

criminals in your Golden Age?"

"Unfortunately, yes." Man 29's face darkened. "Five of us have had to be condemned to forced labor."

"Well, you all are," remarked Binaire, as an aside.

Without hearing, Twenty-Nine continued: "Two are oarsmen in the launch that we use to cross a little bay to the west. The others...."

"Well?" said the doctor.

"There is one man and two women. One of the women fled with the man, who was already her accomplice. They're in the woods. The man is a woodcutter and fisherman. He furnishes us with wood and fish in exchange for other things."

"And what had the woman done?" asked the doctor.

"Oh, she was a great malefactor. She refused to participate in the allocation of the reproduction coupons and their consequences. She refused to...meet...the number designated by chance as the correspondent of her number, under the pretext that she loved the young man who fled with her. He didn't want to take our side...he was an insurgent against liberty, and wanted to do as he pleased. He was dangerous and intelligent. Intelligence is the death of Equality. He defended the young woman and threatened us with his ax. Then they were let alone, but they were deprived of their rights as citizens and could no longer take part in the Parliament—which is a terrible sanction."

"I should think so," said the doctor. "And the other woman?"

"She had a child and wanted to keep it. Naturally, it was taken from her, for it's necessary to do the best for people whether they like it or not. To destroy the woman's evil sentiments, she was condemned after a time to care for all the children of the colony. By that means, we hoped to annihilate her egotistical affection by dispersing it. Unfortunately, after three days, she believed that she had recognized her son and ran away, taking him with her. Afterwards, she came back, saying that she believed that she had made a mistake and wanted to take her real child. She was very excited and threatened to kill us all. We had difficulty getting rid of her. The woodcutter took her in, but she still prowls around, demanding to have her child, whom no one can recognize. She's gone completely mad."

"Damn!" said Pingouin.

"Let's hear about the oarsmen of the launch," said the doctor.

"One is an infamous reactionary. He demanded a pair of trousers larger than other people's, under the pretext that he was fatter. Naturally, they weren't given to him. All our garments are tailored to a median model. There's no reason for some to use more cloth than others, since everyone manufactures the same quantity."

I couldn't help interrupting islander 29. "But by doing more work," I said, "doesn't one have the right...."

He looked at me scornfully. "One can't do more work—that would be unjust, since all men are equal. The wretch knew that very well, and his request for trousers had no other objective but to excite an uprising and the advent of a monarchical restoration."

"Naturally, since not to have trousers and to want them is Royalist," reflected le Rempart.[10]

"As for the fourth"—Twenty-Nine's voice changed—"I can't talk about him without weeping. He was an apostle when we knew him. He was the one who taught us to think and speak. 'You're my equals,' he said. 'Hazard has permitted me to know more than you, and I want to inculcate you with my knowledge.' And he taught us the principles of Justice, Dignity and Truth. He made us what we are.

"Before that, we were a rabble with neither self-control nor liberty. Now...see for yourselves! He's the one who taught us the integral value of the great word Equality. Well, that mind radiant with Light and Truth has succumbed to the most fatal errors. He wanted to betray his brothers. He refused to follow them on the path of progress.

"What insensate desires drove him? Was he dreaming of

10. Le Rempart's sarcasm is based on the fact that the Revolutionary mobs of the 1789 Revolution were known as *sans culottes*.

dictatorship? I don't know, but an accursed day came when, in full parliamentary Assembly, he told us that we were going too far, that we were becoming tyrants to one another, and that there was no absolute equality, and that liberty was doing what one wanted, without hindering the liberty of one's neighbor. He beat his breast, accusing himself of having caused our misfortune and of having rendered us stupid. We were so indignant—especially because he had spoken for longer than his allotted number of minutes, the first step toward tyranny—that we leapt upon him to demand that he shut up. He continued shouting, begging us to forgive him and saying that he was ready for martyrdom. We were obliged to send him to the galleys, in the launch."

"Well done," said Pingouin. "He was the responsible author."

"We've tried to give them amnesty several times," Twenty-Nine continued, "and set them free if they would submit, take their places in Parliament and the delightful exercise of their civil rights, but they've hardened in their criminality. The wood-cutter threatens to kill us with is ax if anyone talks to the young woman who lives with him about reproduction coupons and numbers drawn by lot. The reactionary would like to reenter society, but he never ceases to demand ever-larger trousers. As for the other, he refuses to see us, and has doubtless gone mad, for he constantly repeats: 'The foremost of liberties is the freedom not to be free,' which is incomprehensible."

"He must be a fool," said le Rempart.

"No one is a fool," said the Man. "All men are equal."

"Damn it," said Pingouin, "you're more stupid than nature! Go fetch me an inkwell, or I'll kill you."

Le Rempart seized the arm of the astounded 29 in his iron hand. "You're my equal," he cried, "but that doesn't prevent you from obeying M'sieu Pingouin—or else I'll flatten you like a bug!"

The inkwell was fetched. Coco, climbing one of the masts, had brought down the inscription strip, and, on the captain's orders, I modified it, putting:

ALL MEN ARE BORN AND REMAIN UNEQUAL

We put it up again.

"Now," said Pingouin to Man Twenty-Nine, "tell me your real name. You number disgusts me."

"Du...Durand," replied the other, his teeth chattering.

"Ah! Well, Durand, summon your imbecile companions."

Monsieur Durand, full of terror, blew three times into a kind of hunting horn, extracting the frightful sounds therefrom that we had already heard.

Soon, we saw the islanders coming.

"Go to them; have them assemble in front of me, and tell them to shut up or I'll shoot them," Pingouin ordered.

Durand 29 obeyed, and the others too. They were rather ugly and dirty. A uniform appearance of brutishness gave them a sort of family resemblance. Their clothes were brown sackcloth. The thinnest were floating therein like fish in a creel, the biggest seemed to be wearing swaddling-clothes.

Frightened by our rifles, astonished by the stature of le Rempart, who was juggling with his piston-rod, and tamed instantaneously by the gaze of Julius Pingouin, they gathered silently before us.

Pingouin stood on a boulder and spoke.

"Imbeciles," he said, "look at that inscription. I've modified it in accordance with the Truth. Think about it, such as it is, if your brains are still capable of thinking about anything.

"I could have you slaughtered or shot, but you're more to be pitied than blamed. What it's necessary to change isn't so much the conditions of life as your envious hearts. I advise you to cut off the head, in spite of his repentance, of the man who has filled you full of the nonsense on which you've based your rules of life. I advise you to have yourselves directed by the wood-cutter, who seems to me to me rational. It's necessary to cease the obscenities of your house of reproduction and leave children with their parents, and everyone to the place that suits him. It would be desirable, above all, for you to love one another, but that's impossible.

"I'm going away; I've seen enough. I've said enough to bring you back to life and liberty, if that's still feasible. You need someone to govern you with kicks up the backside—Coco, for example."

"Good Massa, me not want to!" aid Coco, terrified.

"But he doesn't want to, and anyway, I'd rather keep him with me," Pingouin went on. "I'm going away. I'll call in again in a few months, and if things aren't any better, I'll shoot a few of you."

We departed in an orderly manner, leaving consternation behind us. Coco was intoxicated by fear.

We rejoined the *Argonaut* and now, at nine o'clock in the evening, we're sailing freely toward the Future, Hope and the Golden Fleece.

4 December. Splendid weather. Good progress.

Nothing new, except that Coco kept us awake half the night with the frightful howls he uttered in the course of a nightmare. He thought he was the king of the people of the island. He struggled, shouting: "Good Massa, good Massa, me prefer go to guillotine. Me good negro. Not want that stuff!"

We calmed him down, not without difficulty, with orange-flavored sugar-water, of which he drank a liter. This morning, he is still very sad.

5 December. Nothing.

6 December. Violent scene today. It appears that Monsieur Flaum has attracted the enmity of the stoker Cristallin. At about noon, the latter emerged from the engine room and ran into the kitchen. He armed himself with a knife and threw another at the feet of the fat Swiss, crying: "Wretch! I've suffered enough. The time for action has come. Defend your life, and let's dispute the love of Zoé Nèfle like brave men."

The man, settled until then, must have conceived, during

the hours of his ardent labor, a furious passion for the worthy vegetable-seller. The latter not having responded to his flame, he thought he had discovered the reason for her insensibility in her love for the cook.

The latter was terrified. "M'sieu, M'sieu," he cried, trotting back and forth, to the extent that his corpulence permitted, and pursued by the stoker, drunk with rage, "You're crazy! I haven't paid court to Ma'am Nèfle. I have pure morals!"

Cristallin had already seized him, though. Le Rempart, arriving just in time, lifted him up at arm's length, and prevented any mishap. At the same time, Zoé Nèfle intervened energetically.

"My lad," she said to Cristallin, "You need to muzzle your sentiments. You'll do me the favor of returning to your furnaces, in double quick time. It's you who's getting hot under the collar. One isn't jealous of a simpleton like that, and one doesn't compromise an honest woman when one doesn't have any rights over her. If you think that's the means to please me more, you're mistaken. It mustn't happen again, or else I'll talk to the captain about it. I've never seen anything like it!"

And she went away, in a dignified manner, leaving behind the calm induced by the respected name of Captain Pingouin.

"I believe she has a soft spot for me," the undertaker's boy Binaire confided to me, whispering in my ear. "She's a fine figure of a woman!"

Then he turned to Zafolin and doubtless whispered a few light remarks to him, for the chaste fireman drew away, blushing.

The incident was closed, and no one mentioned it to Captain Pingouin, because he doesn't like intestinal disputes.

7 December. Bad news. We're almost out of water. We noticed it this morning. In all probability, it must have leaked out during the tempest five days ago. It's inconceivable that the cook, who's job it is, didn't notice it sooner. The captain has admonished him severely. The Swiss claims that he checked it several times and that all was well. That's quite probable, for he's very regular in his service and no one has anything but praise for him. It's a mystery.

At any rate, it's now necessary for us to land somewhere to renew our supplies. We ought not to be very far from land, and that's fortunate, for the water that remains is scarcely sufficient for two or three days. Bouture claims that we'll be able to disembark tomorrow. He knows this region very well because he's sailed here before.

Same day, six o'clock. Coco has signaled the coast. Bouture affirms that he knows it perfectly. He's steering us toward a little sheltered bay. A lake of fresh water is, it appears, a few miles inland toward the west, and frequently serves to renew the supplies of whaling ships that pass this way. That's how our pilot is able to know how things lie. He's a valuable man and I think that our suspicions against him were ill-founded.

8 December. We're at anchor, off a verdant coast. Hills rise up a short distance away. The lake is in their valley, two hours march due west. The place is deserted and located an immense distance away from any habitation.

The two launches have put to sea, laden with empty barrels and a wheeled hurdle for transporting them, Nine of us will take our places therein, to wit: Julius Pingouin; me, le Homard; the Reverend; the Doctor; Coco; the Fireman; Binaire; le Rempart; and Bayados. The last two are discussing politics in low voices.

Bouture, Flaum, Cristallin and Zoé Nèfle are guarding the ship.

Same date, 9 p.m. We're back—those of us who have come back. I shall never forget this day.

When we disembarked this morning on the coast to which Bouture had guided us, our hearts were full of the joy of life. The land was beautiful and fertile. Between the tall and magnificent trees that sheltered us from the sun's rays, an almost-beaten track led westwards. We followed it, gaily towing our hurdle laden with empty barrels and a few provisions.

The walk wasn't tiring, and when we reached the lake we were able to admire a delightful location. We were in a valley entirely surrounded by verdant hills, the only exit from which was the path we'd just traveled. There was a waterfall descending from the east and pouring into the lake, from which a little river escaped, snaking toward the coast. The lake water was very pure. Birds were flying overhead and it was surrounded by large trees.

Coco seemed very enthusiastic. "Coconuts like coconuts at home!" he cried. "This Coco's land! Coco glad!"

"The works of Providence are comfortably admirable," observed Pastor Tantsticktor, and took out his clarinet.

We had filled out barrels and eaten a meal; it was hot.

"We can take a nap," said Pingouin, "but we need a sentinel."

"Coco will watch," the negro proposed, hastily.

Unfortunately for us, we accepted his offer. Five minutes later, we were fast asleep in the grass. I was woken up abruptly by something stinging my nose. It was a mosquito. I looked around vaguely ready to go back to sleep, but in an instant I was on my feet.

"To arms!" I shouted.

I saw a numerous troop of customs men silently crossing the river to bar our route.

Coco had disappeared, doubtless carried away by his passion for coconuts.

My companions were on their feet in an instant.

Pingouin took stock of the situation at a glance. It wasn't brilliant. Behind us we had the lake; to the right, the almost-impenetrable forest; to the left, the hill; in front of us, liberty—and the customs men barring the route.

"It's serious," said Pingouin. "Too bad—we'll have to leave the barrels. Into the forest!"

We were about to run. Futile. Green uniforms also appeared to the right, surrounding us.

"We're doomed," said Pingouin. "There are at least a hundred and fifty."

"It's that camel Bouture," said le Rempart. He's led us here and tipped them off with his dirty stars. If I could get hold of him! Coco's left us in the lurch—I wouldn't have believed that! Fortunately, I have my piston-rod." And he brandished his iron bar, from which he was never separated.

Meanwhile, the customs men had called a halt. We were in tight formation, rifles shouldered. A negotiator—an officer—emerged from the enemy ranks. He was waving a white flag.

"We need to see what they want," said Pingouin. He lowered his voice. "But listen, Homard—I have the map stitched into a pouch hung round my neck, under my jacket. If I die and you can get to it, try to take it and go on without me."

"Without you! Oh, no, what an idea!" I replied, completely flabbergasted.

"Yes, you have to go. Try to succeed. You have to find the Golden Fleece, no matter what. I'd have loved to go, though, damn it! Anyway, think about the map. I was wrong to bring it—I should have left it on the ship...."

"Meanwhile, the customs negotiator started to shout at us. He made a speech about duty, the horror of rebellion, the mercy of the government. He told us that we mustn't think about defending ourselves. He finished by telling us that we were wanted all over the world and condemned to death as pirates, but he proposed to us, to avoid bloodshed, that he would set us free is we consented to surrender out captain, Julius Pingouin, to him.

"Go to hell!" I shouted.

"The camel!" groaned le Rempart. "If I could get my hands on him...."

Pingouin reflected briefly, and then said to us. "I don't have the right to get you all killed for me. I'm going to give myself up."

"I'll go with you. I'd rather die than leave you, M'sieur Pingouin," le Rempart retorted.

"I'll blow the brains out of the first man that moves," I

declared.

"Come on, Pinguoin, it's not that serious," said the doctor, reproachfully.

"One doesn't ask that of men like us," declare Binaire.

And all the others thought the same.

"We refuse, you son of an ape, you dirty aquatic cop!" howled le Rempart. "And if you were closer, I'd teach you to insult folk, by spitting in your dirty face!"

"Very well," said the officer, red with anger. "We'll finish it."

But then, Pastor Gustav J. K. S. Heysbergeh Tantsticktor elbowed us aside and showed himself in front of us. He was waving his handkerchief. He walked bare-headed, calmly, in the blazing sun. His black garments hung down around him and his blond hair was thrown backwards. He stopped and talked to the customs men.

"Very honorific Military men," he said, "it must not be, for it isn't just. Here you are, much more than a hundred in number, and there are only eight of them. They hadn't done anything before the first attack, back then, to excite it. And then, the man you want to be given up, in one who measures up to the most ancient.

"Remember that the bloodshed will be held against your descendants, and that you will one day stand before the great Lord, who is terrible in his fury. And before him, there will be no badges of rank, nor honors, nor lies, nor prevarications, nor excuses—nothing but your own souls, unclad and in veritable nudity. So, I say this, loudly: Withdraw and let them go on with their occupation without being massacred...."

Thus he spoke—but then, in the ranks of the customs men, some brute who deserved to be burned alive fired on Pastor Tantsticktor and hit him full in the chest. The pastor spun around and fell, crying: "Lord, great Lord, I'm dying!" He made one last twitch, and expired.

"Murderers!" howled le Rempart, and fired his rifle.

"Get down," commanded Pingouin, "and then fire! And forward ho, emptying your guns!"

The volley fired by the customs men passed over our heads, but we were already firing and we were on them. Under our furious pressure, their troop opened up in order to close again and surround us.

Dull thuds were heard, with the groans of the dead and dying. The customs men, all around us, went down like mown grass. I killed twenty myself; le Rempart could count his victims in dozens, and Binaire, the undertaker's mute, excessively cheerful, fought like a tiger. Bayados and the fireman were methodical in destruction, and the doctor remained calm and terrible with his tall stature, his gray hair and his rifle, which he whirled relentlessly, a murderous club. As for Pingouin, he was no longer one man—the ranks of the customs men went down under his assault like ears of corn trampled by a wild boar.

"Forward ho!" he howled. "We're coming through!"

We were, indeed, coming through. Already, between us and the path to freedom there were no more than a handful of men, ready to flee. The rest of the troop, in rear, could not catch up with us, so rapid was our movement, and none of ours had fallen yet. But then, on the path itself, a new enemy troop arrived, at the double, at least a hundred strong. They were on us in an instant. Then, we could see nothing ahead of us but death. We marched to meet it, wanting to increase the number of specters preceding us to the somber edge at ever step. The carnage we created was immeasurable. Every one of us was a killing machine. Pingouin was indescribable. I felt the strength of a multitude in my arm. Le Rempart, covered in blood, taking a stand where the customs men were most numerous, was fighting with the force of an element. His iron bar, in his frightful hand, was whirling around him with a sinister whine, sowing death. But he always had further adversaries.

"When there are no more of them, yet more arrive," the worthy fellow said to me, with tears of rage, at a moment when, behind a pile of cadavers, and covering the doctor, who had been knocked down, we saw a new detachment of adversaries falling upon us. "What I regret, is not being able to pay Bouture back before dying…and aieee!"

And the iron bar slew three of them at a stroke.

Meanwhile, the brave Binaire, having made an immense hecatomb, fell, struck dead, on the body of the fireman Zajolin, pierced by bullets. Pingouin had gone down three times and got up again three times, with blood streaming down his forehead. I received a saber-thrust in the shoulder. We were beginning to tire. The enemy troops were still being renewed.

"There are too many," said Julius Pingoin. "It's the end."

But then, all of a sudden, a terrible howling went up from the woods, and a host of black demons armed with clubs spring forth. At their head raced Coco. They attacked our adversaries furiously, massacring them joyfully.

The customs men, taken by surprise, overwhelmed and terrified, hesitated, and then broke ranks, trying to flee—but the negroes surrounded them, herded them together and cut them down. And we, installed in the very heart of their troop, found new strength. Then the carnage began.

"Mercy! Pity!" howled the vanquished, throwing down their weapons—but we had no pity and we labored without saying a word. When there were no more of them, we stopped, weary and covered in blood.

Coco, well content, came up to Pingouin.

"Good Massa," he said, "you satisfied! Me found friends in great wood and have brought them to defend good Masssa and get booty. Them, dirty beasts"—he indicated the prostrate customs men—"shouldn't have made Coco mad."

Meanwhile, we were washing ourselves in the lake. The water was red with blood. The doctor, recovered from the blow that had stunned him, bandaged our wounds, which were slight.

By then, the negroes had stripped the dead and the wounded. The groans of the latter mingled with the sound of the breeze in the foliage. They were naked and bloody, and the victors were crucifying them.

"No," said Pingouin to Coco," don't make them suffer needlessly."

After that, the negroes were content to cut off their heads.

"Negroes very obedient," Coco told me, "and very brave men. Me have told them good Massa Pingouin be Good God and you great saints.…"

The captain brought us together, in a hurry to leave that place, previously so beautiful, which now resembled some kind of abattoir. We realized then the absence of the engineer Bayados. After searching, we found him, scarcely breathing, under a pile of corpses. The doctor examined his wounds, with a grimace that was a bad augury.

"Well?" said Pingouin.

"Finished," was the doctor's only response.

We were ready to leave, but Coco did not seem disposed to accompany us.

"Good Massa," he said to Pingouin, "good friend negroes have named Coco emperor for military genius. He will found fine dynasty with little women has found. He like better than being emperor of white idiots on island. And Coco not care about Golden Fleece. He not know that. He like better loafing under coconut palms."

"You're going to leave us, then?"

"Yes," said Coco. "Coco like good Massa very much, but cannot disappoint friends by not being emperor, and not want to be emperor of white idiots. Coco will give good Massa six negroes to pull water-carriage, carry Massa Bayados and row launch and go search for Golden Fleece in his place. They need kicks up backside to make work, bit drunk, but good negroes."

We bid him adieu and left. Three negroes provided by Coco pulled the hurdle laden with barrels of water.

"We'll go find Bouture," le Rempart said to me, with a ferocious smile. "Well, M'sieu le Homard, are you convinced that he really is a spy for the Jews?"

"No, the Jesuits," murmured the dying Bayados, carried by the negroes.

"It makes no difference," said le Rempart. "There's an account to settle. I'm disfigured—he has to pay."

Pingouin remained somber.

We reached the launch. Soon, we were aboard the *Argonaut*. There, an unexpected spectacle awaited us, for the pilot Bouture was lying on a bench, tied up. Old Cristallin was standing guard over him, while playing cards with Zoé Nèfle. The stoker told us that, shortly after our departure, the pilot hard ordered him to make ready to take the boat elsewhere, claiming that it was the captain's order. When the stoker refused, he had insisted, and had finally attempted to corrupt him with offers of money. Then Cristallin, aided by Zoé Nèfle, had knocked him down and tied him up.

When the traitor saw us again, there was rage and fear on his face, but he remained calm.

Dusk was falling; we were all on the bridge except Bayados, who was dying in the cabin. There was no wind; the sea was tranquil and we could hear his groans.

Julius Pingouin had the pilot untied.

"Pilot Bouture," he said, "you're a traitor."

"I'm a traitor," said Bouture. "Kill me."

"Yes," said Pingouin. "Men have died. You must die."

"It's all the same to me," said Bouture. "Fifty times I've risked my life for the reward I was offered to deliver you. I regret that the coup went awry, that's all, but someone else will succeed. You'll never get there. The entire world is against you. You'll all die, and I'm glad."

The captain drew his revolver. "Are you ready?" he asked.

"Pingouin!" said the doctor, grabbing his arm.

"Let me go," said the captain. "It has to be done. The man is a traitor."

And he blew his brains out.

"Throw him overboard," said Julius Pingouin, stepping over the cadaver. He went down to his cabin.

We obeyed. The sharks that were circling around the ship shared the corpse.

Now it's ten o'clock in the evening. I'm at the tiller and alone on the deck. The night is stormy and livid. The ship is going at top speed, and I can still hear Bayados' groans as he finishes dying. My wound hurts. I think I'm getting a fever. I'm looking at the sea. Expectant sharks are swimming in our wake. There's a heavy swell and every wave resembles an open sepulcher from which a specter rises up momentarily and then falls back, while the lid closes. I've never seen that before, and I remember old seamen telling me that it's an omen of death. I'm thinking about Bouture's last words: *You'll never get there. You'll all die, and I'm glad.* I'm thinking about all those of us who've disappeared—especially the Man in Yellow, who has perished mysteriously, and whose tomb is somewhere in the Ocean. Above all, I'm obsessed by the idea of what's down below, next to the dying man, tugging at his soul with its arm, to take it I don't know where...now I'm afraid of being alone like this. I'm curling up, my teeth are chattering; I have a mortal sweat on my forehead, and I'd prefer anything at all to the desperate terror that's twisting my heart and taking away the strength to move....

But suddenly, by my side, here's Julius Pingouin, He places his hand on my shoulder and says: "I'm here."

Down below, the groaning stops. The man is dead.

9 December. We're all feeling well and full of courage this morning. Far from depressing us, the frightful events of yesterday have given us new strength, by virtue of the magnitude of the perils overcome and the almost miraculous fashion in which we triumphed. I certainly owe my present energy to Julius Pingouin. Perhaps it's the same for my companions. We're terribly diminished, though.

Of the seventeen we numbered at our departure, only seven remain, to wit: Julius Pingouin, captain; me, le Homard, lieutenant; Dr. Saturnin Plair; Hippolyte, alias le Rempart du Quartier Rouge; the stoker Cristallin; Flaum the cook and the worthy Zoé Nèfle, who loves us all like her children and is truly first-rate. I add the six negroes given to us by Coco; they, unfortunately, can't yet be of much use to us. We employ them as stokers, occasionally as oarsmen, and one of them takes the helm; Pingouin or I relieve him when necessary. They're good fellows, and cheerful, but, as Coco said, rather idle and a trifle greedy.

There's also reason to fear, I ought to report, that we might not have the cook Flaum among us for much longer. The poor fat man is very ill. He's vomiting and choking in an alarming manner. The other day, at the moment when the traitor Bouture died, he fainted because of weakness and emotion. This morning, as he went past me, jaundiced and dragging his collapsed belly, I asked: "Aren't you feeling very well?"

"No, M'sieur le Homard," he said, sadly. "I'm very poorly. I'm going down below decks. I'm going to die, I think. What a pity! I'd rather have found the Golden Fleece with you and Captain Pingouin!"

"Come on, be brave!" I said.

"Yes, I am—but that can't keep alive someone who's going!"

And the poor fat fellow went back down.

10 December. About midday we crossed the path of a big ship that sent us signals. Pingouin replied. They gave us two items of news that are making a stir in the world and they thought we wouldn't know—which was true.

We read:

One: *New world cycling champion is Mémorin. Beat Croisillon by thirty centimeters over course of twenty-five days.*

Two: *President of Republic assassinated by blow of hammer from Republican butcher.*

"I'm going mad," said Pingouin, putting away his binoculars.

Thank you, he signaled. *All well aboard.*

We continued on our way. The *Argonaut* is making good progress. The weather is fine, but our provisions are beginning to run singularly low and we'll soon have to think about renewing them. The extreme Port International is nearly four days away by sea. We're going to land there, with appropriate precautions, and we'll get what we need there. Then it will simply be a matter of going forward. We'll quit the confines of the inhabited world to enter into the unknown, but we have Julius Pingouin and a map.

On that subject, the captain summoned me to his cabin today.

"Homard," he said to me, "I've resolved, after the episode the other day, to leave the map here. To have it on me is dangerous, so I've put it in this little strong-box that's set in the wall. It'll be safe there. To get at it, it would be necessary to demolish the ship—and then again, there's only you and the doctor who know it's there. If anything happens to me, you'll be able to find it. It's necessary that something like that doesn't disappear with one man. The combination to open the lock is 318—the number we had on the Bateaux-Mouches. The catch is underneath to the left.

"Now, let's talk about something else. You know that it's absolutely necessary to lay in provisions, I've thought about it; it's easy enough to call in at Port International, but they know we're somewhere around here, after the last battle. There must be the devil of a lot of police watching for ships. Perhaps it would be better to attack a merchant ship and take what we need. I know it's not very sporting, but in truth, when one has a goal...what do you think?"

At this point the doctor's voice summoned us up above. He had just captured a carrier pigeon that had landed, exhausted, on the deck of the *Argonaut*. The pigeon was carrying the following letter, written in clear on India paper.

Commander of the cruiser Destruction *to His Excellency the Governor of Port International.*

In accordance with Your Excellency's orders, we have sailed to the coast in the waters in which the pirate Julius Pingouin and his ship ought to be found. Disembarking without having been able to discover anything abnormal, we learned from the very mouth of the negro emperor Coco I, the native sovereign of the region, of the recent complete destruction of Julius

Pingouin's company and the death of the pirate himself, slain by the hand of Coco I personally, who had attacked him with his men. We have been able to see, displayed in the sovereign's palace, according to the custom, the heads of Julius Pingouin's principal accomplices, and his own, which we identified with the aid of the descriptions given to us.

The black potentate declared that he had burned the pirate ship Argonaut. *The men who had remained aboard perished there, except for two who had miraculously escaped, who were put into out hands. By virtue of the maritime code, and in spite of the subterfuges which they employed, claiming to be soldiers of the customs and the sole survivors of a troop sent against the pirate and destroyed by him, we had them hanged from our yard-arm.*

In spite of all our research, we have been unable to learn anything whatsoever about the map that Pingouin was said to possess. Either this document disappeared with the ship, or it never existed, and, as is quite probable, the expedition was nothing but a simple enterprise of piracy.

In these circumstances, we thought it our duty to give Coco I the sum of twenty-five thousand francs on gold promised to the man who put an end to the famous pirate and his expedition, a sum for which the monarchy gave us a regular receipt.

We remain Your Excellency's devoted servant.

Signed: *Commander Warrus.*

"Very, very curious," said the doctor. "This Commander Warrus seems to me to be endowed with an uncommon perspicacity and a most enlightened critical mind. His opinion with regard to the map that never existed is particularly ingenious."

"It's Coco who's the ingenious one," remarked le Rempart. "What a neat trick. He good negro, he have good head on shoulders...."

"He's very nearly saved our lives," said Pingouin. "Now we can land in the port in complete safety. We'll let the pigeon rest;

tomorrow morning, we'll release it, and it'll arrive a day and half ahead of us. That's what we need. We'll only have to stick a strip on the stern to change the name of the ship.

"Le Homard will become Captain Litière, Commandant of the *Albatros*—that's the old name of the *Argonaut*, and I've still got the papers...."

"Then, neither seen nor known!" exclaimed le Rempart. "One has a new skin, since one's dead. That's not bad, damn it!"

Meanwhile, the captain went back down to his cabin with the doctor.

"That," le Rempart said to me, "is a king among men; one would have oneself chopped for him. There aren't two like him. He always knows what to do. He knows everything. He's better than Christopher Columbus, who discovered America by standing an egg on its end...."

11 December. All well aboard. Nothing particular to report, except that poor Flaum is getting sicker every day. This morning, he was found unconscious, with his head in a saucepan. The doctor did his best to cheer him up, but he hasn't succeeded in identifying the malady he has, and thinks that the sea air is pernicious to him.

12 December 9 a.m. We've released the carrier pigeon. It took off and immediately flew in the direction of the international port. The *Argonaut* has become the *Albatros*. The captain has had it scrubbed from top to bottom by the negroes and the woodwork of the deck repainted. It no longer looks the same. The ship's papers are ready. Officially, I'm Arsène Litière, commandant of the *Albatros*. We'll doubtless sight land tomorrow morning.

Same day, 6 o'clock. We've just sighted a big merchant ship, with which we exchanged signals. Nothing in particular learned.

13 December. Exactly a month since we set out. To celebrate the anniversary, we supped a little more sumptuously than usual.

Over dessert, Dr. Saturnin made a toast to the health of Julius Pingouin. In his turn, Julius Pingouin made a toast to the crew of the *Argonaut*.

"Comrades," he said, "I raise my glass to you. You're brave men. Death has taken many among us. I salute them, especially Pastor Tantsticktor, who showed us a sublime example. Those who are dead are at rest, we may believe, but we who are alive must fight. The hardest part is still to come, for, after our port of call, it will no longer be men with whom we have to do battle but the unknown. It makes no difference; we shall arrive, be sure of that, and we shall triumph. I have confidence in you; have confidence in me."

14 December. We think the port will be in sight before nightfall, but it's now nine o'clock and there's nothing new.

15 December, 5 a.m. We've just dropped anchor at Port International. I'll pass over the tedious formalities, administrative and otherwise, by which the liberty of everyone to go anywhere is impeded. There were no hitches.

At eight o'clock Pingouin left in the small launch to make arrangements for the provisions. He took le Rempart and two negro oarsmen. Pingouin would like to finish it today and leave tomorrow.

11.30 a.m., same day. I no longer know where I am. Shortly after Pingouin's departure, as we were going tranquilly about our business, an individual brought by a boat rowed by two Malays irrupted on to out ship. He fell upon the doctor, who was reading a newspaper, and in the blink of an eye, compelled him to listen to him.

"Illustrious Monsieur," he said to him, "Knowledgeable voyager, enviable proprietor of this seductive pleasure-yacht, of which I also salute the valiant captain"—that was for me—"permit your humble servant to lay his homage at your feet."

For a moment, he looked fixedly at the doctor, and then continued, without anyone being able to interrupt him: "You're from my homeland, magnanimous man. Yes, I'm sure of it; I know it; my instinct reveals it to me, and my instinct is not mistaken....

"Oh, wretched and culpable are they who, exiled far from their own by destiny, on this Earth too narrow for souls avid for infinity, wretched and culpable are they who can encounter a child of that common mother who is the homeland without their eye becoming moist, their heart beating faster, their arms opening and their voice proffering, stammering with tenderness, the sweetest names. Me, I'm not one of them, one of those hearts of stone"—he beat his breast—"and I have divined you! Blessed by the day that gives me such a sweet joy....

"But I shall cut short my speech, Monsieur and dear compatriot; I must not abuse your precious moments. I shall be brief. I am at your service, in that glorious title of compatriot. It was three years ago, Monsieur, that I quit the mother country, three years in which I have not seen her azure sky, heard her sweet language, fertile in such fertile genius, produced by all mouths, known the joys of amity and amour—for one cannot love far from the country that is your own, especially when one has left one's heart behind with a tender beauty....

"Oh, forgive me—I'm emotional! If you have loved, if you still love, if you have left, far away, the one who...if her tear-soaked handkerchief waved from the jetty...but what am I saying? Perhaps you've brought her? She's doubtless here, in one of those delightful maritime wigwams....

"But forgive me again...I sense that I am indiscreet. It's the joy of seeing someone from my homeland, of hearing its cherished voice. O days of youth, calm and innocence, patriarchal and infantile memories, that are both tender and cruel, in the heart of an exile...!"

He went on speaking without drawing breath, and to think of stopping him would have been madness. It lasted an hour and twenty minutes. I was half-asleep.

Suddenly, the doctor got up. "Enough!" he cried, with all his might. "That's enough! Are you selling something? What? I want to know. Offer your rubbish, and have done with it!"

"Illustrious protector of exportation business," the other replied, benevolently, "I hasten to satisfy you....

"I have the honor of representing, in this international center, one of the most important companies in the metropolis. That company can furnish you, through my intermediary, on the best terms, in the name of publicity—for with a compatriot, I would not like to make it a business matter—the most reputed and the most authentic labels of that product, glorious among all, the name of which has contributed as much as the most brilliant military, political, artistic and commercial successes to spreading the name and consideration of our dear homeland over the entire surface of the world: wine. Wine! That word, Monsieur, ought to be pronounced with the head bare, with composure and respect, with tenderness and passion...."

He went on, victorious and unstoppable. After wine, he talked about napkin rings; he sold them too. Then hosepipes; that was his glory. Then he celebrated the ribs of collapsible umbrellas, capable of doubling as toothpicks, watch-chains or pen-holders, of which he was the only depository. He had everything in his boat....

An hour passed thus.

The doctor leaned toward me. "We have to do something," he said, in a weak voice, "or we're lost. Call Cristallin. Perhaps he'll be able to get rid of him."

Shaking off the mortal torpor that had overwhelmed me, I summoned Cristallin. He came up from the engine-room black with coal-dust. In him our hope resided. Scarcely had he perceived him, however, than the man came to meet him with a soft smile.

"Honorable laborer," he said, "you who, like Vulcan, reign over ardent places in which fire combats iron and engenders powerful steam, your labor is exceedingly dirty! How I bless that circumstance, which permits me to bring you disinterested support—for I cannot make it a matter of business with a compatriot and will act with you in the name of publicity. I am the sole representative of our largest company for the manufacture of soap. That extra product, the glory of our great commercial port, I will furnish you in the best conditions of excellence and price, for, I cannot repeat too often, business concerns are obliterated in me when I am in communication with one of the sons of our beautiful country, of our homeland, which...."

But Cristallin had had enough and went back down the stairway to the engine room more rapidly than he had come up, leaving us alone and without resources. Then the doctor, animated by the magnitude of the peril and the furious resolution of despair, stood up.

"Monsieur," he said, "not another word. You're selling wine? Very well. Give me three cases. There...put them there. Napkin-rings? One can't do better; I'll take two-dozen....beside the wine.... Hosepipe? Six meters, with a nozzle. Collapsible umbrella ribs, toothpicks, backscratchers, etc? Perfect...let's say fifteen.... Soap? One cake.... Is that all?

"Stuffed birds? I've no objection to that. Give me that petrel I can see in your boat...no, not that one, the other one...the one with its wings folded; it won't take up as much room. Put it there.... Thank you very much. That's all for today? Let's get on. How much? Eight hundred and forty-two francs twenty-five? That's nothing. Here's the money. You have a receipt, don't you? Yes.... Well, now, do you see that cannon? Go or there'll be bloodshed here. Go without saying a word, without looking back, and never come back if you value your life, for, word of honor, I'll torpedo your filthy boat before it even gets half way!"

The man disappeared. Very pale, the doctor leaned on the bulwark. "What a session," he murmured, exhausted.

Nevertheless, we're getting ready to meet Julius Pinguoin and le Rempart, for the time is approaching when they'll be expecting us.

Same day, 4.30. I've just come back aboard in the small launch to supervise the loading of the food supplies.

In the meantime, le Rempart must be in the boxing ring. A funny thing happened to him this morning. As he was walking through the port with Pingouin, he met a reporter from a big American newspaper, the *Little Frog*, who mistook him for the famous boxer Duck, who was expected here. Pingouin saw right away the advantage that could be taken of it, for our complete security, and he told le Rempart to go along with it and play the role of the boxer. Our friend has everything necessary for that. The American, delighted to have been the first to spot him, interviewed him right away. Le Rempart, who can't speak a word of English, replied by means of random gestures. Pingouin explained that he'd lost his voice and spoke for him when necessary. The journalist took the champion for lunch, not wanting to let him out of sight for fear that someone might steal him.

A match was organized immediately, for as soon as possible, Pingouin having declared that the honorable Duck had business obliging him to leave the following morning.

At the very moment that I'm writing these lines, le Rempart's boxing. I wouldn't want to be in the shoes of his adversaries.

This morning, at about half past eleven, we joined Pingouin on shore. Remained aboard: Cristallin, who said that he hates walking; and the poor cook, who was too ill. I confess that it gave me pleasure to eat lunch at an immobile table for once. Afterwards, we made our final purchases and I came back to supervise, leaving Pingouin, the doctor and Zoé to watch le Rempart's exploits. It appears that six hundred thousand francs have already been bet on him, merely on his appearance, for he's been exhibited naked to the waist. That's flattering.

When the porters bringing our supplies have finished, I'll go back on shore to rejoin the captain. I hope that we'll be able to leave in the morning.

16 December. We're at sea again. Our one-day sojourn in Port International was rather eventful.

To begin with, when I left the ship, at about seven o'clock,

Flaum wanted to come with me. He seemed to be on the brink of death. Once we met up with Pingouin, who was waiting for us in the harbor, he said in a weak voice: "M'sieu Captain, I'm mortally ill; I barely had the strength to come here in the boat. I'd rather not go with you; I wouldn't be much use, and I'd be a burden. I'm very sorry, for I'd really have liked to accompany you to find the Golden Fleece, but I can't. I'd rather die here. I'm tired of suffering."

"I believe that would be best," said Pingouin, touched. "I regret it—you're a worthy man and we'll miss you." He took him aside. "How will you live? Do you have any money?"

"Not much, but I'll have enough. I've got a hundred and thirty-two francs. I'll try to find your compatriots to get a job if I get better...."

"In the meantime, you mustn't die of hunger. Take this." He gave him some money. "And not a word, to anyone whatsoever, about our expedition. If we triumph, everyone will know; if not, they won't know anything at all."

"Not a word! I swear—word of honor! I'd rather die."

In the meantime, the doctor told us the news about le Rempart. With his terrible fist, and a smile on his lips, he'd caved in the ribs of his first opponent. The second, felled thereafter by a punch in the face, had remained unconscious for two hours.

"And yet, I was careful not to hit too hard," our champion had confided to the doctor.

The third, a negro, had withdrawn without advertising his departure. A delirious and enthusiastic crowd had then carried le Rempart in triumph, acclaiming him with shouts of "Duck forever!" The popularity of the latter boxer has increased immensely without him having any suspicion of it. A superb banquet, not to mention other more advantageous results, had been offered to our friend, and he was presiding there at that very moment, decorated with the belt of honor that he had been awarded. Still mute and responding with gestures to all questions put to him, he had been admirable throughout. Pingouin had told him to be on the quay at ten o'clock precisely, in order to go back to the *Albatros* with us, and in any case, to get back before two o'clock, because we'd be leaving shortly after first light.

"Let's have dinner," the doctor concluded.

The meal was rather quiet. To begin with, it did something to us to leave the fat Flaum—who gave the impression of being at a funeral—ill and alone like that. Then again, I think we were all telling ourselves that it would be the last rest before the great struggle, something like the night before a battle when it's necessary to be victorious or die. And believe me, that rendered us a trifle serious, even though I don't think that any of us is a coward....

At nine o'clock, as we were smoking our cigars, something else happened.

The door of our room opened suddenly, and a man came in. He was drunk, but polite and solemn. He swayed once or twice, recovered his equilibrium, and spoke to me.

"Am Nèfle," he said, putting his index finger on his breast. "Want my wife."

"What?" I said.

"Am Nèfle," he repeated. "Want my wife."

"Oh my God! Antonin!" exclaimed Zoé Nèfle. "What are you doing here? This is too much!"

"Looking for you," the other replied, majestically. "Very glad to see you again...very glad. Sad without you. Holes in socks. Then sister died. Children to raise. Can't do it alone. Put them in shelter, then set off to look for you."

Zoé seemed stupefied. "That's news," she said. "How did you find me? And you're still drunk...."

"Drunk nothing," the other replied. "Despair. You coming?"

"But how did you know that your wife was with us?" I asked.

"Don't know," he said. "Chance. Led by Providence. Electrician on liner." He tapped his chest again. "Disembarked here. Saw Zoé through window, Am very glad...." He added: "Thirsty."

I gave him a glass of wine.

Zoé seemed very agitated. "It's staggering," she said. "To come by chance...and the children? Him, I can do without—I've never been able to stop him drinking—but the shelter...that's disgusting for the little ones.... And then, he's come so far to look for me...without knowing...can't be done...I have to go. But who'll do your darning? And what about the Golden Fleece? Monsieur Pingouin, I'm useful to you, aren't I? I don't want to leave you...no...the pain it's giving me! But that poor man who's so glad to see me...! I don't know any more, Monsieur Pingouin, what I ought to do...."

"Go with him," said Pingouin. "If I come back, we'll meet again." And he embraced her while she sobbed.

"You coming?" repeated Nèfle, who had finished his bottle.

"Adieu!" she cried to us. "Au revoir! I'm going!"

And she ran away. Nèfle followed.

We remained in silence.

"It's ten o'clock," said the captain, suddenly. "Let's go."

Le Rempart wasn't on the jetty.

"Let's go back to the *Argonaut*," said Julius Pingouin. "He'll have been held up. He said that he'd come back alone later on, if he wasn't here on time."

More adieux—those of Flaum, our cook.

"I'm very sad," the fat man repeated, wanting to embrace us all.

Our boat drew away from the deserted jetty, from which the Swiss was gazing at us, over the calm sea.

"Captain Pingouin!" he suddenly shouted in a loud voice, when we were forty meters away.

We stopped.

"Captain Pingouin," he repeated, at the top of his voice, "you've tried to persuade us that black is white, mistaken men for heroes, and me for an imbecile—but I'm not stupid and I know your secret! Don't come back or I'll call the police, who are very close by. Now I'm going to set up a company to find the Golden Fleece. Look at your map!" And he waved a piece of parchment.

"Damn it!" said Pingouin. "Go back!"

"Don't move!" cried Flaum. "I'm the stronger. I'm warning you, so that...."

The sentence remained unfinished. An athletic form loomed up behind him, a hand snatched the map from his hand, and le Rempart's fist descended like a thunderbolt on the traitor's skull, staving it in. Flaum stretched out his arms and fell into the sea like a pole-axed ox.

"Lucky for you I got here on time, old chap," said the hoarse voice of le Rempart, who dived in head first and swam toward us, with the map in his teeth. He gave it back to the captain, who shook his hand without saying anything.

"Had a good day," le Rempart confided to us, seemingly a trifle tipsy. "The man who'll get the better of me hasn't yet been born. They threw me a really first-rate party. I've won something like forty thousand bullets and a nice little belt of honor. One could make a living at that game."

Soon, we were back on board. Pingouin observed that the strong-box in his cabin had been opened. Cristallin hadn't noticed anything, having been asleep the whole time.

Pingouin folded up the map and put it back in his leather pouch.

"I won't be parted from it again," he said. "I wonder how the other was able to open the safe. Truly, le Rempart arrived just in time."

We got ready to leave right away, even though half our coal supply was still lacking. I ought to add that two of the negroes supplied by Coco had deserted.

Now it's ten o'clock in the morning. We lost sight of land some time ago. We won't be landing again at any known location. Guided by our map and Julius Pingouin, we're heading straight for the Golden Fleece. The captain thinks that in a month or so, we'll reach the region where it ought to be. For that, it's necessary that our voyage shouldn't suffer any hindrance, but we have to take into account the unknown difficulties of these extraordinary seas into which no navigator has advanced so far, as yet, and from which it's said that no one returns.

We're full of confidence and strength. There are only five of us—not counting the negroes, it's true—but those five, sure of one another and of themselves, fortified by ordeals and the magnitude of the difficulties overcome, are worth a hundred, let it be said without flattery. Flaum and Zoé, although their disappearance is inconvenient from the point of view of service, would doubtless have been an encumbrance in the long run.

Old Cristallin, the indefatigable stoker, is particularly satisfied with the execution of the cook; the latter, it appears, at the time when Cristallin was smitten with Zoé, had had him sign a resignation of his share of the price of Golden Fleece, in exchange for a necklace of fake diamonds with which Cristallin hoped to win the laundress's love. I didn't understand much of the rather confused story that the stoker told me about that, but the strangest thing about it is that Flaum, not having the item of jewelry on him, didn't have to deliver it until after the voyage.

17 December. Last night, in clear weather, we briefly perceived the flashing light of a powerful lighthouse, which is certainly that of South Cape. It's doubtless the last manifestation of human existence that we'll be able to salute for a very long time, perhaps forever.

18 December. Nothing. Nor on the 19th and 20th of the same month.

21 December. We've been singularly inconvenienced by a swarm of insects, which, since this morning, have covered the deck of the ship. They're reminiscent of flying lice, which a violent squall has hurled upon us like a thick cloud, and a pestilential odor invaded us at the same time. The doctor seems very anxious about the phenomenon. The infection dissipated significantly after an hour or so, but the flying lice have persisted in large numbers, in spite of our efforts, and their commerce is unpleasant.

22 December. Yesterday, toward dusk, we were all gripped by an outbreak of a bizarre fever, engendered, according to the doctor, by the flying lice, which are now almost all dead. In some of us the attack of the malady has been slight, but Cristallin and two of the negroes suffered a great deal for nearly two hours, with vomiting, delirium and loss of consciousness. The doctor showed great devotion until he was afflicted himself, with so much violence that we fear for his life.

Same day, 11 o'clock. The fever gripped us again this morning with a terrible energy for some of us. Cristallin and two of the negroes are seriously ill. The doctor and the third negro are, on the contrary, much better and can walk. Pingouin, le Rempart, myself and the fourth negro, having suffered relatively lightly again, are now in a tolerable condition, if not entirely back to normal.

Same day, 4 o'clock. One of the negroes has just died. He was immediately thrown in the sea. One of his comrades is not much better, and Cristallin is almost unconscious. The doctor, still weak and shivering, is very anxious about the strange malady. All the expeditions that have ventured this far before us have been struck by this terrible epidemic, engendered by the same causes, and have been sorely tried. Some have been totally wiped out.

The sharks, which have devoured the first negro, are following the *Argonaut*, in the hope of further nourishment.

The sky is now strangely coppery. Toward the horizon, in the calm atmosphere, mists are rising in spiral eddies, and everything suggests that the wind will get up. There are only four of us to combat the threatened tempest.

23 December. The wind has not been as bad as we feared. The night, however, lacked security. In the end, though, we've been able to keep going without any serious damage, and the danger has passed. At about two o'clock, the negro who seemed to have got better suddenly died. His comrade, by contrast, is completely out of danger, as is Cristallin, who has been able to get up and walk. The doctor is well, although still suffering from stabbing pains.

24 December. The temperature is mild. A light breeze is pushing us in the right direction. We've deployed the sails and they're assisting the progress of the ship greatly. We're making at least fifteen knots, which is considerable. The invalids are entirely recovered, and our morale is satisfactory.

25 December. We're still plunging further into this unexplored sea. The weather is fine, but gets colder toward dusk. It's Christmas today, and I remember the Christmases of my childhood, and that makes me emotional. It's many years since I thought about that sort of thing.

26 December. Sea calm and glaucous. Many birds, which seems to indicate the proximity of land. No coast on the horizon.

27 December. Last night, we passed within sight of a huge volcano crowned with a ruddy plume. It must be Gelboe-Hor, whose existence, identified by a few navigators, has been strongly contested.[11] No expedition has advanced any further— or at least, none has returned to say so. Moreover, the place is frightfully dangerous because of its reefs, through which the *Argonaut* is moving with difficulty. The passages are so narrow and the sea so violent that it's a miracle that we haven't been

---

11. Mount Gelboe and Mount Hor can both be found in the *Catholic Encyclopedia*, where the names are attributed to extinct volcanoes mentioned in the Old Testament. Gelboe is also mentioned in the apocryphal *Travels of Sir John Mandeville*. As Pingouin's expedition appears to be somewhere in the Antarctic Ocean, however, the identification has to be reckoned dubious. Le Homard might be thinking of the two Antarctic volcanoes observed by James Ross in 1841 and named (after his ships), Erebus and Terror. Then again, the Antarctic region featured in Poe's *Narrative of Arthur Gordon Pym* is afflicted by volcanic mists.

wrecked and sunk at any moment.

Julius Pingouin is at the helm, and huge foaming waves are howling around us.

28 December. We're out of the reefs and advancing into a tranquil and somber sea under a rainy sky. This morning, the doctor was gripped by a slight return of the fever, but it didn't last long and wasn't serious.

29 December. Weather poor. Nothing special.

30 December. 11.30 p.m. Something has just happened that I need to talk about. At about nine o'clock, Pingouin, the doctor and I had been together in the cabin for a short while, leaving one of the negroes to look after the helm. Le Rempart was asleep in his hammock. Cristallin and the other negro were in the engine-room.

We were talking, I don't remember what about, when suddenly, the door of the cabin opened and the negro we had left up top hurtled in. His face was the color of ash. He babbled in his incomprehensible language and made signs bidding us to come up on deck. We followed him. Then, in the tranquil and livid darkness, the negro pointed to the bow of the boat—and there, sitting in his old place, smoking his pipe exactly as he had while alive, was the Man in Yellow.

For a second we stood there, motionless. Then Pingouin launched himself toward the apparition of the man, who had drowned on a stormy night. When the captain got close, it flew to the other side. Pingouin threw himself after it. It returned to the first location. Ashamed of my hesitation, I ran toward it, but when I got close to it, it was no longer there. Then I felt a painful nausea, for I could smell the odor of his tobacco, and none of us had smoked for days.

Pingouin took me by the arm and we went to one side with the doctor, who was still standing there, white-faced, with his hair standing on end. In the bow, there was the Man in Yellow again, impassively smoking his pipe.

"It's an omen of death," I said to Julius Pingouin, in a low voice.

"I know," he replied. He remained silent momentarily. "I think he's come for me, but he won't get me like that. If he succeeds, however, listen to me, Homard: you'll go on toward the Golden Fleece with all your might. When it's found, and you've brought it back in triumph, then I want you to keep, at home, one of those birds that bears my name. You'll give it the best place, and the first, and put a golden collar around its neck with a little bell, and you'll let it go wherever it wants. And every year, on the anniversary of our departure, you'll throw a big party for it, where it will be crowned. That's what you'll do, in memory of Julius Pingouin, whom you'll have known...."

Suddenly, the doctor burst out laughing, and pointed to the bow, where the Man in Yellow had disappeared. That laughter was succeeded by a voice that we had difficulty recognizing as that of the scholarly doctor Saturnin Plair.

"That's a bit too much," he said. "What's the explanation? Give me one, if there is one! I want to understand! That we've seen him is a sign that we have good eyes, all well and good. But that he's gone, without saying goodbye, that surpasses my understanding. I've seen many astonishing things, and I've always understood them logically. But this? Oh, no, no! It's a bit too much. Even more so than our expedition. You old imbecile—at your age! Why aren't you sitting quietly by your fireside? Nothing's as good as a nice dinner, a nice bed and a pretty woman.... Science is a fraud; discoveries are a fraud; the Golden Fleece is a fraud...!"

"He's mad," Pingouin whispered in my ear, in a voice so low that I could barely hear it.

"Not mad at all!" howled the doctor. "Cured, rather, of the malady we've all had, and that has killed so many of our comrades! Ha ha ha! The Man in Yellow, and Joseph, and Bouture murdered, and the Pastor, and the customs men, and all the rest—all for you....

"They're all there, I tell you, in the wake, in the clouds, in the wind. Listen to them calling, Captain Pingouin. Given them your iron soul—go on, that would be better! No, I'll go in your place; I'm a hero too...."

He was raging furiously. We took him back down below, and he finally went to sleep. Now I'm writing this, and soon I'm going to replace Pingouin at the helm and see the Man in Yellow again, who's come back.

31 December. For hours I've stayed at the helm, with that astonishing figure sitting tranquilly in the bow.

This morning, the doctor seemed calmer, but as soon as he spoke we saw that his reason had gone forever.

Our voyage continues without material perils. The weather is mild, but the sky is exceptionally cloudy.

Same day, evening. At nightfall, the Man in Yellow came back. We were expecting him, if I can put it like that.

"We shouldn't disturb him," Pingouin had said, "and we should keep as far away from him as possible."

In spite of our efforts, the doctor went to sit down beside the figure in the bow and talked to him in a familiar way. The other didn't budge, and continued smoking. The odor of his tobacco drifted toward us on the light wind.

"Give it to me," said the doctor insistently, talking about something unknown. "What are you going to do with it? Come on—you can't have any use for it out there; give it to me. Be a good chap—come on, give it to me. You know full well that they need me, here, and that without it, nothing will work out. I'll give it back to you afterwards, I promise. When they reach the end and can overtake me. When one reaches the end, one stops and comes back: you'll find me again then. It's a few days of credit, you can do me that small favor. Don't be so demanding. Think how painful it is no longer to have it with me. I'm used to it; I've had the use of it for such a long time. You know very well...."

He lowered his voice and we could no longer hear him. Thus, he spoke to the apparition, which had nothing terrestrial about it, I think, and didn't want to let itself be persuaded.

After a long time, the doctor came back to us, leaving the other.

"I've done everything I can to get it back," he said, without explaining what he was talking about, "but he won't listen. He's got a wooden head. It's not my fault." He lowered his voice. "Tomorrow, I'll make my preparations in advance…and I'll have what's needed to give him pause for thought.…"

1 January. Nothing in particular. The boat's going well.

The doctor has spent part of the day shut up in his cabin. He no longer seems to be in control of himself. He told us, in a very reasonable fashion, that he felt slightly indisposed and tired, but that it was a residue of the fever and that he'd prepare a potion to take this evening in order to relieve it.

Pingouin hopes that the fit has largely dissipated, and won't be renewed.

Same day, 9 o'clock. As night fell, smoky and livid, like all the nights in this region, the Man in Yellow came to occupy his usual place. His coming was already familiar to us. He's so similar in all respects to what he was before his disappearance that I sometimes think.…

As I was writing the previous lines, the doctor appeared on deck and advanced toward the figure sitting in the bow.

"Well," he said, "have you thought about it? Are you more reasonable than yesterday? Come on…hey? Come on, give it to me; go on, be kind, you won't lose anything by it. I'm only asking for it for an hour…only an hour, there, so that I can put my affairs in order. An hour—you can't refuse me that…you don't know how you're making me suffer.… You're not thinking at all—take care. You see this phial…it's me who prepared it and it's diabolically nasty, I warn you.… Well, I'm going to count to ten, and if you haven't given it back to me…you understand what I mean, don't you?

"I'm beginning: One, two, three, for, five, six, seven, eight, nine…ten. There it is…are you going to? No! Well then, take this and go to hell."

And Dr. Saturnin Plair emptied the phial, and fell down dead.

We ran, but there was nothing more we could do for him except throw his body into the sea, which we did.

Then the Man in Yellow went away, and didn't come back.

2 January. I've just noticed that, since yesterday evening, we've been in a new year. I hadn't paid any attention to it, and, after all, it's of no importance. The world of men no longer exists for us. Believe me, one leaves it behind easily.…

Now we've been reduced to four by the doctor's death.

Our two negroes are beginning, it's true, to render us many services. They're intelligent, and are now very nearly able to understand us, and jabber a few words. For greater convenience, the stoker Cristallin, whose role they take over by turns, has given them names: one is Bergami and the other Frise-Poulet. It's impossible to know why he chose those names, of course.

3 January. Since yesterday we have been passing through a bizarre strait, closely confined by two high walls of red stones, and so tortuous one can't see more than a hundred meters in front or behind. The rocks are frightful, bare and sinister. Between them the waves are seething.

Above the walls rests a thick cloud that hides the sky from us, and through which we sometimes seem to glimpse small living figures leaning over to observe us, but perhaps that's just an illusion.

There's a rather sharp chill in these low latitudes, where the sun never sets and a cruel malaise makes us yearn to see the open sea soon.

4 January, 5 a.m. The summer night is still so intensely dark that we were only advancing with the greatest prudence through that unknown passage, between those ramparts that accompanied us until four o'clock this morning. We realized then that we were in open water again.

The obscurity is still as complete, but the danger has almost dissipated.

"We've kept moving all night in spite of the peril," Pingouin said to me, "because at the opening of the strait there's a terrible whirlpool, a hundred times more powerful than the Norwegian Maëlstrom, and which can only be crossed, given the movements of the tide, at the exact moment that we came through."

"How do you know that, Captain?" I asked him, astonished.

"I know it," he said, and went below.

It's probably on the map. Without that miraculous document and without Pingouin's direction, no expedition in the world could have dreamed of doing what we've done—and I'm proud, even if I have to die without ever being able to reach the Golden Fleece, of having accomplished such great things.

Same day, 10 o'clock in the morning. All of a sudden, at about six o'clock, the darkness vanished and gave way to the complete clarity of daylight. We were, and still are, in a truly singular marine region. The sea is uniformly salmon pink and the sky, everywhere, apple green. There's no sun or any cloud, but the same raw green light in every direction.

"It's funny, you know, that sea," declared le Rempart.

"It's ridiculous," I said, discontentedly.

"It scares me," said Cristallin, and went back down to his engine.

However, these unexpected waves are inhabited by a quantity of utterly imbecilic beings. Scaly rats are playing, leaping and spinning around in our wake; enormous turtles with necks three meters long and mobile eyes on stalks are moving gravely over the surface of the water without sinking into it; large seaweeds are opening gelatinous flowers, where flying mollusks are gathering pollen. Multitudes of aquatic bats and winged fish are describing curves around the ship and already settling on our masts to couple there and construct nests, deafening us with their discordant songs....

I'll pass over all the rest, which is even more stupid.

"It's extremely odd," said Pingouin. "We ought to drop a sound; we might perhaps dredge up something interesting."

We dropped a sound. The depth is medium. The sound brought back unexpected objects.

Firstly, a milky white bivalve mollusk. It opens, showing us a face with closed eyes that reproduces human features, always mobile and different, over which pass resemblances to a host of people that we have known.

Secondly, a very elegant corset in violet silk, with frills, rolled up in an issue of the *Journal Officiel*.

"Well, there's been some governmental adultery hereabouts," said le Rempart, who seemed greatly amused.

Thirdly, a reddish mass having some analogies with a sponge; it swells up progressively, producing soft music, then bursts infectiously.

Fourthly, a damaged iron horse, which measures fifty-three centimeters from one horn to the other.

"That," said Cristallin, "has been fabricated for a beast before the deluge—a Stone Age nag, so to speak...."

"An iron horse from the Stone Age? Idiot—why not the Age of Mud? That's the right word, with our dirty government."

Fifthly, nothing at all. A voracious monster of the depths has doubtless swallowed our sound and made off with it, for the line was torn from our hands and snapped. It's a pity.

"Perhaps it's the honorary pimp," said le Rempart. "Yes, indeed, the Man-Fish who was seeking the Truth...he must have a bed down there."

"Let's continue on our way calmly," said Pingouin. "We're on the right course. Then again, it's necessary not to get excited if we encounter extraordinary things. It's only because we're not used to them that they seem so...."

"Remember the Man in Yellow. We did very well there."

The sea is still salmon-pink and the sky still apple-green, and we're in an insensate carnival. Now the turtles walking on the surface of the water are standing up on their hind legs, reading newspapers and leaning on canes; seals are appearing with long hair and violins, which they're playing.

Gelatinous books of some kind are floating like parachutes; ducks with shiny tin-plate heads are paddling everywhere; neat little squares, like those in big cities, well-swept and deserted, can be seen afloat.

Gigantic yellow turnips are emerging, spinning with vertiginous rapidity, sometimes spreading delightful perfumes and sometimes stinks that are beyond description.

Bright blue children are forming lines to either side of the ship and playing cup-and-ball with their heads, which are attached to their tails by braided cords, and which they're catching with their necks.

A troop of baboons with fins, decorated all the way down the back, are varnishing the surface of the sea with paint-brushes, with a pretty pink lacquer, and grimacing because they're hurrying. Protecting their work, a placard on the end of a pole bears the words: *Animal Society of the Fine Arts.*

Two octopodes are opening large dreamy eyes and brandishing little flags at the end of their tentacles. I can see *Eight Hour Day* written on them.

Enormous crayfish are running foot-races; others are urging them on with frightful screeches; the winners receive medals.

A sea-serpent is playing a Barbary Organ with its tail.

Cod are holding a meeting and shouting: "Long live the King!" Indolent rays are deploying their squirrel-like tails like fans; multicolored conger eels are playing the trumpet; two hippocampi as big as giraffes are fighting a duel with lances; a sea-pig is drawing a bow; a frog dressed as a postman is distributing letters; a sperm-whale emerges from the water and takes flight.

Above it all the most varied mollusks are buzzing....

All that is terribly funny, and makes us split our sides laughing, but deep down, I don't know that it's as amusing as all that.

"We're on the right course," said Pingouin. "Let's keep going."

We're going on—but darkness is falling, like a cloak, as rapidly as the daylight came.

A pale blue heavenly body, which we assume to be the moon, is visible on the horizon, half-drowned in the sea, into which it soon sinks. Obscurity grips us, and at the same time, a furious wind gets up, continuing until morning.

5 and 6 January. Violent wind and struggle against the elements. The sea is normal but very rough. The sun, which has risen with a sickly yellow glare, is projecting very little light and heat. We're still going forward, but our supply of coal is getting low.

7 January. The wind has eased somewhat, giving us some rest. Around us, there's nothing but sea. Nothing to pick out. Past events, even the most recent, are floating at a prodigious distance for us. It seems to us that ten years have gone by since our passage through that pink sea under a green sky. It seems to us that a thousand years have fallen upon us, drop by drop, since the evening of our embarkation. And I wonder whether, in truth, we've lived the adventures that I've recounted, which are no more than shadows in my memory.

9 January. We're in regions so remote and so unknown that human sentiments are prey to supernatural movements here. We're aware of vague and inexpressible impressions, and they certainly have no relation to the sensations of the inhabitants of the Earth. However, we're still going forward, without weakening....

12 January. I despair of rendering the sentiments engendered by this fuliginous sky, this trailing mist, as vicious as a damp cloth, this oily sea with soft waves....

What's the point of trying to express them, since I don't have the words....

My companions are weary....

I don't know why I'm writing this. No one will be able to read it....

The days of my human life have been thrown back into a fabulous antiquity. I think that centuries have passed in this voyage, which I've noted as days....

We're at the limits of the world, and I wonder in amazement how we were able to get here....

15 January. The wind is dead. We're advancing. Evil thoughts assail us as we gaze at that uniform sea, which never ends, and that deserted sky under its ragged curtain...and astonishing noises are floating and echoing voices that we know in our ears....

Now, in this powerful fog that surrounds us, there are faces that contemplate us and vanish....

One was especially odious, which trailed after us for hours... an apparition with white hair....

There's a bleak indifference around us. Day and night have finished here....

A progressive shadow is descending by the hour....

At present, I can no longer remember what brought us here....

I know that we'll never get out of these crushing vapors, which, in this illimitable ocean, lead to nothing else, nothing at all, and that's all the same to me.

I sense that my soul has changed and also, doubtless, those of my companions.

17 January. A new peril has constrained us to the energy and the effort to save our lives. In the indecisive obscurity, in the distance, toward the horizon, there were two twin white lights, variable in intensity but always growing. We realized that they were two volcanoes, separated by a narrow channel.

Pingouin leapt up on the deck.

"Stand up!" he shouted. "Prepare yourselves. We have to

pass between the volcanoes. It's the only route!"

In an instant, we were at work, installing the hand-pump to flood the deck. We got closer. The volcanoes were in furious eruption and all the gleams with which they were streaming, the torrents of their lava and the prodigious fiery columns that they were launching into the radiant sky with the same uniform glare were as white as snow.

"Forward ho!" cried Pingouin. "Courage!"

"We're going to get warm," sniggered le Rempart.

The ship advanced at top speed. The captain took the helm. Cristallin was with his engine. The two negroes were handling the pump, the jets of which I was directing, and le Rempart was inundating all of us with a bucket.

Then, into the tumult and the din, into the vaporous whirlwind and the convulsive sea, under the rain of fire and death, we had to hurl ourselves, and the terrible furnace seized us. The heat became frightful; the masts were ablaze; our skin was roasting; we were breathing nothing but mortal fire. One of the negroes was killed by a flaming boulder....

"Faster!" commanded Pingouin, above the racket. "Faster—we're almost in the middle."

But Cristallin appeared on deck. "There's no more coal," he said.

"Damn it!" howled Pingouin. "Use the axes! Burn the ship, burn the masts, burn the food, the oil, the tar...we have to get through or die!"

Already we were taking the *Argonaut*'s bulwarks and deck-houses apart with huge blows; we felled what remained of the masts. Hams and oil crackled in the furnace. The engine roared furiously. We kept going. The wood was added.

In flames, the *Argonaut* was razed like a pontoon, but it was moving with a prodigious velocity, and we got through. The fires on board were extinguished, not without difficulty, and the white lights of the volcanoes was already becoming distant. Our speed was slowing down, though. Then old Cristallin reappeared.

"There's no more coal," he said. "There's no more wood; soon there'll be no more ship. We have to stop. Me, I've had enough...."

"Courage," said Pingouin. "All's well, we're on the right route...."

"It's too late," the old stoker replied. "There's nothing left. We have to stop. Me, I've had enough." And he sat down on the deck, putting his had in his hands.

I took him by the arm, but his body slumped sideways heavily and escaped my grip. We realized that his soul had abandoned it.

We couldn't stay on the *Argonaut*. We lowered the big launch into the water, which hadn't suffered too much, and was loaded with everything useful we could carry. I took the present Ship's Log with me. We set fire to the old ship and abandoned it. Julius Pingouin was the last, and as he got down into the launch I saw a kind of despair in his face.

The *Argonaut* burned, illuminating our path through the darkness with its ruddy glow.

Julius Pingouin said to us: "It's now that it's necessary to have a strong heart. Of those who set out, only three of us remain... we have to reach the goal. If we die before, so be it. I don't regret what I've done. I believe you think the same. Whatever the result, we've accomplished what no other human being has ever accomplished."

"What if we were to throw a bottle into the sea with these notes?" I said.

"No," said Pingouin. "If we triumph, people will know everything.... If not, there's no point."

"And we'll triumph!" howled le Rempart. "M'sieu Pignouin, I'm yours till death. And hey—we can still row; that'll keep us warm!"

All three of us shook hands with assured hearts, and also that of the brave negro Frise-Poulet, who was rowing with all his might.

And now, for hours, we've made ourselves as comfortable

as possible in the launch. The darkness around us is profound; only a single lantern scarcely illuminates us, because we have to conserve oil.

Pingouin is holding the tiller and consulting his map. We're taking turns rowing, with only one idea, that is like an intoxication: to go forward.

20 January. We're still rowing. The sea is like soot. It's extremely cold. No noteworthy incident.

28 January. Yes, I think it's 28 January, but the captain's watch stopped suddenly and I have no means to measure time in the middle of this constant and frightful darkness, which grips us ever more cruelly. The cold is extreme.

Hours and hours, days and days have certainly gone by while we've been floating like this in this sea. Our compass is now motionless. We don't know anything. We're wandering at random through ever-more-profound darkness. The water itself is the color of ink.

We're rowing desperately in order to go forward, without knowing where, without daring to stop, without thinking and without hope. By the feeble light of the lantern, Julius Pingouin consults his map, which can no longer tell us anything....

More time....

With mute accord, we've stopped the futile labor of rowing. Sometimes, one of us grips them in a fit of furious terror, but he soon stops and falls back into silence and immobility.

A discouraging fatigue has overwhelmed us. The cold is more pitiless than I've ever suffered.... We feel that there is no longer any life around us. The darkness is a garment of pitch, stifling us.... The white patch that our lantern makes is doubtless the only thing keeping us from dying, but soon, we'll no longer be able to feed it....

It's a long time since I've had the courage to write. A long time.... Days...? Weeks...? We're numbed by a deathly calm. We've put the last drops of oil in the lamp, and they'll be used up before long.... Julius Pingouin is no longer saying anything to encourage us.... Now a frightful snow is beginning to fall on us, which is as black as the darkness....

It's falling relentlessly, burying us with an icy suffocating slowness.... The eternal silence is crushing us....

I think the final hour is coming, for the light of the lantern's now gradually weakening...and these lines are doubtless the last ones I'll be permitted to write....

The light went out. With it died the negro Frise-Poulet. Then, for us, it was a matter of the intoxicating wait for death.... But a noise became audible in the distance, which increased with prodigious rapidity. Already, there was a black liquid mountain upon us, roaring with the voice of thunder, and which carried us away, exhausted and unconscious, in its vertiginous course....

Afterwards, there was a shock, and immobility.... And around us, a coppery light fell from the clouds into a valley where we were lying.... Julius Pingouin called out to me. The floor of the valley was red and polished, like coral; the hills were similar, and similar too the trunks of the trees whose leaves were crystal and whose large flowers were black velvet.

"This way," said the captain, pointing at the highest of the hills, which was crowned by a ruddy cloud.

We climbed for hours, with a terrible fatigue. We fell, our feet bloody and the sharp leaves breaking in our flesh. We looked at Pingouin. Torn and bloody, like us, he seemed transfigured.

"One more effort!" he cried. He gripped up by the arm. His strength entered into us. The summit was reached, and the cloudy mass crossed.

The cliff was blindingly white. It circled to the right and the left, and we were at the top. There was a sky as pale and luminous as diamond, and in the distance, an unknown star from which splendor streamed. And a motionless sea bathed the foot of the cliff with its supernatural waves, which were pure gold.

Julius Pingouin had the face of a god.

"Forward ho!" he cried. "Forward ho! Into the sun!"

He threw himself from top to bottom and was swallowed up. Then, in the movement, the sound and the light, everything spun and ceased to be for our eyes.… And I knew no more.

Now, le Rempart is a god, because of his strength, among the savage populations that subsequently picked us up on the sandy beach of their desolate isles. Personally, I've come back, and it took me a very long time, for the place where we woke to the life of the Earth is at the very end of the world.

(24 December 1901.)

EVENTS OCCURRING IN THE VICINITY OF SCAFFOLDS

It is night. Snow is falling. At the extremity of the old city is the place of executions, which the living avoid but where those that the hand of the executioner has hung by the neck constantly remain.

The place is a large area situated on the edge of the river. The banks are elevated; at the bottom, the black waters run silently. On the far side, the long wall of the cemetery bars the extent; a little gate is visible in it; above the wall leafless branches twist and grimace, and one can make out the tops of funerary architecture and the crowns of yew trees. To the right, the area is limited by a vast abandoned building, which extends its decrepit façade obliquely. A palisade, with a closed barrier, extends as far as the cemetery wall. To the left, there is a wooden hangar, in front of a confused heap of rubble, which is the collapsed ruin of one of the towers of the old city wall. Brushwood and a few trees grow in the vicinity.

Toward the middle of the river-bank, at the top of the slope, three gibbets raise up their identical forms, each one clinging, with the uniform gesture of its stiff arm, to its hanged man. The middle gibbet carries a lantern, which awkwardly projects a moving light. The heads of the dead men are inclined over their breasts. They seem to be meditating, their feet joined together, their hands behind their backs.

At the back of the open space, under the hangar, three very old, exceedingly ugly and exceedingly wicked witches are going about their business. Their great cauldron is warming over a peat fire, emitting prodigious fumes. One of the witches is carrying a black cat on her shoulders, the second an owl on her head and the third a snake around her neck. That last witch is stirring the mixture in the cauldron and grimacing.

In the open space a dead tree is visible, lying on its side, along with a staved-in boat and a heap of stones.

Over everything, snow is falling from the black sky. A wan light emanates from the ground where it is piling up. Its tenacious descent mingles the darkness with a blurred net that catches the eye and plunges into the water, scrupulously covering everything. Sometimes, a gust of wind agitates the lantern, scattering the snowflakes, causing the chains to creak.

Crows arrive from beyond the river. They circle above the open space obliquely, croaking, then land on the gibbets.

A CROW

Are you asleep, comrades?

FIRST HANGED MAN

No one sleeps here.

THE CROW

Except Death.

SECOND HANGED MAN

Who works hard has the right to rest.

ANOTHER CROW

The sleep of Death must be very light.

THE FIRST CROW

Get away! It's as deep as a well, damn it!

A WITCH

Silence, bird of ill-omen! Your blasphemies are coagulating my philter.

THE CROW

Why are you complaining, witch? If your philter turns, you'll drink it.

THIRD HANGED MAN

God's Bowels, my feet are freezing in my boots.

SECOND HANGED MAN

What's the matter, brave thief? Can't you tolerate that petty inconvenience?

A PLAINTIVE VOICE *rising from the cemetery*

It's very cold in the tombs!

SECOND HANGED MAN

Listen to the augural voices prophesying the future. Oh, the destinies aren't joyful!

A CROW

Don't complain, Masters—your destiny is worthy of envy. Your sepulchers are alive, vigorous, winged! Your sepulchers will be our famished entrails!

FIRST HANGED MAN

Detestable bird, do you dare to eat our flesh, the image of God the Creator?

THE CROW

I do indeed dare!

SECOND HANGED MAN

The image of the Creator is not the body but the soul. The ignominy of human desires and thoughts proves that.

FIRST HANGED MAN

Blasphemer, since Hell will char your heart for all eternity! The perfection of the human soul renders it mistress of the world, and its virtues will lead it to heaven.

SECOND HANGED MAN

Its virtues! Ha ha ha! They're particularly developed in you, aren't they, and its in recompense that Jo Rouge, the executioner, has hanged you here?

FIRST HANGED MAN

Like the majority of men you're talking about matters of which you're ignorant. My execution was engendered by the most astonishing adventure that has ever demonstrated the force of human intelligence and the malicious power of the Devil.

SECOND HANGED MAN

Oh, really? It's the Devil who hanged you?

THIRD HANGED MAN

That's a lie! He was hooked up before my eyes by old Joël of the Red Hand, the executioner, and he was already beating time with his feet when I was still down below, on firm ground!

FIRST HANGED MAN

Yes, such was the fruit and conclusion of all my lifelong studies....

SECOND HANGED MAN

Would you care to tell us this marvelous story?

THE CROW

That's it! Tell us your story, old man, to charm the hours of this long winter night!

FIRST HANGED MAN

My story is simple. I have always studied, believing in God, loving humans....

A CROW, *interrupting*

Dear child!

THE HANGED MAN, *paying no heed*

At sixty years of age I knew everything that it is permissible for a man to know in the mechanical and physical sciences....

A CROW

Except to regulate your own person!

A large white phantom silently appears above the wall of the cemetery.

THE PHANTOM

Continue—the specters are listening to you!

Another phantom appears, beating its breast.

THE HANGED MAN

I acquired a universal reputation. I fabricated apparatus and automata more astonishing than had ever been imagined before....

A WITCH, *shouting in a loud voice*

Fume, fume, fume, cauldron mixture! Drive your fumes all the way to the Moon!

SECOND HANGED MAN

Shut up, loudmouth!

The two phantoms descend from the wall and come across the open space slowly, one behind the other. In the middle of the space there are suddenly three of them. They come to the river and jump in.

A CROW, *to the first hanged man*

Speak, then!

THE HANGED MAN

Why is it necessary for me to speak? In retreat in that city, where I was unknown, after four years of labor, I constructed that which was my life's goal: a man made entirely by my own hands, with the inanimate substances of the earth, with metal, wood, leather, glass, wax and stone. When I had finished, he walked, talked, worked—I was content. One day, he thought... yes, he thought, for he came with a dagger to kill me in my bed. I struck him repeatedly with an ax as he was imploring and threatening me. His screams were frightful. The police arrived and their torches illuminated a body on the ground, from which blood was flowing, from which entrails had spilled, whose brains had splashed the walls and which was quivering, panting, still alive. It was him. Then I was bound. No one wanted to understand. Now I've been hanged.

SECOND HANGED MAN

My word, that's good! Why involve yourself in imitating the work of God? It's bad enough as it is....

FIRST HANGED MAN

You lie! I would never have dared attempt....

A PHANTOM, *passing its head through the cemetery gate*

Crimes are heavy!

SECOND HANGED MAN *to the third*

What does the comrade think?

ANOTHER PHANTOM, *appearing at the window of the abandoned building*

The house of the dead makes the living afraid!

ANOTHER, *keeping a lookout on the roof*

There's a drowned man floating in the river! Drowned man, have you met in the course of your journey the Seven Sleepers following their dead dog?[12]

A CROW, *circling*

Drowned man, where are you going so swiftly, floating on the waters swollen by the snow, with your belly bloated, your face rotting and your head down?

THE DROWNED MAN *in the river*

I haven't seen anything in my journey; I no longer have any eyes. I'm going to find my murderers—my wife and my brother. In order to enjoy in peace their shameful love, to enjoy in peace their filthy vices, they threw me in the river with my throat cut, since I lay between them.

SECOND HANGED MAN

You're ignorant, then, of the forgiveness of offences?

---

12. The legendary Seven Sleepers of Ephesus feature in both Christian and Islamic legend, although the latter version does not specify a number; it is the Islamic version, however that also mentions a dog asleep at the entrance to the sleepers' cave, routinely mistaken by passers-by for a watch-dog

A WITCH

Crow, fly over the drowned man, open his breast and rip out his heart, all burning with vengeance, and bring it to me!

THE CROW

Madame, I'm your respectful slave, but I can't do as you command.

THE WITCH, *angrily*

I'll pluck you alive, vile eater of cadavers, and cook you in my pot!

ANOTHER WITCH

Silence, witch! The Work's darkening!

A CROW, *flying around the third hanged man and brushing his face with its wing*

You're very taciturn, companion!

THIRD HANGED MAN

For the Devil's sake, why wake me up, ambulant carrion?

THE CROW

Damn! The man with the black beard's energetic in his language!

SECOND HANGED MAN

Vehement words are appropriate to the brave. Were you dreaming about all those you've sent beyond life, comrade in bloody labors?

THIRD HANGED MAN

I was dreaming about all the pretty girls I've violated, or who loved me....

SECOND HANGED MAN

The last one was very beautiful, eh?

THIRD HANGED MAN

If you know my story, why disturb me?

THE CROW

What he knows is nothing! We're the sole confessors here. Recount your lusts—go on, we won't hold them against you!

THIRD HANGED MAN

It doesn't matter to me! At every dagger-blow my hand struck I thought of the gibbet and its crows, with neither fear not anxiety. To finish like this or some other way is all the same to me. I only miss a few things: the clink of gold on gaming tables, the taste of wine, the odor of blood, the blades of swords and the loins of women! Outside of that, life is stupid.

FIRST HANGED MAN

Wretch, don't you fear God?

THIRD HANGED MAN

Silence, old man! When I speak, I speak alone. Fear God!

That's what the old usurer Profernal told me, who was my last victim. He, who killed by despair or hunger more creatures than I killed with my knife, begged me when I asked him for his gold, invoking God's justice! Ha ha ha! A thousand demons! I dragged him through his house by his hair, scorched his feet to roast them at his miser's stove—he didn't reveal anything! It was then that his daughter came, getting out of bed. God's blood, she was beautiful! Her breasts were whiter than her chemise and her lips redder than blood. I knocked her down on the stone floor— she was a virgin—her teeth clicked under mine, her skin was as cold as death and her wide eyes were weeping with horror and sensuality! Ha ha! She enjoyed herself with me; I felt her loins quiver! Bloody hell, she was too beautiful—I forgot everything. The Jew had dragged himself outside to die there shouting for help. I was still on top of her when they arrested me!

SECOND HANGED MAN

Calm down, my friend—your regrets are carrying you away.

THIRD HANGED MAN

I have no regrets! She's dead too—because she loved me! I saw her this morning when I was climbing the ladder. Her eyes were burning in the crowd. As I launched myself for the last dance she blew me a kiss and plunged my dagger into her heart!

At that moment a nearby clock chimes midnight from the height of a bell-tower. The resonances fall away slowly, deadened by the snow.

THE PHANTOM *at the window*

At this hour, as at any other, can suffering souls resign them- selves to their pain?

THE WITCH WITH THE OWL

Misfortune, thrice misfortune, to all those who perform some good deed in the course of the day that is being born!

THE WITCH WITH THE BLACK CAT

May the power of evil increase and be fortified!

THE WITCH WITH THE SNAKE

A curse upon the young and the old, on the good and the bad, on men, animals and things!

THE THREE WITCHES, *in chorus*

Accursed be the day we're entering! Thrice accursed and spell-bound, by the effect of the charm seething in the pot!

Time passes, in silence.

THE PHANTOM *on sentry duty on the roof*

Necromancer, where are you flying off to?

A VOICE

I'm not a necromancer. I'm a prisoner's dream. I'm flying straight ahead, intoxicated by space.

Another silence.

THE PHANTOM

I see living beings coming through abode of the dead.

SECOND HANGED MAN

Open the gates! Light the chandeliers! Pour the wine! Here come our gracious companions, marching on the clouds, sustained by the angels, covered in snow!

The gate of the cemetery opens slightly, and two nuns slip out, furtively

THE PHANTOM *on the roof*

Sisters, are the shades of the victims appeased?

THE FIRST NUN, *a young woman*

Who spoke?

THE SECOND NUN, *who is older*

I don't know. Night creates strange forms and voices. We're free!

FIRST NUN, *leaning on the cemetery wall, oppressed*

I'm trembling. Our flight through those tombs has terrified me. I thought I heard the voices of the dead.... (*She shivers.*)

SECOND NUN

Courage, Giselle. Don't let anguish overwhelm you. We're safe. They can't catch us.

Behind them, a phantom closes the gate, gently.

FIRST NUN

This place frightens me. What are those motionless forms under the snow? How shall we get over them? Can you hear the crows?

SECOND NUN

It's nothing. Think of the one you love. Your return will be his happiness.

FIRST NUN

Let's go, I beg you.

SECOND HANGED MAN

Come this way, my beautiful child!

FIRST NUN

Who spoke?

A SPECTER *on the rubble*

The voices that speak will shut up!

SECOND NUN

I don't know....

THE PHANTOM *at the window*

Virgins, have you prayed to God?

FIRST NUN, *frightened*

The Devil is master here!

SECOND NUN

No, the night is fine—look.

For the eyes of the living it seems that a veil has suddenly been removed. The specters, the witches, the hanged men and the crows are visible.

There is a multitude of little white phantoms passing back and forth in the ruins, many carrying lamps whose flames they are protecting with the flaps of their shrouds; others are kneeling on the stones. Winged apparitions are flying in the sky. Old sardonic monsters clicking their teeth are hiding in the boat and behind the scaffolds. Lights and shadows can be seen wandering around.

A WITCH *to the young nun*

Let's leave together, little one. I know an old man who'll give you a thousand gold pieces.

SECOND HANGED MAN

I am the Christ on the divine gibbet—kiss my feet!

FIRST HANGED MAN

Blasphemer, may Hell burn your tongue!

SECOND HANGED MAN

You'd repeating yourself, old fellow!

A CROW, *flying around the young woman*

I'm very cold, my child. Warm me up between your breasts!

TWO OTHER CROWS

We're the birds of God! Our eyes pierce the night, we confess the dead. We're discreet, you know. Tell us how your lover possessed you!

THIRD HANGED MAN

By the loins of the Virgin, she's more beautiful than anything I've ever seen! Young woman, come here to me—I'll defend you!

SECOND HANGED MAN

Ha ha! (Imitating the other.) *Young woman, come here to me—I'll defend you!* Not bad!

More numerous specters, gesticulating in the half-light, are marching gravely, striking their breasts, wringing their hands, unrolling and reading parchments, threatening unknown enemies with their fists, running away, and disappearing. Plaintive mocking laughter resounds, with blasphemies, sobs, whistles and appeals.

FIRST NUN, *terrified*

We're in the domain of Hell! Better our slavery than that—let's go back!

She runs toward the cemetery gate, but sees that it is closed. A phantom is standing between her and the batten.

THE PHANTOM, *in a deep voice, raising a hand*

Those who have emerged can no longer return!

SECOND HANGED MAN, *shouting*

Servant of the Lord, come and take me down!

THE FIGURE OF A MAN, *naked, in an excessively obscene condition, advancing toward her, extending his arms.*

Madame, the snow is soft, we'll enjoy ourselves very well! Lie down on your back, lift up your robe, and open your legs!

SECOND NUN, *pursued by a menacing monster*

In the name of God, get back! (*She makes the sign of the cross.*)

A WITCH

What! You're invoking the name of God while quitting his service?

FIRST NUN

Repentance washes away all sins.

A FEMALE FIGURE, *thin, clad in a split tunic, tugging the young nun's sleeve*

Look at my hands, look at my mouth. If you knew...my tongue is burning or frozen. I know profound caresses. Let me undress you....

SECOND NUN, *replying to the witch*

We have fled what was for us a prison. I sought liberty, my companion sought love. They are divine aspirations.

A PHANTOM, *rising above the rubble*

You'll find the tomb!

FIRST NUN, *driving away the phantoms surrounding her with her outstretched hands*

Let me pass, infernal shades, my fiancé is waiting for me!

A VOICE

He's no longer waiting for you. He loves another.

ANOTHER VOICE

That's a lie. He's dead.

A CROW

Embrace me, Giselle!

SECOND NUN

The Hanged Men frighten me less!

She flees toward the scaffolds.

SECOND HANGED MAN

Why did you quit the convent, venerable lady?

THE NUN

What voice spoke?

THE HANGED MAN

Mine! My companions are taciturn—they were too chatty not long ago.

THE NUN

If you have some power, I implore you, in the name of God the Creator, to come to our aid; enchain the demons that are attacking us.

THE HANGED MAN

They're not demons. Answer my question first.

THIRD HANGED MAN

Leave us in peace, you! My God—the lady's still good. If you care to take me down, my beauty, you can boast of having a lover who'll know how to reward you. What is it you lack?

THE NUN, *replying to the other*

I wanted to recover my liberty. My heart and mind have been agonizing for twelve years in captivity. The child who is accompanying me offered to share her escape toward the man who loves her. We fled through the chapel and the cemetery, marching straight ahead, without further reflection....

THE HANGED MAN

In fact, it's all the same to me.

A PHANTOM

Throw yourself in the river!

THE NUN

The river?

ANOTHER VOICE

There's no way out. You've seen the flight, you haven't see the result. What will you do in the World?

A PHANTOM

Only the dead know repose.

THIRD HANGED MAN

That's a lie! Before, when I had worked well, I went to bed and slept like a beast. Now, the whole world wakes me up and torments me. It's unjust, and if I were free.... (*To the first hanged man.*) What do you say, old man?

FIRST HANGED MAN

Let me be. I recognize in the shadow the Image of God, which is rising with the morning.

THE YOUNG NUN

(*In the midst of the specters tormenting her she sees the resemblance of her fiancé passing, and hurls herself forward.*) O my love, save me!

A MAN'S VOICE

Giselle, I'm dead!

A WOMAN'S VOICE

Get away! He's my lover!

THE MAN'S VOICE

Giselle, behold my tomb.

At the young woman's feet a stone sepulcher is gaping. A name is engraved on the displaced stone.

THE VOICE

Read my name by the gleam of the snow!

THE WOMAN'S VOICE

Look at your spouse in my arms!

THE YOUNG NUN

(*She sees her fiancé passionately embracing a half-naked woman, who laughs voluptuously and puts her arms around his neck.*) Save me, my God! My soul is suffocating with anguish... I'm going to die...I'm suffering....

THE MAN'S VOICE

Come into my tomb. I'll sleep better wrapped in your white arms....

In the sepulcher there is now the apparition of a dead man, buried, his face uncovered. The young woman recognizes him, and collapses, with a sigh. The witches immediately utter loud cries, tipping their cauldron over on to the fire.

THE WITCHES

Malediction! Malediction! Malediction! She's died of love, our Work is wasted!

They fly away on broomsticks.

The young woman is lying in the snow, dead. Snowflakes cover her. Phantoms kneel around her, as if desperate.

A VOICE

She's dead! What a misfortune! She was so pretty! I would have liked to caress her a little....

ANOTHER VOICE

She'll go to Hell. She perished in a scandalous manner!

SECOND NUN

My child, my child, you're dead! Oh God, everything is finished for me!

A PHANTOM

Throw yourself in the river!

THE NUN

I'm damned. She's dead, for my sin. May God forgive me!

SECOND HANGED MAN

You know more than you're saying.

The nun runs toward the bank and throws herself into the river.

At the same time:

THIRD HANGED MAN

Wouldn't you like to take me down? I'm very robust.

THE PHANTOM *at the window*

Think of me during your voyage, Sister

SECOND HANGED MAN

Come back when you're a shade. We'll set off for the clouds together on horseback, to travel the world.

For a moment, silence reigns. A vague light is born on the horizon.

FIRST HANGED MAN

Greetings! I salute you and I adore you, Spirit of God floating in the Light!

THE PHANTOM *on the roof*

The light of day is odious to our eyes!

He precipitates himself toward the ground and disappears. All the shades vanish with plaints and shrill cries.

A CROW, *to the hanged men*

Have you said your last words, Masters? Have you thought your last thoughts? Here's the dawn, and we're hungry!

SECOND HANGED MAN

Hanged men, it's necessary to die!

THIRD HANGED MAN

You too, Comrade.

SECOND HANGED MAN

Me? Ha ha ha! I'm only the simulacrum of a shade!

FIRST HANGED MAN

What is that shade?

SECOND HANGED MAN

Old man, the chagrined spirits, perverse or familiar, which haunt battlefields, cemeteries and places of execution are the guests of the night, and vanish when day comes!

He disappears, carried away by a furious gust of wind, which chases the clouds and the nocturnal nightmares from the sky. The snow is no longer falling; magnificent and serene; it dresses the open space; it is the shroud of the virgin who died for love. Dawn brightens the horizon. The river flows on, its taciturn waters higher. The crows eat the hanged men.

CONVERSATION BETWEEN A POET, TWO UNDERTAKERS AND A PROSTITUTE

The room is vast, low and irregular. A small window open at head height to the night, allows a livid mist to penetrate, which vaguely reveals the poverty of things. The walls seem pallid. At the back, in the corner to the left, there is a bed on which a sheet covers a human body. Near the wall to the right a little stove raises its tortuous flue. Hanging clothes form a dark patch. In the center of the room is a table surrounded by chairs and stools. There is a door opposite the window. A cupboard door stands ajar.

The increasing sound of footsteps and collisions is heard, mingled with stifled oaths, seemingly coming from a staircase behind the door. Then there is a pause, the groping of a key, and the door opens. A light appears. The room appears even poorer; the walls are decrepit and dirty, the brick floor-tiles are dislodged in places, the table is a shutter on two trestles, and the stuffing is coming out of the chairs.

The first undertaker comes in, holding a lighted candle and a key. Bottlenecks emerge from his bulging pockets.

FIRST UNDERTAKER, *his voice thick and hoarse*

Wait a minute, wait a minute! The door's too low. I'll help you.

He deposits the objects on the table, with his black top hat. The candle falls off and almost goes out. He picks it up and replaces it. It falls over again.

Damn!

He bends down again.

SECOND UNDERTAKER, *his voice slow and measured, but raucous*

No need, Monsieur Trouilleby, no need; I can get in easily on my own. Just be careful of the bottles.

He comes in, bent over, carrying a long pine coffin on his right shoulder. He stumbles in a hole in the floor, swears, and eventually deposits the coffin along the wall under the window. Straightening up, he sneezes twice and resumes speaking.

Cursed fog! Stupid precaution of keeping this window open! This cold will preserve the body for a week, and we'll likely come down with galloping consumption.

He closes the window. Then, to his comrade:

Do you think, as I do, that a little fire would be in order—would be particularly cheerful and healthy?

FIRST UNDERTAKER

He succeeds in mastering the candle and fixing it in the neck of an empty bottle found in a corner, and closes the door, replying:

For sure, Monsieur Mame. There must be some coal here.

He goes to open the cupboard and peers in.

Here!

He takes out a bundle of kindling and some coal, and lights the stove.

SECOND UNDERTAKER, arranging the bottles on the table

Rum, whisky, rum and rum again. Perfect! With a saucepan, we could make an admirable punch. The old man must have one.

He goes to the cupboard, rummages inside and extracts a small cast iron bowl.

This'll do very well, Monsieur Trouilleby; it's superlatively appropriate to that usage—veritably superlative!

In a grave and self-important fashion he sits down to the right of the table. He uncorks the bottles and pours large quantities of whisky and rum into the receptacle. He adds a few gray sugar-lumps taken from his pockets and goes to place the bowl on the stove, which is humming.

FIRST UNDERTAKER

Lucky there was coal—it's getting better now.

He rubs his hands together and sots down next to the table. For a few minutes he watches his comrade's actions silently, as the latter stirs the alcohol from time to time with a long-handled iron ladle. Suddenly:

It's time, Mame! It's time—light up!

SECOND UNDERTAKER, a trifle coldly

I know how to make punch, Monsieur Trouilleby!

He lights a twist of paper with the candle, approaches it to the liquid and sets fire to it. He picks up the bowl and sets it on the table. The two men stand to either side, vigorously illuminated by the alcohol flames. The first, Trouilleby, is short, plump and negligent. The circular ruddy face is decorated by gray-tinged russet side-whiskers. His forehead is bald; his habitual expression is jovial. Mame is tall, pale and clean-shaven; his top hat covers his head and his frock-coat is buttoned up. A well-formed knot secures his muslin cravat. The excessive majesty of drunkenness reigns over his face.

To himself:

It was indeed, the moment, neither too soon nor too late.

He stirs the punch and lifts out ladlefuls, streaming with a hectic flame, which he immediately tips back into the receptacle, where they are swallowed up with a splash of igneous globules and high cracking flames. Moving and magnified shadows agitate on the walls; the silhouettes of the undertakers take on the appearance of epileptic gorillas. Mame soon ceases stirring the alcohol. The flame dies down, runs rapidly over the liquid and, after one or two renewals, goes out. Obscurity resumes its semi-possession of the distant parts of the room. Trouilleby brings two glasses; he mixture is partially poured into them. The undertakers drink. The glasses are emptied.

FIRST UNDERTAKER

Superior! Monsieur Mame, you have no equal for the confection of punch.

SECOND UNDERTAKER

You flatter me, Monsieur Trouilleby, you flatter me. Perhaps I do have ability, but there are certainly artists who surpass me.

What I can say is that I accomplish the task according to the rules....

He fills the glasses. Pipes are stuffed and lit; smoke spreads abundantly.

FIRST UNDERTAKER

Damnation! Without punch and fire the night would have been hard—harder for us than for him (*He points to the dead man.*) Anyway, as we are, it will work out. A funny idea, all the same, for us to stand guard over the old man. It appears that the heir didn't want to do the job himself. He's rich, and the old man left nothing but debts. Then again, he wasn't a credit to his family, you know—let a disreputable life; he drank, dressed in dirty clothes and...I don't know! Anyway, he had bad habits. But in my opinion, what annoyed the heir the most is that the old man made writings, contrivances that were printed....

SECOND UNDERTAKER, *scornfully*

Oho! Monsieur was a writer!

FIRST UNDERTAKER

Exactly. You understand, then; when a man's well set up, it's annoying for him to see an old madman like that making use of his name for a heap of rubbish. All the same, that doesn't alter the fact that it's harsh to have let him die like that, all alone, and then not even come to see him—to put up people like us, of whom people make mock, and only because he couldn't do otherwise, because there'd be an outcry if he left him all alone. No, personally, I wouldn't like that. Might as well be a dog!

SECOND UNDERTAKER

No matter, Monsieur Trouilleby, no matter! You have infantile prejudices. What difference can it make, once dead, to be alone or not, to be burned or thrown in the sea? They're childish, your ideas, childish, nothing else.

He drinks.

FIRST UNDERTAKER, *showing signs of intoxication*

Childish, possibly. Prejudices, possibly. That doesn't affect the sentiments. At any rate, we arrived a little late—eleven o'clock instead of eight. Still, that's the way it is. Better late than never, eh, you old rogue?

He aims a slap at Mame's belly, which is too far away.

SECOND UNDERTAKER, in a dignified manner

Monsieur Trouilleby, Monsieur Trouilleby, I'm pained, veritably pained, to observe that the slightest dose of spirits suffices to annihilate in you any sentiment of propriety. Your words and your gesture are coarse, I must say, and that astonishes me— what will you do in an hour's time? Our profession is almost a priesthood, Monsieur Trouillbey, and demands qualities of education that you seem to be forgetting. You're outraging your dignity and mine. I'm pained, pained!

FIRST UNDERTAKER, astounded

Me, I'm forgetting my qualities of education? I'm outraging my dignity and yours? You don't think that, Monsieur Mame—say you don't think that! Such a little thing...to you, an old friend. We've been burying together for ten years, Monsieur Mame, don't forget that, Monsieur Mame—such things render people almost brothers. (*He seems upset.*)

SECOND UNDERTAKER

Calm down, Trouilleby, calm down. Don't upset yourself. Your faults are great—every man has them, alas—but your qualities are superior. Shake my hand at let's take a glass of punch together as a sign of reconciliation.

They shake hands. Trouilleby blows his nose noisily into a vast checkered handkerchief. They drink. Mame continues:

I haven't forgotten, and never will forget, that we've been carrying coffins together for ten years. The affection that I've contracted for you in the course of those labors, pushes me to observations that displease you. You know that I was once part of the noble corps of education! Yes, I was a junior master at the celebrated boarding-school known by the name of the Maison du Salut, kept but the honorable Monsieur Rugbool. I would doubtless still be there if fatal accidents to undisciplined young pupils had not caused that unparalleled establishment to close down—a great injustice. Then, being as fortunately endowed in physical capacity as mental capacity, I entered into the liberal corporation of which we are not, I dare say, the most unworthy members. (*He makes a gesture to stop Trouilleby, whose modesty protests.*) You too, Trouilleby, you too, and it is in recognizing in you the finest qualities, and in memory of the years of youth (*he sighs*) that I have undertaken your education, and am convinced that, before long, I shall make a perfect gentleman of you. But be careful of dignity and reason, Trouilleby—be very careful of them; that's the main thing. With dignity and reason, a man rises above all the insults of life. Look at me—I'm dignified; I'm reasonable—always dignified and reasonable—and people respect me, and honor me, if I might express myself thus in my own regard.

At that moment three distinct knocks sound on the door. The undertakers shiver and, unconsciously, correct their attitude slightly. Before they have replied, a hand raises a latch, the door opens, and a fat woman comes into the room, with the dirty, brazen and rascally appearance of a low-class prostitute. She gathers up her dress to the side, displaying her muddy shoes and the base of a stout leg clad in a red stocking. She is carrying a bag and an old umbrella.

The undertakers look at her in astonishment.

THE WHORE

Honorable Monsieurs, my little darlings, it's cold outside it's raining, it's pitch dark and I'm thirsty. Oh la la! Here there's a fire, rum and honorable company; that's why I've come.

MAME, *to Trouilleby*

She's a beauty!

THE WHORE, *having heard*

A beauty—too true. Ask that old man there. He wouldn't have loved me if I hadn't been beautiful....and I can boast that he adored me. (*She laughs.*) He did everything I wished; he gave me all his money, which wasn't much—so little that I had to commit infidelities...oh, not for vice, but, after all, it's necessary to live. Oh la la! How I changed him during the time we were seeing one another—what, every day! At the beginning, he was young. Oh la la! He wrote, he declaimed—what do I know? He was jealous, he said to me: if I have a woman, whatever she might be, who loves me and is faithful to me, that will compensate me for everything; then he told me that I had a simple nature, unpolished—what do I know? He didn't want to understand, he never understood what I really was (*she snig-*

gers), what I was for him. Oh, but he changed, my dear friends, he changed, I beg you to believe. Oh, I don't boast of having done it all on my own. It's the rum, especially, that became his old friend and whispered advice in his ear.

I'm explaining all that so you'll understand that I have a right to be here and to stay here—I have more rights over him than anyone else. Ah! I want to see that he'll be well buried. (*She laughs.*)

SECOND UNDERTAKER

Of that you can be sure; we're not children, Monsieur and I. Anyway, there's no need for explanation; a beautiful lady is always welcomed by two gallant gentlemen.

FIRST UNDERTAKER

For sure.

THE WHORE

You're polite—that's good. Well. I'll settle in.

She puts her umbrella down in a corner, and takes off her hat and hangs it on a nail. She seems bloated, and even more repulsive. Mame contemplates her admiringly and invites her to sit next to him. He pours her a glass of punch and moves even closer.

SECOND UNDERTAKER

Well, here's a very agreeable mortuary vigil—one could wish that every night was similar, eh, Trouilleby?

FIRST UNDERTAKER

For sure, Monsieur Mame. (*To console himself for the appro-priation of the whore by Mame, he pours himself a large glass and drinks it.*)

SECOND UNDERTAKER, *to the whore*

Then old Samuel was lucky enough to....

THE WHORE

To sleep with me? Yes, and I can assure you that he was solid for a man of his age, but vicious. Oh la la!

SECOND UNDERTAKER, *lit up*

Oh! He was keen?

THE WHORE

For sure! He told me that there was nothing better with rum... and he took full advantage of it!

SECOND UNDERTAKER

Moreover, when one has the good fortune to be loved by a woman so...advantageous...it's only just....

THE WHORE

Loved? Oh la la! Me, love him—you can't imagine! But I had to stay with him, and I stayed...he knew me well, all the same, and I wasn't always as genteel as I am now, you know, my dear. He detested me then; at times, he was afraid of me. Ha ha ha! Idiot!

MAME, *beginning to get drunk*

That doesn't matter! Lucky are those who've been able to please you, adorable woman! (*He kisses her.*)

THE WHORE

That's not what Samuel said. And yet, he always came back to me—he had to! Anyway, if it pleases you....

She allows herself to be drawn on to Mame's knees. He is drinking in large gulps and his face is gradually becoming pale. He puts his right arm around her. The whore is half turned toward the back of the room. A fragment of underwear emerges from her unbuttoned bodice, and her dress is lifted up to the knee. Mame is very cheerful. Trouilleby moves to the back of the room with the bottle of whisky.

THE WHORE

Feel me up, my dear—one more, one less, I don't mind.

FIRST UNDERTAKER

A pleasant evening, in God's name...am content! But the dead man, at five o'clock...need to bury...at five o'clock...neither sooner...nor later...mustn't forget...(*sobbing*)...poor old man... must be bored, like that on his bed, without a drop to pass the time. To endure that, believe me, will drive him to drink.... (*He sniggers.*) What do you think, Monsieur Mame?

SECOND UNDERTAKER, *preoccupied*

About what?

FIRST UNDERTAKER

About giving a drink to the old man, getting bored all on his own!

SECOND UNDERTAKER

Do what you like, Trouilleby, and leave me in peace!

THE WHORE, *to Trouilleby*

Indeed! You're suffering, my lad! Give a drink to a corpse! Behave yourself!

Trouilleby does not hear. Half-filling a glass with whisky, he goes to the bed.

SECOND UNDERTAKER

Madame, when a man wants to do something, women shouldn't interfere!

THE WHORE

Oh! Now you're annoying me.

She draws away slightly. Mame clutches her tenderly.

At the bedside, Trouilleby hesitates, arrested by a scruple.

FIRST UNDERTAKER

Don't you think, Monsieur Mame…don't you think that it's… not very respectful to him?

SECOND UNDERTAKER

Monsieur Trouilleby, if the whim took you to pour alcohol into the jaws of a dead dog, would you hesitate?

FIRST UNDERTAKER

No, but....

SECOND UNDERTAKER

So, do it, if it amuses you. Repudiate all your vain prejudices. A dead man, a dead dog—it's the same thing, no longer anything but a vile carcass!

Fortified by this assurance, Trouilleby staggers toward the bed and pulls back the sheet, uncovering a livid head bristling with a stiff gray beard. He leans over the cadaver.

FIRST UNDERTAKER

How are you, eh? (*He feels the forehead.*) Cool, isn't it?

He sniggers, parts the dead man's lips slightly, and pours the draught of liquid through a gap left by a few missing teeth into the throat. The effect is immediate and unexpected: the body is shaken by a spasm, which launches the arms forward toward the terrified Trouilleby, throwing the undertaker into a panic, so that he starts running hither and yon, green about the gills, no longer possessed of any dignity, searching for an exit or a hiding-place. He does not find one, and crouches down behind the little stove, sticking out to either side of it. He stays there, only the chattering of his teeth disturbing the silence. The whore leans tranquilly on the wall, contemplating the dead man, who has opened alarmed eyes and thrown back the sheet.
He is half-naked, solely wrapped in a chemise in poor condi-

tion, which allows his bony thinness to be seen. He looks around him vaguely and, without speaking, grabs the sheet that was his shroud and wraps himself in it. Then he advances into the room. Seemingly unconscious, he sits down at the table, takes a full glass and drains it. He puts his head on his hand and remains motionless. Meanwhile, the whore approaches him slowly and puts her hand on his shoulder.

THE WHORE

Bonjour, Samuel!

SAMUEL, *shivering and looking around wildly*

Ah! Still there, even now! No matter, I know you too well… my soul is overloaded with filth. If I weren't dead, I'd commit suicide.

THE WHORE

That's stupid! (*She turns to Mame and appeals to hi*m.) Listen to that, Monsieur, eh! The old lecher says he'd commit suicide if he weren't dead!

Mame stands up, his drunkenness augmented by emotion. He has recovered slightly, and is ashamed. A certain rage against the cause of his terror is also invading his brain. Looking at Samuel, he speaks to him.

SECOND UNDERTAKER

What do you expect, Monsieur? What does this conduct signify, to which we haven't been accustomed on the part of your colleagues, who generally retain an appropriate stance! I don't want to criticize your behavior, but, after all, this fashion of brutalizing my colleague, the virtuous Monsieur Trouilleby…

where is Monsieur Trouilleby? (*He catches sight of him huddled on the floor. He goes to him and shakes him.*) Get up, Trouilleby, get up. You might have killed him, Monsieur—in the prime of life! I don't understand your actions at all. When one is dead, one remains quiet!

THE WHORE, *sniggering*

When one is dead, one remains quiet! My word, well said! Isn't it, old Samuel?

SAMUEL

Dead? I've been dead to hope for such a long time! What death is redoubtable except that one? (*He pours a glass of rum and drinks it.*)

THE WHORE

Oh la la! More grand phrases! But he doesn't forget to drink!

SAMUEL

To drink, to drink to forget, since the dead remember! Am I dead or alive? Who can tell me the truth?

THE WHORE

Come on, enough stupidity, old man! You know full well that you're dead, since these gentlemen are here to bury you, and here's your coffin....

FIRST UNDERTAKER

Five o'clock in the morning...no later...no sooner...mustn't forget!

He drains a full glass, sits down and leans on the table.

SECOND UNDERTAKER

It's certain that the physician has certified you as dead, that your heir has visited you and said: "It's not too soon…I'm finally rid of him, the old madman!" and that here's a brand new coffin made expressly to take you to be buried at five o'clock in the morning and to take you to frequent the roots and earthworms. So, you're dead!

SAMUEL, *distractedly*

It's possible that I'm dead. It's possible that my miserable and vile old body has finally died. It's possible that my flesh is rotting already under the kiss of the worm and that I'm already blossoming in flowers in the meadow. It's possible that my name has disappeared from human memory—I don't say the memory of those who loved me, for there were none. Anything is possible, in truth, but it's certain that my immortal soul exists, and aspires, with the folly of hope, finally to know happiness in the great ideal heavens!

THE WHORE

Shut up—you're making me sick! I'd rather make love to my darling undertaker.

She looks at Mame, who has sat down again and is preparing large glasses of whisky and rum for her and for him. Mame draws her toward him again, sniggering.

SECOND UNDERTAKER

Well, old man, when one is dead one isn't jealous, eh? (*He takes the whore on to his knee again. The old man drinks, muttering indistinctly.*) I propose a toast! I drink to beautiful women—and to Madame, who is their representative among us! Well, Trouilleby, are you asleep? Drink up!

Trouilleby, his head in his hands, groans inarticulately. The whore thanks Mame with a noisy kiss. Samuel seems to emerge from his torpor and suddenly stands up, a full glass in his hand.

SAMUEL

I too want to propose a toast!

Listen, everyone, friends of past days, companions of my youth who applauded the flowers of my dreams and clasped with so much sympathy the hand of the man you were to abandon so soon! Listen, women from whom I received avowals of love, so sweet and so deceptive! Listen, O days of drunkenness and illusion when I sensed the crazed ardors of genius, passion and glory burning in my soul—listen! I raise my glass and I drink, with hope and respect, with terror and adoration, to the immense force that vibrates in the human mind, which it tortures and consoles! I drink, in the sincerity of my living and tormented soul, in the bitter consciousness of what was my life, in the eternal memory of all that I have lost irrevocably, in the eternal dolor of having been myself, in the name of all that I have dreamed, I drink recklessly to the Ideal!

THE WHORE

Well! What about me? I'm jealous. So you no longer recognize me, your old companion of days and nights, whom you kissed so many times on the mouth, with despair and disgust, with the rage and shame of sensuality? Ha ha ha! Samuel, old poet, old vagabond, I'll assume my true face: look your life in the face.… I really exist, and I'm your mistress! Come, in order that my arms might close around you, that my warm flesh might live beneath your body, that you can savor your vice once more!

Reject the imbecile Chimera, and come and enjoy Reality!

SAMUEL

Back, prostitute—this is not your moment! My immortal soul belongs entirely to the ideal lover that my mind imagines! She is made of my dreams, my hopes, and my love of beauty. She is more seductive than a divinity, she is pure and faithful—she is the virgin that smiles, adorable and pensive—in the depths of hectic ecstasies, the soul of envisaged Paradises!

The joy of an internal vision seems to transfigure him—but a moment later, he falls back in his chair. The impact is transmitted to the table and the slumbering Trouilleby.

FIRST UNDERTAKER, *his voice thick*

What time is it?

SECOND UNDERTAKER, *emptying his glass and consulting his watch*

Half past five! Devil take us, we're late! Hey, Trouilleby! It's time to nail Monsieur in.

FIRST UNDERTAKER

Of course! Five o'clock exactly! Neither sooner...nor later... mustn't forget! I've got it! (*He gets up. He drinks a large draught. He looks at Mame anxiously.*) But...he's moving.

SECOND UNDERTAKER

Don't bother me with details—let's hurry, we're already late!

THE WHORE, *sniggering*

For sure—and you have to catch up!

SECOND UNDERTAKER, *furious*

Shut your mouth, you! Has one ever seen…? (*He grabs Samuel by the shoulder; in the meantime, Trouilleby brings the coffin into the middle of the room.*) Let's go!

SAMUEL

Extracted from his torpor, he seems to have lost all discernment. He whimpers: Eh? Eh? Don't hurt me!

SECOND UNDERTAKER, *abruptly*

Come on, come on! Hurry up!

He and Trouilleby seize the man brutally and drag him.

SAMUEL, *struggling*

Let me go! Don't hurt me! Oh la la! Help!

SECOND UNDERTAKER, *hitting him*

Damnation! Shut up!

SAMUEL, *pushing him away*

No, no! I don't want to! My soul isn't dead! I don't want my immortal soul to be buried in a coffin where it will suffer! Let me go! My mistress is waiting for me!

THE WHORE

Your mistress? Old debauchee! So I'm not sufficient for you? It's true that we're leaving one another, eh?

SAMUEL

Who's talking about leaving? All my hopes have left me. *To the undertakers, who have grabbed him again and knocked him down*: No, I tell you! My soul is immortal, it's flying in the sky, cradled by the evening breeze! Oh, God, help! They want to kill my soul!

The tumultuous group approaches the table, which, bumped, vacillates. The bottles fall, the candle goes out. The obscurity is feebly combated by a nascent gleam, pale and icy, which passes through the window. The silently struggling group is scarcely discernible; then a dull thud resounds, and muffled groans.

SECOND UNDERTAKER

Relight the candle, Trouilleby!

Trouilleby obeys. Mame is seen crouching over the coffin and leaning on the heavy lid, agitates by somersaults.

SAMUEL'S VOICE, *no longer excited, strangled by sincere horror*

Oh God! I'm dying! What are they doing to me? I'm not dead! I'm not dead! Can't they hear me?

FIRST UNDERTAKER, *kneeling on the lid.*

The hammer, Monsieur Mame.

Mame gives it to him. He begins nailing the lid down. Punctuated by the persevering rhythm of the hammer, cries are still emerging, and becoming weaker.

SAMUEL'S VOICE

They can't hear me! They don't want to hear me! But I remember—the bed, the shroud, my madness! Oh! The prostitute! So she was there! What can I do? Oh God, what can I do? Is there no help? Listen to me—I'm alive; let me out; I'll give you money, I'll give you.... Help! Help! Help! Oh, no one will hear me! I'm suffocating! Malediction! I'm suffocating! Isn't it a nightmare? No, she was there, it's real! Help! Help! Oh...I'm dying...oh....

SECOND UNDERTAKER, *sitting on the lid*

That's all right, he'll shut up. Fortunately, the cemetery isn't far, the grave's already dug, we'll fill it in ourselves...and then he won't say anything more...otherwise they might think that we'd buried a man alive. (*He laughs.*) A singular idea, all the same! Believing oneself to be alive when one's dead! With others, that might have succeeded, but not with us, eh, Trouilleby?

FIRST UNDERTAKER, *deferentially*

With you, Monsieur Mame, with you.

SECOND UNDERTAKER

With us, with us! Not so much modesty, Monsieur Trouilleby! Veritably, in these unfortunate circumstances, your conduct has been praiseworthy—praiseworthy, I'm pleased to recognize!

The coffin is nailed shut. The cries have ceased. Nothing more can be hard but a vague groaning.

FIRST UNDERTAKER

All's well. (*He stands up, looks at the bottles and swallows a few drops that remain in one of them.*) Now, forwards!

They lift the coffin on to their shoulders.

SECOND UNDERTAKER

He's devilishy heavy. Dirty old swine—if they were all like him....

FIRST UNDERTAKER

If you ask me, he was drunk.

They go out. The woman who came to oppress until death the man she had always oppressed has now disappeared. The room is empty. The smoky flame of the candle pales in the light of dawn.

SCENES IN A TAVERN

DRAMATIS PERSONAE

The Innkeeper
A Taciturn Man
An Old Jew
A Scoundrel
A Man
A Poor Drunkard
A Regular of the Tavern
Five Deserting Sailors
A Naval Officer
Marine Soldiers
A Young Woman with her Child
A Drunken Old Woman

The room is square. The low ceiling is supported by black-ened beams from which two smoky copper lamps hang, to the right and the left, lighting the whole room weakly. The walls are covered with dilapidated roughcast. The one to the right is pierced by two narrow windows, very close together, sealed by heavy wooden shutters behind their dusty and broken lead-framed panes. Between the windows is an arched door made of dark wood and garnished with iron; every time it opens its bolt resonates and it grates noisily. Along the walls there are wooden benches, massive tables and stools. A stove extends its crooked flue through the room. At the back stand two enormous oak barrels, almost black; a long ladder is propped against one of them. Barring the space between them, a high and dirty counter extends, laden with bottles. In front of the left-hand barrel, a closed trap-door is outlined on the floor.

Behind the counter stands Jonas Thripp, innkeeper, an immensely large fat man endowed with a prodigious abdomen over which his plump hands can scarcely join up. He is clad in violet, beige and pink check trousers, and a matching waist-coat charged with a heavy gilded chain, which is unbuttoned, allowing sight of a blood red flannel shirt, over the collar of which descends the yellow rind of his cheeks, bristling with brick-colored hairs. On the innkeeper's head is jammed a double-brimmed cap, as multicolored as his trousers.

Jonas Thripp is seated on an exceedingly high stool, smoking his pipe. Sometimes he gets down to serve a drink or to circulate about the room, waddling like a duck.

In the far corner on the right, the Taciturn Man is sitting on a bench. He is thin, clean-shaven and staring wide-eyed into the void. His clothing is somber. In front of him is a half-empty bottle of whisky and a full glass. From time to time he drinks, and then returns to immobility, his hands flat on the table.

On the same side, sitting on a stool, half-turned toward the door, is the Jew. He is red-haired, old and grotesquely incarnates the type-specimen of his race. He is dressed in a sordid frock-coat.

At the next table is the Drunken Old Woman. Her ruddy face seems swollen. In the middle protrudes a singularly livid bulbous nose. Her eyes are haggard, her mouth allows her inferior jaw to droop slackly, revealing violet-tinted gums and a few teeth. The old woman is wearing a large and lamentable plush hat garnished with frayed bonnet-strings and pretentious but pitiful plumes, which hang down over her face, mingling with a few unkempt wisps of hair. She is clad in a ragged striped shawl, wrapped over rags. She is drinking gin.

At the table furthest away from the counter on the left is the Regular of the Tavern. He is a tall and solid individual, rela-

tively well-dressed. His face, by virtue of its uniform pink tint, little eyes submerged in fat, and stiff white hairs, is reminiscent of that of a pig. He is smoking a short-stemmed wooden pipe, and has a bottle of eau-de-vie in front of him.

The room is silent. From time to time, from outside, squalls of rain can be heard pattering on the ground, and the grating of the chains mooring boats to the edge of the nearby river. Suddenly, the door opens and the lamps flicker in a gust of damp wind, which enters at the same time as Jim Chassuy, the poor drunkard. He is soaked, thin, clean-shaven and ragged. He closes the door carefully and shakes himself.

JIM CHASSUY, *obsequiously*

I wish the honorable company a good evening. Detestable weather, in truth! (*No one replies. He sits down at the table nearest the counter.*) How goes it, Master Thripp?

THE INNKEEPER *disdainfully, not moving*

Well enough.

JIM CHASSUY, *humbly*

Give me a glass of gin, Master Thripp; I'm frozen.

THE INNKEEPER, *still impassive*

Have you the money this evening?

JIM CHASSUY

I have a penny, but I need to keep it to be able to sleep at the night-shelter. It's too cold to stay outside.

THE INNKEEPER

In that case, no.

JIM CHASSUY

Just one glass, I beg you, Master—just one glass.

THE INNKEEPER

Not a drop; it would be unfair to my family.

JIM CHASSUY, *desperately*

Well, I'll work to unload your barrels, if you wish—I'll do it as I did last month—you can pay me when you wish. If you remember, I did the work well—so well that I was ill for several days, for I can't carry such heavy things. I was determined never to do it again, but truly, it's too cold this evening and I'm too unhappy. Anything's preferable to the absence of gin. Give me gin, I beg you! I seem to be drinking joy and I become a different man! Without gin, it's frightful!

THE INNKEEPER

If you work to unload my barrels, I'll gladly give you gin this evening—but only sixpence for all the work, and not for the day, because you're too slow.

JIM CHASSUY, *hesitantly*

What, only sixpence for more than one day? Such hard work!

THE INNKEEPER

Yes, only sixpence, not a penny more, and it'll be the last time

I employ you, because you make me lose at least a demijohn. If you don't want it, you can go elsewhere.

JIM CHASSUY

Yes, yes, I accept! It's agreed.

THE INNKEEPER, *bringing him a glass.*

Above all, get here early.

JIM CHASSUY

Yes, yes, without fail....

At this point the drunken old woman begins to make herself heard. Her wide eyes staring into the void and her hands flat on the table, she mutters the words of a hymn, but her voice is so low that one can scarcely grasp any of them.

JIM CHASSUY, *drinking with a sigh of satisfaction*

Delightful stuff! A thousand thanks, Master Thripp!

Bang! Bang! Bang! With violent blows of the fist, the taciturn man shakes the table. The innkeeper raises his head; with a movement of his chin, the man indicates his empty bottle; the innkeeper comes and fills it. He is returning to his place when a group of sailors comes in, jostling one another.

FIRST SAILOR

Shut the door, then, Isaac.

Isaac obeys. They all come to take their places around a table facing the door, between the Jew and the Old Woman. They are wearing reefer jackets and dirty hats, torn and covered with tar.

FIRST SAILOR, *tapping the table with a silver coin*

Rum, comrade! Lots of rum!

The innkeeper serves them.

SECOND SAILOR, *slapping him on the belly*

Still fat, then, old Thripp! Still as solid as a post!

They drink and stuff their pipes, the smoke of which rises up toward the beams, combining with the tar-saturated vapors that their damp clothes exhale. The room fills with a heavy and odorous mist. There is a pause.

THIRD SAILOR, *in a low voice*

Are we safe here? There's no fear of being caught?

FIRST SAILOR

No fear—the tavern's isolated, as you've seen, and its light doesn't show outside.

FOURTH SAILOR

It's none too soon, all the same—accursed Press Gang.

FIFTH SAILOR

You said it, Isaac: accursed, and thrice accursed Press! To work for the king and not a sou—to get yourself killed for nothing is no bargain. And in the meantime, the children die of starvation or their mother is obliged to…brrr!

FOURTH SAILOR, *laughing*

Oh, that not what stops me.…

FIFTH SAILOR

Of course not—you're a bachelor. But ask Harry and Bob whether they don't think the same as me.

FIRST SAILOR, *with conviction.*

Too true!

THIRD SAILOR

Me, I don't have a wife and don't want one. It's cumbersome and expensive. But even so, the king's navy really is too hard—the cat-o'-nine-tails and the bastinado for nothing. And it's a lucky man who retires, for the rope's always there if the bullets forget you. One word too loud and there it is: insubordination! And then, not a minute of liberty to amuse oneself. Oh no, it's not for good lads! Commerce is the thing! Beware of the Press!

A pause.

THE REGULAR

Hey, Jonas—brandy!

THE INNKEEPER, *serving*

There you are, Your Honor

THE JEW, *mysteriously, to the sailors*

Would you like to buy any of the pretty things I have here?

He brings out of his pockets mirrors, razors, knives, pipes and other miscellaneous objects. I don't sell them dear—not dear at all. *To the first sailor*: A pretty knife?

FIRST SAILOR

No, old man—I have my own, and you don't have one like it. He brings an enormous cutlass out of his pocket, capable of slaying a rhinoceros.

THE JEW

A good pipe?

FIRST SAILOR

No, no, you can see that we have our own.

THE JEW

Well, these nice little rings, for your girl-friends, eh?

He smiles like an old figurine sculpted in chestnut and exhibits brass rings.

SECOND SAILOR, *impatiently*

Leave us in peace, old man, Go back to your bazaar. We've got other things to do.

THE JEW

Oh, yes—the Press. That doesn't prevent....

SECOND SAILOR, *angrily*

What? The Press doesn't prevent…imbecile! Do you even know what it is?

THE JEW

No, I don't—I've never come here before.

SECOND SAILOR

Well, old man, this is what the Press is: when good lads like us have left a corvette or a frigate, and it's known where they are, when dusk falls, marine soldiers throng the streets and go in everywhere to capture deserters, as they call us. And then, all those who are taken are embarked! And a week in irons, and years on a cruiser so agreeable that if one doesn't die of hunger it's by special protection. Have you seen the port's flag tonight?"

THE JEW, *astonished*

No, I haven't seen it.

SECOND SAILOR

Well, you'd have seen that it's yellow, which means Press, as blue means No Press. It's to warn the inhabitants to shut themselves indoors. As they're doing, see. (*He indicates the drinkers.*) That's what the Press is, you old rogue. Now buy me glass of gin—I've talked enough for two.

THE JEW, *embarrassed*

I'm very poor.…

SECOND MATELOT

That's a good one! He shrugs his shoulders and takes a swig of rum.

THE OLD WOMAN, *still drinking in her solitary corner, becoming excited*

Praise be to Christ! Glory to the Lord! In a high-pitched, hoarse voice she intones a hymn: Honor to Jehovah/Let's proclaim his praise/And detest the mire/which his hand washes away/Let us gather behind/behind his banner/who subjugates our hearts, with gentle ardor/He is so fine/the white lamb/He is so fine/He is so fine!

The anxious sailors look at her from the corners of their eyes. The Innkeeper seems discontented. The old woman continues, more loudly:

I have full confidence/For my heart is his/But protect us well....

She is interrupted by the door, which opens. The sailors start in alarm, but it is only a lone man. He is tall and bony, clad in an old frock-coat and coiffed to the eyebrows in a large, extremely battered gray top hat. His hair, almost colorless—as is his beard—falls in wisps to either side of is face.

The unknown man comes in at a deliberate pace, slow and majestic. Without looking around or pronouncing a word, he goes to the back of the room and, over the counter, puts his right fist under the innkeeper's nose. The latter get down from his stool and emerges from the counter. The interested sailors form a circle. The unknown man puts his hat on the ground. He and the innkeeper stand face to face, each in a boxer's stance, in the middle of the room. The fight is ready to begin.

Without budging, the Old Woman continues singing, to accompany the exploits of the boxers with her hymn.

THE OLD WOMAN

Let us be mistrustful/And of cynical wickedness/And of vile immodesty/By which are insulted/My laudable purity!/He is so fine/The white lamb/He is so fine/He is so fine!

THE REGULAR, *standing up and serving as referee*

Lay on!

Blows are exchanged. The innkeeper shows more agility that such adipose development appears to permit. He jumps to the right and the left, making the parquet tremble and proffering hoarse grunts. His adversary, motionless, lands numerous punches. Thripp ripostes vigorously. Already, his right fist, falling on his adversary's face, has bruised it, causing him to spit out two teeth and a mouthful of blood.

THE REGULAR

Good hit, Jonas!

THIRD SAILOR

Warm up, lads! Oh, nice riposte!

That approval is won by a skillful stratagem on the part of the unknown, who, feigning to leave an opening, flattens his adversary's nose with a violent punch. Blood spurts. A one-minute truce is declared. The combatants drink. The innkeeper, with Chassuy's aid, ties a blue handkerchief horizontally around his head to stop the blood flowing from his nostrils.

SECOND SAILOR

They're well-matched, Three shillings on the tall man's ripostes.

THE REGULAR

I'll take it! Hurrah for Jonas' fist!

THE JEW, *to himself*

I'd like to bet, but I don't know which is the stronger.

The door opens, and Skerres, the scoundrel, appears. He is short, thickset and dressed in a coarse velvet frock-coat. He is wearing a cap. He looks around, and comes toward the Jew.

SKERRES, *to everyone*

Don't disturb yourselves. *And to the innkeeper*: I'll drink at any time.

He sits down beside the Jew and embarks upon a discussion with him in low voices, showing him various objects under the table, which he takes from his pockets. Golden gleams are glimpsed.

THE OLD WOMAN, *singing*

Open the widows/and the door of Zion!

THIRD SAILOR, *irritatedly*

Shut up, you old sow!

THE OLD WOMAN, *imperturbably*

My gaze penetrates there/From my lions' den!

The pugilism resumes, but this time Thripp immediately seizes the advantage with a straight blow that bruises the unknown man's left eye, with a flaccid sound. Immediately, the eyelid swells and is surrounded by a wide aubergine-colored aureole.

THE INNKEEPER, *his voice stifled by his handkerchief*

Take that, fellow!

THE SAILOR *who bet on the afflicted man*

Damn!

The bout is coming to an end. The unknown man is manifestly inferior. His arms are slack. He can no longer see clearly and his face is turning blue under blows. Finally, he falls, covered in blood.

THE OLD WOMAN

He is so fine/The white lamb/He is so fine/He is so fine!

THE INNKEEPER

Had enough?

The man on the ground makes a negative gesture. He wipes his face and drinks a glass of rum brought to him by a sailor. Finally, he gets to his feet. There is a further resumption. It is brief. Three times, with a dull sound like a laundry-beater, with a remarkable propulsive power, Thripp's fist strikes his adversary's face; the latter totters but remains upright. Finally, a fourth blow at the base of the sternum hurls him, unconscious, to the ground. A sailor picks him up, supports him on his knee and makes him drink a mixture of rum, gin and pepper that the victor has prepared. The invalid is shaken by a violent commo-

tion. He stands up, and without a word, picks up his hat, puts it on, throws a silver coin on the table and goes out. The sailor who bet on him pays the winner, without comment.

The innkeeper, placid and jovial, takes off the handkerchief, His nose has the form and color of a tomato.

THE INNKEEPER

Every month, the same thing.

FOURTH SAILOR

What, every month?

THE INNKEEPER

Yes. Last spring that man came here to tell me that, exactly a month before, I had trodden on his foot in a crowd. He had only waited to get better and wanted a boxing match for the insult. One can't refuse such a thing.

FOURTH SAILOR

Certainly not.

THE OLD WOMAN, *singing louder than ever*

The angels in rapture/Are beating their drums/And the sweet sound caresses/The hearing of my love!

THE JEW, *unable to hear what Skerres is saying*

The old woman is being very annoying.

THE INNKEEPER

Then we boxed. And since then, every month, on the day when I wounded him, he comes back, without ever forgetting, and we box. I don't mind, because it takes the rust off, and he's a worthy fellow. I've already broken a dozen of his teeth like that—another two this evening makes fourteen. I'm keeping them to make a necklace. (*He laughs.*)

THE OLD WOMAN, *screeching*

He is so fine/The white lamb/He is so fine/He is so fine!

SECOND SAILOR, exasperated

Curse you and the lamb! Shut your mouth, you old saucepan!

SKERRES, shouting

A pint of ale, Innkeeper! And make that old tramp shut up, damn it! We can't hear ourselves.

The old woman only interrupts her hymn, each verse of which she has recommenced several times, to drink. She is dead drunk, sitting stiffly on her bench, with her hat oscillating at every quiver and spilling its deplorable feathers in every direction.

THE OLD WOMAN

But the glories of the world/Want to shackle me/And without respite/As perfidious as the waves/They come in troops/ Forsaking all modesty/They hold out their cup/To my dear candor/He is so fine/The white lamb/He is so fine/He is so fine!

THE INNKEEPER

Mistress, I dare to say that I'm religious and a friend of the children of Christ, but you really are intolerable. Shut up or get out!

THE OLD WOMAN, *bellowing at the top of her voice*

Yes, but Christ is my goal/Beware my soul?/He crowns my flame/For I have not drunk!

The innkeeper attempts to grab her, but she escapes and hurls a bottle at his head. Thripp avoids the missile and the bottle breaks on the wall. Tumult. With the aid of Chassuy and two sailors, the Innkeeper gets hold of the old woman, who struggles, knocking over stools, putting up a desperate resistance and vociferating her hymn terribly, mingled with the insults and blasphemies of the clawed and bitten sailors. Simultaneously:

THE OLD WOMAN

Ah! I glimpse Heaven/Gleaming through the spite!/Hurrah for the spectacle/For evil it's catastrophe!

THE SAILORS

Damnation, she's scratching me!
Valley of Jehosophat, the old scab!
Hold her, Bob!
Oh, damn. She's got away!
I'm bleeding—my God, what a harpy!

CHASSUY, *screeching*

Oh la la! She's put my eye out!

They have, however, succeeded in getting her to the door as the verse ends. Violently, they throw her outside into the heavy rain. Vaguely, one can still hear:

He is so fine/He is so fine!

Less than a minute has gone by, however, when she comes back in, covered with yellow-tinted liquid mud; her hat is flattened and absolutely detestable. She tries to come down the steps but misses the first and collapses to the floor, where she remains immobile, snoring powerfully. The innkeeper rolls her to the wall with his foot.
A silence.

SKERRES, *loudly, thumping the table*

No, no, no and no! You won't take me for a fool, Solomon! If you're a Jew, I'm an Irishman—that compensates.

THE JEW, *trying to shut him up*

La, la...shh! Don't get carried away like that. I really can't go any higher.

SKERRES

Then it's all for nothing that I've...? Come on, you old crow, you can devour me when I'm dead, but in the meantime, be conscientious and don't steal from me beyond the permitted limits. *A pause.* So that's it—you won't put up any more. You know that I'll go to see Abraham.

THE JEW, *embarrassed*

Little man, little man! Let's see—wait until tomorrow evening; I'll think about it until then. Let's see—ten o'clock...."

SKERRES

All right, but it's the last minute, you know. Make up your mind, and no tricks! Watch out!

He crosses the room, heading for the door.

THE JEW, *shouting*

Your pint! Your pint! He hasn't paid!

SKERRES, *sniggering*

It's on your account, you old rogue.

He goes out. The Jew groans. A few minutes go by.

FIRST SAILOR, *to the innkeeper*

What time is it, comrade?

THE INNKEEPER, *consulting his watch*

Half past eleven.

THIRD SAILOR

Damn! It's now or never, the danger of being caught!

FOURTH SAILOR

Bah! There's nothing to fear here. Give us rum, Master Tripp.

Suddenly, Annie comes in rapidly, her child in her arms. She is a young woman, seemingly no older than twenty or twenty-two years old. Her face is thin and pale, pretty enough with its large unhealthily shining eyes and thick dark hair, unkempt beneath a black bonnet. She is dressed in a frayed skirt and a ragged bodice. The skin of her neck and arms can be seen through the holes. She is soaked, as are the rags that make a formless package of the child. Scarcely has she entered than she is seized by a violent fit of coughing. She places the child on a bench near the door. A few feeble whimpers escape the package, but they are drowned out by the mother's coughing. Finally, Annie gets her breath back and is able to speak.

ANNIE, *in a hollow and muffled voice*

Give me some gin, Innkeeeper?

THE INNKEEPER, *coldly*

Mistress Annie, you've already drunk here on credit for nine shillings two pence—it would be unfair to my family to give you any more to drink without money. Do you have money tonight?

ANNIE, *excited and breathless*

What, you won't give me anything? And you think that I can go without gin? Ha ha! You're funny. I'm frozen, dying of hunger and you think I can do without gin. Ha ha ha! *She coughs as she laughs and goes on angrily*: You'll give me gin, I tell you! You'll give me some! It's only gin that's keeping me alive. It's only admirable gin that warms me up and cheers me up. I'll sing you something if you want, but I want gin right away. I want to get drunk to cheer myself up. I want to forget everything for the short while I have to live!

She coughs and wipes her bloody lips with a piece of cloth.

THE INNKEEPER, coldly

I can no longer give you any more to drink without being paid right away, Mistress. I can't, not any more!

ANNIE

You can't, any more? But come on, it's impossible that you're refusing me! Master Thripp, I beg you! Think—my husband was hanged last week! He was a blackguard, but I loved him. My child's ill now, and I'm all alone. Think! All alone and without a sou...what do you expect me to do without gin? Jut one glass—come on!

THE INNKEEPER

It's futile, Mistress; what's said is said.

He gets to his feet with the evident intention of throwing her out. The sailors have followed the scene, sniggering or sympathizing. The Regular of the Tavern gazes attentively at the young woman with an appreciative half-smile. Annie's headscarf is loose and allows a glimpse of her throat. The fat man makes a sign to Thripp.

THE REGULAR, *to the innkeeper*

Wait, Jonas! *To Annie*: Come here a moment, beauty! Let's see you!

Annie turns round, sees the man and initially recoils, but then blushes deeply and comes nearer.

ANNIE

How can I be of service to Your Honor? Would you like to pay for the gin? (*She laughs.*)

THE REGULAR

Hee hee! Why not? A pretty girl can always find a kind fellow to offer her what she needs, if she's not too hard to reach an understanding with him. Hee hee. (*Brutally:*) You're free this evening?

Annie hesitates for a second, then makes a gesture of indifference.

ANNIE

Free, your honor; entirely at Your Honor's disposition. But get me a drink first. When I'm drunk, I'll do whatever you want.

She sits down at a corner of the table. At a sign from the Regular, Thripp brings gin to the young woman, who drinks it in large glassfuls. The Regular does not know what to say but feels compelled to speak.

THE REGULAR

My word, you drink well. One can see that you like gin. (*He laughs.*)

ANNIE

Gin, rum, whisky, everything that causes drunkenness, forgetfulness, generates joy and warmth. I need it! (*She laughs, and drinks.*)

Bang! Bang! Bang! The Taciturn man's habitual thumping demands a further supply of drink. It is served.

THE REGULAR

You need it?

ANNIE, *becoming animated*

My God, yes! My life, especially now, is so gay that I'll soon go mad if I don't die sooner.... (*She begins to get drunk and to talk unconsciously, her elbow on her knee, her chin in her hand, swinging her foot.*) It's singular, the marvelous luck I've had since I became a woman. Before, I was happy in my tranquil little town. I worked a little, all went well. But then a man told me he loved me. Good, I loved him too. I was very young, I marry him. And two months later, I learn that my dear husband is a murderer already condemned to death. Funny, isn't it? Moreover, he continued. Instead of going far away, as I wanted him to, he brought me here. He consumed all that I had. It's true that he taught me to drink! (*She laughs.*) And when he no longer has a sou, he stole again. There's a new way of living happily! He was caught, and last week, hanged. Hanged—I can still see it...now, since then, I'm dying of starvation. I'd got the habit of drinking with him, I continue, and, this evening, in order to be consoled by the powerful gin, I'm going with this fat and ugly gentleman.... (*She nods her head toward the fat man, who has not heard the whole sentence.*)

THE REGULAR

Yes, that's right. Let's go.

He pays and goes out with the young woman, who is singing an old refrain in a low voice.

THE INNKEEPER, *sniggering*

Good night, Your Honor!

The old woman is still snoring under the table. The sailors are half asleep and the Jew, vexed at having wasted his evening, is getting ready to go leave when the dull rhythmic tread of a marching troop is heard. The sailors jump to their feet, in unison.

FIRST SAILOR

Damn! Here come the soldiers!

FOURTH SAILOR, *running madly back and forth*

Malediction! Malediction!

THIRD SAILOR

Quick, let's hide—you have a hiding-place, don't you, Jonas?

THE INNKEEPER

The cellar, if you like!

He opens the trap-door in front of the right-hand barrel, revealing a hole into which a ladder plunges. The sailors hasten to go down. The Innkeeper closes the hatch again. Scarcely has he done so than the door opens violently and a uniformed naval officer appears. He is red-haired and ruddy-faced, tall and scornful. His saber swings and resonates.

THE OFFICER

You have deserters here! Where are they? (*The Innkeeper opens his mouth, about to reply.*) No point denying it—I'm sure of the fact I know them personally: Bob, Harry and the others. Come on, come on, where are they?

THE INNKEEPER

Your Honor is mistaken. No one but these gentlemen. (*He indicates the drinkers.*) No deserters!

THE OFFICER, *impatiently*

Come on, I'm in a hurry. I don't have time to search the whole house. Two guineas to the man who can tell me where they are!

THE JEW and THE INNKEEPER, *simultaneously*

There, Your Honor! (*They point to the cellar door.*)

THE OFFICER

Very well! (*He makes a sign. Soldiers come in and open the trap-door.*)

THE OFFICER, *leaning over*

Bob, Harry, Isaac, Ben and Williams! You're discovered—your host has sold you; it's futile to persist in staying down there, and even more futile to resist—it can only procure you a rope at the end of a yard-arm, or at least memories of the cat-o'-nine-tails. Be good lads, come out of your own accord.

Noises are heard in the cellar; then the head of a sailor appears. He climbs the ladder. A second comes after him, and all five emerge successively. They are chained to a wooden bar that is passed under their right arms. They seem dejected and allow themselves to be attached and led away without saying a word. However, as they reach the door, the third turns round abruptly, half-waving his arms at the Innkeeper.

THIRD SAILOR

Au revoir, Master Thripp!

The Innkeeper shrugs his shoulders. The Officer throws two gold coins on the ground and leaves. The Jew launches himself forward and picks them up, but the Innkeeper tears them away from him with a rapid gesture and shoves him back.

THE JEW, *angrily*

There's no justice! I should have half, at least. You're a thief!

The Innkeeper looks at him, then seizes him by the collar, drives him to the door with kicks, throws him out and closes the door again.
Bang! Bang! Bang! The Taciturn Man's position has changed; he has slipped part way under the table. The Innkeeper serves him.
Suddenly, Annie comes running back in, head bare, her clothes in disarray. The fat man comes after her, congested, seemingly stupefied, and extremely discontented.

ANNIE, *shouting*

My baby! My baby! I've forgotten my baby! (*She runs around the tavern like a madwoman, looking everywhere.*)

THE INNKEEPER

It's inconceivable—one doesn't forget one's child. (*He shrugs his shoulders.*)

ANNIE

Where is he? Where is he? My dear baby! My dear little baby!

(*She finally discovers him under the bench where she put him down. She unwraps him rapidly. The little face is violet, the eyes vitreous. Annie looks at the infant fearfully.*) What's wrong with him? What's wrong with him? He's frozen! Ah!

She utters a loud scream and launches herself toward the door, the child in her arms.

THE REGULAR, *trying to stop her*

Come on, come on—calm down, Mistress!

ANNIE, *shoving him away*

Curse you! Let me be!

THE REGULAR

But where are you going?

ANNIE, *pulling away*

Where am I going? The river!

She runs out, and soon the muffled sound of a fall into the river is heard. Jim Chassuy goes toward the door with the Innkeeper and the Regular.

JIM CHASSUY

Let's take a look. It's true, all the same—she's drowned herself.

THE INNKEEPER, *placidly*

It's the best thing she could do now, because, for her, letting her drink on credit, I'd never have done that again—really, never again. It wouldn't have been fair to my family.

THE REGULAR

Stories like that are very disagreeable, very disagreeable....

They go out. At the same moment, the Taciturn Man empties his bottle of alcohol at a single draught. His head is level with the table. Still holding his bottle, he raised his arms to the heavens at the exact moment that the door slams shut, in a furious gust of wind that extinguishes the lamps. Profound darkness. A solemn voice is then heard. It is that of the Taciturn Man.

THE VOICE

Life is an excellent thing. Oh, excellent! I bless the good God!

Glasses break in the darkness, and a heavy fall is heard: that of the Taciturn Man, who slides under the table, dead drunk.

And that is all.

THE AQUARIUM

It was a Friday in an aquarium.

Outside, the tedious downpours of an April afternoon were streaming from the damp sky over the muddy park.

Inside, along the gallery of artificial rocks, the enervated atmosphere of hothouses reigned, and the vaporous shadow that the green water and panes of glass were filtering.

There was a musky scent of exotic flowers. There was the distinguished scent that a lady perfumed with white-rose was emitting. There was the lady herself, elegant, young and fallible. There was also, with the lady, a gentleman, very chic, stupid and seductive. There were the fish behind their glass walls. There was, between the gentleman and the lady, a banal little new-born phantom that was making sly grimaces, in order that he might be mistaken for Cupid.

There was also the sweet and sour sensuality of captious spring.

At any rate, the gentleman and the lady were together in front of one of the glass walls, and they were not married to one another—which resulted in them looking far less into the green-tinted water than one another's eyes. In consequence, their hearts felt something like a nip of anguish and a penchant for mystery and harmless peril, with a small quantity of the romantic.

His words impassioned, in the solitude of the aquarium, the gentleman was murmuring them in an enchanting voice, and was not adequately repressing gestures that were the prelude to those which are forbidden....

Meanwhile, when she dared not look at the gentleman, the lady daydreamed, or feigned a reverie, by vaguely contemplating, without actually seeing, the fish on the other side of the glass.

Every time that some inconvenient visitor appeared in the aquarium, however, the gentleman ceased his gestures and changed the subject of the conversation. And he began, for the entertainment of the lady, a continually-interrupted lecture on the natural history of fish—about which, moreover, he knew nothing.

And the lady, who had shivered and taken a step back, pretended to be listening while putting on a shrewish expression, but with a hint of embarrassment.

Then, when the visitor had gone, the gentleman drew closer to the lady and rapidly reverted to inflamed rhetoric, pressures of the hand and other seductive manifestations....

And the lady, after a few sighed remarks about their imprudence and everything that she was risking for him, once again—for she was fallible—vibrated in unison.

And they went on like that.

Now, on the other side of the glass, in the sea-water, there was a family of fish who were watching the gentleman and the lady with as much interest as the gentleman and the lady pretended to have for them when people went by. That family of fish, happy and united, was composed of a father, a mother and three children. Each of them had an enormous head, large frightened eyes and a small tail.

The father fish, for the education and pleasure of his sons, was telling them fine stories about those funny human beings who had been there for an hour on the other side of the glass without seeing them; and he commented in his own fashion on the words and actions of those beings. He taught his sons many things by that means, but in his teaching, as in all teaching, there was far more falsehood than truth, and far more personal appreciation than perspicacious observation. It was, however, good education.

Thus, in the solitude of the aquarium, the gentleman seducer said to the fallible lady: "Lucile…oh, Lucile! Your hand…give me your hand…I adore you.…"

"I'm trembling," said the lady. "It's madness…if my husband.…"

And the father fish explained to his sons: "Examine those two closely, children. I've shown you some quite similar, but these constitute the type specimens of the genre. For an hour they've been there, doing nothing and repeating the same words. It's a malady from which theirs species suffers. It's generally manifest by their becoming red or pale, tremulous, excited and stupid. It's contagious; when someone catches it, he immediately tries to give it to the person who has contaminated him. That doesn't always succeed. It varies in its seriousness. It's necessary to let the disease take its course, but it gets better on its own.…"

"Papa," said the youngest fish, a baby still ignorant of the facts of life, "why does one of them have two legs and the other a big bell instead?"

"I've already told you that, little scatterbrain," the father replied. "The one with two legs is a male and the one that has a bell is a female. In this disease, which they catch two by two, there's always one with two legs and another with a bell.…"

"But how does that one move with a bell instead of legs?" persisted the bay, stubbornly.

"It doubtless runs on wheels, or something similar," the worthy father replied, a trifle embarrassed. "But listen to what they're saying."

"Lucile," cooed the gentleman, in a concentrated and convulsive fashion. "Lucile, oh, Lucile! I.…"

"Shh!" said the lady, stepping back. "People are coming.…"

Indeed, a pregnant maid and a fireman appeared, both wet and mud-spattered. Hand in hand, in front of everyone, they went through the aquarium.

"Lucile," resumed the gentleman, who did not think it worthwhile to resume his lecture on ichthyology for so little, gazing intently, "Lucile…I.…"

"Papa, Papa!" cried the eldest of the fish sons. "Look at his eyes—the man with the two legs.…"

"It's an indication that the disease is reaching its apogee," the father explained. "It's what the ill-mannered individuals of his species call 'dead fish eyes'—as if one of us, even dead, has ever looked like that.…"

"My God," said the lady, "I think that's the maid of the cousin of my old piano teacher. If she recognized me, I'm doomed… my husband.…"

"Lucile," purred the gentleman seducer, "Lucile, I adore you.…"

Thus, for them, the time passed agreeably.

Outside, the rain was still inundating the muddy garden, falling from the white sky. Inside, the soporific air was even heavier, and possessed of a sicklier and more imperious sensuality. And the lady became increasingly fallible, and the gentleman increasingly seductive.

"Come here, children—don't look at those two any longer," said the scandalized mother fish, taking her sons away.

A Cook caravan charged into the aquarium like a whirlwind, preceded by a tour-guide, sweeping everything out of its way. For a few terrifying minutes the gentleman seducer, holding on to the rail, supported his companion with one arm, struggling against the avalanche that had taken him by surprise in the middle of a sharp explosion of sentiment. And the gentleman, wishing to save appearances in the eyes of the Cooks, who were filing past, bellowed zoological terms in the tumult.

"That one," he proffered, indicating the father fish behind the glass to his frightened companion, "is a *Polychelles ferox*.[13] When one takes it out of the water, its swim-bladder comes out of its mouth."

"And you!" cried the irritated father fish. "And you, imbecile,

---

13. *Polycheles* (with one *l*) is actually a genus of crustaceans.

if you're taken out of the air, does your bladder come out of your mouth?" And he turned his back.

"My God," moaned the lady, "I'm doomed."

Meanwhile, with their noses in their guide-books and indifferent to the external world, the Cooks had passed by.

"I want to go," said the lady. "I want to go...."

"Lucile, I adore you," sighed the gentleman seducer.

She stayed.

The shadows of the damp evening were oscillating under the trees; and the keepers were thinking that they ought to close up; and the father fish was taking his sons home for dinner; and the gentleman seducer was obtaining, with a kiss, a promise from the fallible lady for the following day, when there was a kind of tumult at the entrance to the aquarium.

"I'm going in, I tell you!" roared a voice, hoarse with rage.

"My husband!" cried the lady, feeling ill, leaning on the shoulder of the gentleman seducer.

"Help!" cried the latter, putting her on the ground and running hither and yon, in a panic.

"It's becoming amusing!" said the father fish. "Come and see, children!"

"Treacherous woman! You make me sick!" howled a fat man, furiously, as he ran up at top speed. "Perish, wretches!"

And he fired two revolvers, with which his hands were armed, simultaneously.

There was a frightful noise. A muddy deluge sprang forth, inundating everything.

"I'm dead," moaned the gentleman seducer, who had not been hit.

"I'm soaked," groaned the lady, who had fainted momentarily. She got to her feet, streaming, and added: "My dress is ruined."

"The glass is broken, the aquarium destroyed!" roared a keeper, taking hold of the fat gentleman.

"Thus perish all thieves of honor!" the latter pronounced, nobly, striking a slightly oblique pose. "I am the hand of justice!"

"Savage beast," coughed the father fish, who was dying on the floor with his entire family. "You've missed your target and hit the innocent, as your kind always does!"

And he rendered his last sigh.

A MANUFACTURER OF HUMAN DOUBLES

This factory exists in America, and supplies the entire world. It is directed by Mr. J. C. Turkey, an honorable gentleman who founded it several years ago and has been able to give this important creation the energetic and intelligent direction that the complete development of such an important venture requires.

The products of this peerless company are utterly superior and defy all competition. It is impossible to do better work of this sort. Mr. Turkey has created his industry from scratch and had taken it to the extreme limits of perfection. The admirable subjects whose collaboration he assures for a high price are capable of assuming the most difficult characters, confronting the most visible situations, and playing the most delicate and complicated roles, without one having to fear the slightest weakness on their part. They are able to double the most well-known individuals, the most eccentric personalities as well as the dullest, without being distinguishable from the real thing by the most intimate friends or the most vigilant enemies of those they incarnate.

Mr. Turkey is a gentleman in the prime of life, distinguished, phlegmatic and clean-shaven.

"I can't tell you precisely," he explained to me in answer to a question—we were sitting in his study, with cigars and whisky-and-sodas. "I really can't tell you…it's a long time since I had the original idea. It first came to me on seeing how merchants make money by selling fakes as the genuine article—from works of art to holy relics.

"Then I set about it too. I've sold everything, I can assure you, but only the apocryphal. I've sold no end of historic souvenirs—it's Napoléon who's most in demand. I've sold, bone by bone, for all the places of pilgrimage in Europe, I don't know how many skeletons of the same saint who was much in vogue ten years ago: Saint…to tell the truth, I can't remember any more. But it was in occupying myself with zoological rarities that I found my vocation. It's true that I met Street. He was an amazing fellow who fabricated whatever he wanted in the way of animals. He knew how to construct a bird with nothing but three feathers and a bit of beak. He rearranged things like no one.…

"For instance, a collector came to me who wanted a moth he lacked—a certain *Bombyx* for which he would have paid a fortune because no one had one. It's only found in Borneo, it appears, in the heart of the island, where there's cholera and endemic fever and the Dayaks play bowls with the heads of explorers.

"Naturally, I undertook to furnish the moth. There was to be no expense spared, and I went to find Street. 'It's not worth the trouble of going to Borneo,' he told me. 'People don't come back. At any rate, they won't bring the moth back because it doesn't exist.' He added, coolly: 'But I'll make you one…'

"'What do you mean, make one?' I asked.

"'Yes,' he said, 'I've made many other things. I've constructed beasts that never existed for the Museum. They have Latin names and are displayed in glass cases. They do very well, because they're unique specimens, you see. I've made all sorts of curiosities—birds, quadrupeds, eggs, everything. No one knows anything about it. It's my hobby. If I had the time I'd manufacture, in accordance with scientific descriptions, the great anthropoid ape of the Malay archipelago. If I had the time, I'd fabricate humans.… As for the moth, it's trivial. Leave me the description. Your collector will be content. In six months you can supply the *Bombyx*—the time's necessary for the supposed voyage—along with a detailed account of the expenses.'

"He kept his word and made the moth. Shortly afterwards, he died, because he drank too much, but his idea of manufacturing humans never left my mind...and I wanted to try, in my own way."

"What!" I said. "Humans!"

"Yes," said Mr. Turkey. "Humans—fake humans. Oh, not the way Street meant. I haven't constructed humans with bits of other humans, as was done, it appears, in the Middle Ages. Nor have I manufactured them as one builds a machine, although... but let's pass on. No, I set up a factory of living human doubles. It's perfectly simple. Do you remember a story by a French writer, Jules Verne? I can't remember the title,[14] but it was set in America before the war for the abolition of slavery, and there are two brothers who resemble one another perfectly and take advantage of it to commit all sorts of crimes, each time creating for one another an apparently-indisputable alibi. Well, perhaps that only gave me a part of the idea, and I had the rest on hearing the complaints of people in the public eye who were unhappy because they don't have a minute's peace. I thought of all the advantages one could get out of the two things, and immediately set to work. It was long and difficult, I can assure you. It required a considerable financial investment to set the business up on a suitable footing, to carry out discreet advertising and to be able to respond in a perfect fashion to the initial orders. It was necessary, above all, to procure reliable, devoted, honest and intelligent collaborators....

"The clientele was created, I must say, very rapidly, almost of its own accord. People are so overstretched by social obligations, excursions, dinners, chores of every sort that they don't dare refuse, out of human respect, that the majority of them have welcomed the offers of my representatives enthusiastically. A few people were suspicious at first, but when they understood

---

14. *Nord contre Sud* (1887; tr. as *Texar's Revenge; or, North Against South*).

how worthy my employees are of confidence, when they have seen, in a drawing room, one of their friends come to sit down beside them and talk about familiar matters, without suspecting for an instant that it was a double that I had furnished, they were won over. And as all the employees I procure are discreet, zealous and delicate, and as all my clients—who are, moreover, from the top drawer of society—maintain complete silence regarding our relationship in their own interest, well, my enterprise is flourishing...."

"Might I ask how you operate?"

"How? It's very simple. Here's a new client who comes to me, asking for his double. Naturally, he's a very rich man, and generally, given that I'm now established in solid manner in society, he's an ambitious man. You get my drift? He's found himself in the public eye, in some fashion. Then, it's necessary for him to go out, to show himself, to go to society occasions, to dine out. That's the only means, according to popular opinion, to sustain one's glory and increase one's renown. Whether it's true or not, people believe it. But work suffers, and health too, in consequence of the permanent fatigue and the dietary excesses that go with grand dinners. It's then that it's necessary to think about having a double. The newly famous man contacts me and I put him in touch with one of my artistes, who is almost the same height and build. If I don't have what he needs to hand, I carry out a search and find it. And after two months—three at the most—my employee, who has been in touch with my client throughout that time, has gradually acquired his external characteristics; he has adopted his mannerisms, his gestures, his manias. Naturally, he has similar clothing. He represents him very adequately at official ceremonies, weddings, funerals, even solemn dinners, and, in the meantime, the other works in peace at his fireside, in his dressing gown and slippers.

"Naturally, for intimate visits, and conversations about personal affairs, that can't be sufficient. We can contrive to replace anyone at all, believe me—but it requires an enormous amount of work and money to achieve a perfect result. I've always achieved one, however, and no failure has tarnished my reputation. Some of my old subscribers have their own double, who only works for them, and who has succeeded in getting into their skin to such a point that even I can't tell them apart. I've obtained amazing results, I can assure you."

"But nevertheless, the conversation...."

"Ah!" said Turkey. "The voice? Yes, that's the most difficult thing, but with work, one can arrive at a perfect result. One can apply make-up to speech, jut like the face...."

"That's not what I mean," I put in. "I'm talking about the intelligence, the education, the inimitable charm that doubles can't have...."

"Ah!" Turkey continued. "It's possible, but no one has ever noticed that. When someone has the reputation of having intelligence, one always finds it in him, you know....

"Well, now you have an idea of the immensity of our enterprise, eh? You see that we can answer any demand. We can furnish anything: men of science, artists, writers. We've furnished doubles, just between the two of us, for husbands weary of their wives or desirous of going on the spree while proving an attachment and constant fidelity to their spouses, We've furnished doubles—and they've paid very dearly for them—to certain worldly seducers whose were beginning to tire of their role as Don Juan and wanted to rest, while conserving their reputation...and even in those delicate functions, we've never had to deplore a fault, an error, a misunderstanding, or an indiscretion. Our agents, I tell you, are superior men. Just think that we have had the honor of supplying crowned heads and Heads of State...."

"What?" I said.

"Yes," he said, "naturally...for example, in order that the King of England could go to France, during his official voyage, in 1903, or, at least, that he could go everywhere he was taken... and would you believe that in Russia.... There are, you see, sovereigns who are believed to have been assassinated, who are living quietly, retired to the peace of some pretty countryside.

But let's pass on; that's touching on diplomatic secrets. Simply know, my dear sir, that we supply the entire world, and that one never knows to whom one is talking...."

"Have you never had treasons, competition among your employees?"

"Once," he said. "Just once. A...presumptuous man. He had been troubled by various misfortunes. He was one of my former chiefs of staff and his action constituted a treason in my regard. He wanted to set up a competing company, making use of our methods. But I took care of it personally. I knew him well, didn't I? And he was arrested for a crime. Twenty people had seen him. He protested in vain that he was away traveling that day, but all the evidence was against him. He was condemned...."

"To what?" I asked, a trifle shocked.

"To electrocution—that's how it's done here, you know. Apart from that, there haven't been any serious mishaps...."

"And none of your collaborators has ever thought of taking over the identity of the man for whom he was doubling permanently?" I asked.

"Never, to my knowledge," aid Mr. Turkey. "However... one of two of our agents, who were operating on the continent, haven't come back and haven't written to us for a long time. And a manifest evolution has been remarked in the politics of one Head of State...and an influential minister. But that doesn't bother anyone, and we continue to receive payment of our bills on a regular basis, so all's going well....

"But I can see that you want to leave. Thank you for your visit, my dear sir, and goodbye...."

"Goodbye," I said.

"Goodbye," repeated a voice behind me, exactly similar to mine.

I turned round, astonished. I thought at first that there was a mirror in the doorway, for, coming toward me, I saw a human creature exactly similar to myself...it was complete identity. To the extent that mirrors permit me to know, I was seeing my own face, facing me.

The apparition greeted me with a soft smile, and went past.

"Excuse, my dear sir," said Mr. Turkey, urbanely, "the insufficiency of that reproduction of yourself. I wanted to give you a slight idea of what we can do, but I only had a mediocre employee to hand, and there wasn't much time...."

I took my leave.

THE MIRACLE OF THE IVY

The young man sang endearments beneath his beloved's balcony, with the aid of his guitar.

The hour and the place lent themselves to it, for they offered all the characteristics of the most frantic romanticism, such as one only finds in a few small provincial towns. Everything was there: the beautiful summer night, the complicit pale moon; the nearby bell-tower and the solitary square with mysterious gardens, with old walls and mossy pavements, between which poetic grasses grew.

And beneath the cherished balcony, carefully framed, on the flank of the family dwelling, by very fortunately-planted ivy and wisteria, sighing toward his beloved, was the young man. And he fitted very well into the landscape, with his hat pulled down over his black hair, which he was agitating, and his Spanish cloak, which was keeping him warm but could scarcely have been more decorative....

Beside the young man, lying patiently on the ground, was his faithful shadow, which had accompanied him from home, in the moonlight, doing everything that it could to make him to give up his extravagances and go quietly home to bed...but he did not want to, and continued with his endearments.

His sang softly, in a prudent voice, careful not to wake anyone, and only to be heard by the one who was the elect of his heart and the indispensable flame of his life....

He had not known her three months before, but had encountered her one Sunday in spring at mass, and, as he was twenty-two and she was pretty, he had experienced the thunderbolt. Thus, from the first instant, he had awarded her his life and the enviable rank of elect of his heart. Since then, he had delivered himself furiously to all the manifestations usual in such cases, without hesitating before the most excessive, for he was a young man who was acquainted with literature.

Now, in spite of everything, on the flank of the family dwelling, the window of the beloved had remained obstinately closed. The beloved, however, who was eighteen and had candid eyes, was dying of the desire to open her window, for, independently of the fact that the heat in her closed bedroom was suffocating, it has to be admitted that there was everything that was required for the young woman to be impressed by the pathetic suitor in the Spanish cloak.

She was impressed, in fact, and forcefully, for it was her first debut, and the young man, who did not hesitate to assume such appearances in such a décor, had come at the right moment....

Nevertheless, the window remained closed, for the beloved's aged aunt, an austere guardian, was asleep and snoring in an adjacent room.

Furthermore, with the young woman, and holding her back with all his might on the fatal slope down which she was sliding, was her guardian angel, who was not at all impressed by serenades, or young men in Spanish cloaks, being a skeptical old hand who had seen everything in the course of his previous and successive sentry duties beside young women whose surveillance had been consigned to him throughout the ages since the days of the lost paradise.

Now, midnight came, and the bronze bell vibrated for the romantic hour that, twelve times reborn, took flight toward the unknown catacomb of the hours that have done their duty....

A guitar chord sobbed in the shadows like an afflicted heart....

The young man's voice modulated a supreme amorous appeal to his beloved....

It was too much. Persuasive perfumes were swimming in the

nocturnal air. A nightingale was singing with all its might. The beloved, to the annoyance of her angry guardian angel, opened the window and, a white form with long hair, appeared on the balcony.

"Angel," murmured the young man,

He was on his knees and unchained.

Accompanying himself with gestures on his faithful guitar, he wailed all that was passing through his head, in the form of a declaration of eternal love, burning like the sun and as profound as the sea. In the space of ten minutes, he compared the beloved to everything that a woman can be compared to, in the style of frenetic enthusiasm, passing from stars to flowers and flowers to birds with an astonishing fury, running at top speed through the vast fields of the most contrasted similes, in order to play better, and without taking account of any plausibility. He offered her his life sixty-two times and implored her more than three hundred times, with spasms, to tell him that she loved him, without waiting for or receiving any reply. To finish, scornful of the law of gravity, he affirmed to her that she was floating in the heavens, along with a thousand other idiocies of the same sort, as old as the world and the human race, which everyone employs, with varying success, but with the serene certainty that no one has ever employed them before, and that they are the brilliant fruit of the inspiration of the moment.

After that, his emotion and the efforts he made not to proclaim his flame too loudly—which might have woken the aunt whose vigilant snoring was perceptible—suffocated him, and he calmed down for a while. His shadow was asleep at his feet.

"What an imbecile!" murmured the irritated guardian angel. "I never heard such a string of nonsense. Close the window, then, you little fool," he ordered the young woman.

"No," she said, disguising her sentiments. "It's too hot in here. And then, I want to hear what he saying. It's amusing...."

The unfortunate down below, having got his breath back, began again. That lasted ten minutes. This time, he talked about the future, and proposed various modes of abduction, as impracticable as they were ridiculous. In addition, he recited lyrical extracts from all the poets.

That worked, for the young woman stopped laughing, and the angel became seriously annoyed.

"Do you love me?" asked the young man, for the thousandth time.

"Yes," the beloved murmured, in a sigh.

And at that moment, it was true.

He wanted to know if she loved him a great deal, and again she said yes, and then, whether she loved him more than anything else in the world; with some difficulty, she agreed.

The angel's face was a sight to behold, he was so furious.

Then the young man, weary of words, wanted to move on to a few inoffensive and agreeable actions.

"If I could only," he sighed, "O beloved, if I could only touch your hand and your hair, and kneel to kiss the hem of your white dress...."

"Ah!" she said, shivering. "No, you mustn't...."

"And then, fortunately," muttered the guardian angel to himself, "there's the distance from the pavement to the first floor...but it's only a postponement: that creature has a persuasive voice and a memory full of seductive nonsense. I fear that the little one might be pinched....and there's nothing I can do...."

"How can I get up there? What can I do?" moaned the amorous young man, agitating down below. "Oh, if only I had a silken ladder, like Romeo! Or, even better, if we were in pagan times, I could offer a sacrifice to the gods in order that they might change me into that fortunate ivy that's enlacing the balcony...."

"Change into ivy," said the angel to himself, slapping his forehead. "That's a good idea...." To the amorous fellow, he said: "Would you really like to be that climbing shrub?"

"Would I like it! Would you not welcome me, sweet love of my heart?" the latter demanded of the young woman.

"Oh," she said, swooning. "Come!"

"That ivy!" he cried, recklessly, down below. "If only I were that ivy! To brush that charming head with my leaves! To see her night and day! Rapture!"

"That's simple and easy," said the angel. "You're a good lad—I'll work a miracle for you."

"My eternal gratitude" cried the young man.

"Master," said his shadow, waking up and tugging at the bottom of his trouser-legs. "Don't do that, Master—it's too dangerous."

"Cast off your cloak," said the angel. "Put down your guitar. Set yourself against the wall, extend your arms into the air...."

"Master! Master! Don't do that! Don't leave me!" begged the poor shadow.

But the passionate young man had already obeyed the angel's instructions.

And the miracle happened.

"He's doomed!" groaned the shadow. "I'm alone in the world."

"Ah!" said the young woman, throwing herself into the branches of the ivy, which hugged her recklessly to its heart....

"Amour...," murmured the breeze, agitating the leaves.

"My God!" said the young woman, recoiling, with three caterpillars in her hair and a host of aphids on her neck. "You're full of beasts...."[15]

"Naturally," said the angel. "Besides which, he's an imbecile. Let's go back in, my daughter. You can't espouse a bush, even a climber. The registry clerk that your aunt has in mind for you, will fit the bill much better...."

"That's true," she said. "And this one is full of beasts."

She went back in.

"My God, what a dirty little ingrate! She's typical of her sex, that one," murmured the shadow abandoned by the young man, down below, sadly returning home with the cloak, the hat and the guitar—vain spoils.

Around the balcony, the breath of a nascent storm agitated

15. There is a crucial pun here, which does not translate. The French noun *bête* [beast] also serves as an adjective, meaning "stupid."

the twisted branches and the eternal and plaintive foliage.

"I'm dying where I'm attached," sighed the poor ivy.

Later, he was cruelly pruned on the orders of the registry clerk, who, having married the young woman, to the satisfaction of the guardian angel, did everything she wanted.

She thought that the ivy was impeding her clear view, and besides which, it was full of beasts.

A PHANTOM

It was ten o'clock in the evening when, full of resolution and ready to confront the most extraordinary perils, Anatole Douvre arrived at the haunted house.

Thanks to the descriptions that he had been given, he identified it without difficulty, isolated as it was in the deserted side-street by the walls of the adjacent gardens, and bearing a huge TO LET sign that did not tempt anyone.

"This is it!" Anatole said to himself, seemingly a trifle excited, and examining the ensemble with an investigative eye. "Watch out for tricks!"

He had a key to open the door at the top of the front steps. In the large vestibule, by the light of a wax taper, he headed toward the stone staircase.

"In the big room to the right on the first floor," he murmured, as he climbed the stairs. "That's their rendezvous, it seems. Let's go…if they think they've scared me, with all their tales of witchcraft…."

He reached the first floor, and by the dying light of his taper, he groped around a door in the vicinity of a brass knob that did not want to turn.

"Come in," said a faint voice from inside.

"Huh! There's someone in there," murmured Anatole, astonished, as he opened the door.

A large fire in a huge fireplace, and two candelabras on a table, illuminated the room, which was vast and comfortable. There were bottles of liqueurs on the table, and glasses. Next to the table, which occupied the middle of the room, sitting in a green armchair, a little old man, bald and well-dressed, was warming his feet and holding an unfolded newspaper, while considering Anatole through his spectacles. He had put his top hat down next to him, with his scarf and gloves inside, and his silver-handled cane was beside him. His overcoat was lying over the back of a chair. The old gentleman was smoking a cigar and smiling agreeably.

"Come in, my dear Monsieur Douvre," he said to Anatole.

Why, he knows me—so who is he? the latter said to himself, as he came in, a trifle disconcerted. Aloud, he said: "I...I beg your pardon. I didn't know...."

"Sit down, then," said the old gentleman.

"Thank you." Anatole took his place in an armchair that seemed to be waiting for him. "Excuse me for disturbing you," he went on. "I didn't know...in fact, as you're surely aware, the house is said to be haunted, and as it belongs to my friend Pont...do you know Pont?"

"Very well," said the gentleman, "Very well. Have a glass of cognac."

"In that case," Anatole said, "I'm astonished never to have met you at his home. No, no sugar, thanks. And you're here?"

"A cigar?" offered the old gentleman, pushing a box.

"Gladly. I was saying—wasn't I?—that I'd come for the haunted house. Pont didn't tell me that there'd be two of us spending the night here." He emptied his glass and filled it again immediately, for he was rather fond of spirits. "I'm charmed, though," he added. "Were you expecting me?"

"Yes," said the other.

"Pont really might have warned me," Anatole observed, in a cloud of smoke. "He really should have...."

"But he did," said the old gentleman.

"Well, I didn't receive anything...and it's a trifle embarrassing to arrive as an intruder...."

"Not at all, not at all...." And the old gentleman smiled more agreeably than ever.

"Yes," Anatole declared, with dignity. "It's embarrassing when one doesn't know...." He paused, hoping that his interlocutor would name himself.

The latter said nothing, and Anatole, to hide his disturbance, emptied his glass and filled it.

"Exquisite," he said "Ex...quis...but since we're here, in a...scientific experiment...I can ask you whether you have an opinion on the subject of ghosts. People have mentioned the phantom of an old imbecile of a former tenant.... At any rate, no one wants to rent it, and those who have tried to spend the night here, as we're doing, have never done so again. But what is it, exactly...that people say? By what, or by whom, is the house haunted?"

"By me," said the little old gentleman, looking at Anatole over his spectacles.

"By...*you!*" Anatole strted. "What a joke!"

"No," said the old gentleman, "it's not a joke. It's the truth. I'm the one to whom you referred just now as 'the phantom of an old imbecile of a former tenant.'"

"The Devil you say!" murmured Anatole. "The Devil...!"

"No," said the old gentleman.

"What do you mean, no?" asked Anatole.

"No, I'm not the Devil. I'm a specter, that's all: a phantom; a shade; a spirit...whatever you please...but not the Devil."

"That's...that's good," confessed Anatole, anxiously. "But I don't understand." And he took another glass of cognac.

"You will understand," said the specter, condescendingly. "I came to live in this little house fifteen years ago, alive and well. I died in it four years ago. Then I was in the other world, but, for personal reasons, I wasn't able to stay there; so I came back here, and in order to be tranquil, I've been obliged to scare away all the people who wanted to live in it, haven't I?"

"I...I understand," said Anatole.

"That doesn't astonish me," said the phantom. "You're very intelligent, and that's why I thought I could welcome you like this, politely, as a friend, with no formality, avoiding all those stupid chains and flames, only good for frightening janitors. But you're not drinking...."

"Yes...yes," said Anatole, pouring a lethal mixture of kirsch and chartreuse into his glass. "But forgive me—you say that you weren't able to stay in the other world. Why not?"

"I said that it was a personal matter," the specter observed, reservedly. "All the same, I can confide it, under the seal of secrecy, to a gallant man. When I died, I was given a ticket to Paradise, wasn't I? For I'd been a good man in life, with a virtuous heart, pure in my mores, protecting widows and orphans. So, I went to Paradise, and...."

"And?" Anatole queried, fixing his interlocutor with eyes that were beginning to moisten with tears of intoxication.

"And Paradise," said the obliging phantom, "isn't tenable. Always music, all the time, relentlessly and pitilessly. And nothing but great art! Opera, my dear chap, the most terrible opera, with I don't know how many performers, who all go at it full tilt, without even the relief of a false note from time to time. Frightful! And the audience! All there is of the worst in virtue, people fleeing from no matter what...it made me disgusted with my honorable life. In brief, I lasted as long as I could—four months and eight days—but I became enraged, and I got out. And I could see that poor St. Peter, who opened the gate to me, would have liked to do as I was doing. As I left he said to me, enviously: 'You've had enough, eh? You're off? I wish I could do as much. Listen to them over there with their damned orchestra—eighteen hundred years they've been making my head ache with that....'

"Then I went down to Hell...."

"Ah!" said Anatole, very interested, swimming in the delights of the most exquisite iced kummel. "And is Hell amusing?"

"Yes," said the specter, bitterly, "very amusing, but naturally, there's no room. It's full up. I had a serious recommendation and I put in my request to obtain a position as a junior demon, but the head of personnel told me frankly that I shouldn't count on it. There are eleven million, seven hundred and eighteen thousand, two hundred and twelve candidates ahead of me—not to mention those who have serious entitlements. There are three popes still waiting, and seventeen kings, two of them negroes; that's the long and short of it...."

"You said it," said Anatole, sympathetically, the kummel having a powerful influence on him.

"Then," the poor revenant continued, "having been chased from Paradise by the music, evicted from Hell by the lack of career prospects...."

"Purgatory?" observed Anatole.

"Closed for a long time," said the other. "Conditions became impossible there. So I had nothing better to do but come back to earth, and this house, which I'm obliged to defend against all the idiots who want to live in it. I've delivered myself to the most hackneyed farces to gain a little tranquility. I've played death with a skull and veils for a stubborn old woman, and it scared her to death. I've rattled chains and written on walls with fire for a braggart of a doctor. He left—or, rather, he was taken away, very ill. It's true that what I wrote was intended to trouble him. I extinguished lights and opened doors silently in front of a phlegmatic Englishman who went to look for me in the loft. After the third candle and the sixth door he was no longer phlegmatic, or in the house. I whispered in the ear of a young woman who was playing the piano—the horror!—and pulled the legs of her father, an old retired colonel, while he was asleep. They fled too....

"All that's poor and banal, isn't it?—but it's not tiring, and then, when one does it well, it always works. So, I've succeeded in getting a little peace, and this evening, I've told you all that, my dear sir, as an intelligent man, albeit a little drunk...."

"I haven't touched a drop," said Anatole, drunk and offended.

"Intelligent, albeit a little drunk," the specter repeated, "in order that you should convince your friend Pont that his house in uninhabitable because of the spirits infesting it."

"That's not true," said Anatole, becoming familiar, "You're no spirit!"

"What?" sad the specter.

"No," declared Anatole, majestically, speaking with difficulty. "Specters aren't like you...they're scary...and you...you don't scare me...."

"I don't scare you, imbecile?" said the phantom, irritated.

"No," said Anatole, "not in the least. But...don't insult me.... .that makes me...hurt.... You're very kind.... You're a bit of a drunk, but very kind...."

"What a brute!" murmured the phantom. "He's as idiotic as the others. It's necessary to play the buffoon again...."

All of a sudden, the light of the fire and the candles dimmed. All sound died away into a mortal silence. And in front of Anatole, there was the old gentlemen, magnified to the point that he was touching the ceiling; and his head was that of a flayed sheep with sinister teeth; and his red eyes shone like accursed beacons in the horrible darkness that descended upon the room.

Anatole, sobered up, his hair standing on end, his face convulsed, remained motionless and mute momentarily, suffocated by terror.

The phantom extended a livid and tentacular hand—but Anatole was already howling with fear, in a voice that was not of this world, and running for the exit. He rebounded from the corner of the fireplace, demolished the corner of a side-table with his shoulder and, unable to find the door, leapt through the window. He reached the pavement easily by that method, and lost consciousness there with no other damage than a broken femur and multiple large bruises.

"When I think," murmured the specter of the old gentleman, who had resumed a polite appearance, "that it's always necessary to revert to the old melodramatic means...and they say that people are becoming skeptical!"

THE TALKING DOG

(A STORY IN THE ENGLISH VEIN)

It was the respectable old gentleman's turn to tell us a story, and he did not need any more pleading than was strictly necessary. He passed his hand through his sparse white hair, settled his neck comfortably in his collar and expelled a sententious cloud of tobacco-smoke.

"The story I'm going to tell you, my friends," he said, "is both instructive and touching: instructive, because it shows what treasures of genius a man at grips with the difficulties of life can deploy to procure what unjust fortune has refused him; touching, because it informs us how delicate are the sentiments of those devoted companions that Providence has given us in the person of dogs, and how necessary it is to be careful never to let them suffer lack of regard, or unjustified abandonment, which harden their tender little hearts and lead them to scorn the venerated master to whom they have devoted their love—a love more disinterested than any other on earth...."

The old gentleman stopped and put his hand over his eyes, as if choked by emotion. We were all impressed, and maintained a respectful silence.

After a few moments, he continued....

The heroes of my story were named Barfin and Azor. Barfin was the master; Azor was the dog. They both loved one another very much, but, deep down, Azor loved Barfin more than Barfin loved Azor, as the subsequent story will prove.

You've heard mention of Barfin, haven't you? He was an intelligent man—too intelligent, in fact, which is dangerous when one doesn't have enough money. He was cleverer than anyone else and had done surprising things, but perhaps he never showed more genius than with the Talking Dog, and no one has ever done better, before or since.

To bring off that coup, it's first necessary to be a good ventriloquist, and then to have a dog—the breed doesn't matter, as long as it looks good and doesn't bark. It then remains to find the partner with whom men like Barfin play, without saying so, and without ever losing—an innocent who goes through life with his eyes shut and his mouth open, mistrusting straws and bumping into beams. People like that, however, can easily be found with a little sharp sight.

As a ventriloquist, Barfin had no peer, and his dog Azor was a mongrel, but an odd one, reminiscent of an owl when one looked him in the face and a pike when seen in profile, and he grimaced with his muzzle when Barfin winked at him, but no one ever heard him bark.

So, one settlement day, Barfin went into a restaurant near the office where he had to pay his rent at about half past two. There was no one there by one worthy fellow, some sort of rural land-owner, who was eating on his own, with a contented expression. Barfin sat down at the next table, and Azor got up on a chair facing him.

Barfin ordered his lunch and began eating while reading a newspaper. Suddenly, Azor, who as looking at the food as if he was hungry too, started talking.

"What about me?"

"Shut up, Azor," said Barfin.

"What?" replied Azor, angrily. "I should shut up? You're sitting there stuffing yourself, while I don't have anything! That's disgusting!"

"Shut up, Azor," Barfin repeated, severely, lowering his newspaper. "I've forbidden you to talk when there are people about."

"I'd have waited till the fellow had gone," Azor ssaid, "but I'm dying of starvation...."

Barfin gave him some bread dipped in gravy. To the side, the worthy provincial had stopped eating, and he was contemplating Azor intently, amazed."

"Come on!" said Azor, suddenly, his mouth full. "How does that fat elephant expect me to swallow when he's staring at me with eyes as wide as napkin rings?"

"That's not nice," said Barfin.

"Pardon me, Monsieur," put in the worthy man, in a strangled voice. "That dog can talk?"

"Yes," Barfin replied.

But Azor, at whom his master winked, and was behaving himself perfectly, thought he ought to get involved. "Of course I can talk!" he exclaimed. "Why shouldn't I be able to talk?"

"Well...no reason...obviously," said the gentleman. "Did you teach him?" he asked Barfin.

"Yes," said Barfin, coldly.

"Pardon me if I'm indiscreet, but it's so surprising...how did you do it?"

"Oh," said Barfin, with a bitter smile, "it's a secret to which I've devoted fifteen years of my life, and all my fortune—you'll permit me to keep it to myself."

"Certainly—forgive me. But excuse me again, no one but you, until now...."

"No," Barfin explained, modestly. "I only have the glory of having rediscovered it. Antiquity brought it into usage. Pliny the Elder talks about it."

"Indeed, indeed," said the fat gentleman, who did not seem to be intimately familiar with Pliny the Elder. "It makes no difference...it's admirable. You haven't shown off that prodigious animal?"

"No one knows about it—you're the only one, and I'm counting on your discretion as a man of honor...."

"I've finished," said Azor. "I want something else. And you'd do better not to gossip about me."

"That's a bit strong," said Barfin.

"Permit me," the gentleman interjected, leaning toward Azor benevolently. "My friend, would you permit me to offer you whatever you please, and ask you a few questions?"

"I'd like chocolate éclairs and coffee with cream," said Azor, "but as for chatting to you, I don't want to know—your face is too dirty."

"Exquisite!" cried the fat man, bursting out laughing, while Barfin was scandalized. "Exquisite! Charming! Ha ha ha!"

He ordered the chocolate éclairs and the coffee with cream, and resumed eating with a pensive expression. Barfin had resumed reading his paper, and Azor swallowed his cakes.

Suddenly, the fat gentleman put down his napkin and spoke to Barfin. "Is he the only one you've taught?"

"No," said Barfin. "I have two others. They're better than him. They can talk argot and sing songs in English."

"Better than me" Azor put in, indignantly. "How can you say that? To begin with, it's me who taught them, by dint of patience...."

"He's a teacher too!" said the gentleman, full of admiration. "That's extraordinary...." To Barfin, he added: "Monsieur, I'll buy him from you."

"Monsieur!" Barfin replied. "Never!"

"Very good," said Azor, and to the gentleman: "Buy me? What do you take me for?"

"I'll buy you," the other continued. "Which is to say, we'll be partners. I'll put up the expenses for a luxurious exhibition, and the most astonishing advertising. I have a head for business...."

"Not another word," Barfin put in. "I won't dishonor my ancestors by descending to the rank of an exhibitor of phenomena."

"Very good," Azor approved. "Show me off like a juggler. Have you ever heard the like?"

"Monsieur," said the worthy fellow to Barfin, "one can march with one's century without dishonoring oneself. One shouldn't sell oneself short. One doesn't turn down, with a light heart, an opportunity to make millions—for your dog has millions in his throat."

"I know that," said Barfin, hesitantly.

"Isn't it only just," the other continued, more insistently, "that all the trouble you've taken in this superhuman work should be rewarded?"

"Perhaps," said Barfin. "I've thought of going overseas to exhibit my pupils in the great cities of the Union...."

"Monsieur," said the fat man, "you don't need three subjects. Sell me Azor. Go with the other two. I believe I can tell that you're in straitened circumstances...."

"Monsieur...."

"Don't take offense. The price I'll pay you would facilitate...."

"I don't want to!" howled Azor. "Don't sell me! You know full well that the entrepreneur of spectacles that we saw yesterday promised to advance you what you needed."

"Monsieur!" the fat man almost shouted. "Entrepreneurs of spectacles are thieves! This one will exploit you. You'll create a debt that will follow you like a ball and chain. By selling me Azor, you'd remain your own master. Providence has placed me beside you for our mutual benefit. I have daughters to marry off...." He no longer knew what he was saying, intoxicated by the fortune that he believed he had to seize at that moment, or never.... "How about five thousand?" he said

"No!" howled Azor. "The other one offered you ten thousand, just for traveling expenses. Don't sell me! I want to go to America!"

"It's not a question of money, Monsieur," said Barfin.

"Monsieur," said the other. "Eight thousand....."

"Think of your debts!" cried Azor. "Keep me. I'll always be good. I'll make parliamentary speeches, if you want...."

"Monsieur," said the fat man. "All right, ten thousand...."

"No!" howled Azor, heartbroken. "No! I don't want to! Don't sell me! Don't sell me!"

"I have to," said Barfin. "Monsieur, I accept. It's my duty. That way, I can pay my debts without mortgaging the future, which is God's. Give me ten thousand francs and take Azor, my beloved child...."

"There it is! He's done it!" bellowed Azot. "Are you a Judas, then, to sell your friend?"

"Come on, calm down," said Barfin. "Monsieur will be very good to you..."

"You'll be the master in my home, my dear little chap," the fat gentleman protested.

But Azor started turning round and round, swearing like a trooper—but the other was exultant, and the coarser Azor became, the more content he seemed.

The bargain was concluded, and the gentleman counted out ten thousand-franc bills—which he had obtained that morning, he said.

He put Azor on a lead, and the three of them went out.

Azor tugged on his lead as hard as he could, and shouted in the deserted street that he wanted to go with Barfin.

The fat gentleman stopped a cab. He got in, holding Azor in his arms, and gave Barfin one last handshake. The carriage moved off, but Azor—who, we must suppose, was waiting for his chance—leaned out of the door toward his former master and shouted to him, peevishly: "What you've done to me, the two of you, is too dirty! To punish you, I'm not going to talk any more!"

And, indeed, he never said another word.

A PHILANTHROPIST

(A PLAUSIBLE AND TRUE STORY)

Médar-le-Vieux—I shall conceal its real name; you'll understand why as you continue reading—an ancient pretty little town constructed on a hill, the principal town of a canton in Seine-et-Oise: 1150 inhabitants, a gendarmerie, a Mairie, a Gothic church, a hospital, feudal ruins, etc.

Such was the small town of Médar-le-Vieux in 1886, when Monsieur Aubergeois came to take up residence there. Such it still was when he died there seven years later....

Since then....

At the time when Monsieur Aubergeois arrived, as I've said, the town had only 1150 inhabitants, virtuous and peaceful laborers. Mendicity was almost unknown there, the poor numbering only eight. The surrounding countryside is attractive, and the air of a rare purity. Monsieur Aubergeois, who had retired from the commercial struggle with a considerable fortune and the desire to enjoy it in peace for as long as possible, was completely seduced by the attractions of Médar-le-Vieux, and in the month of July 1886 he bought a very fine property overlooking the town. Below his property was the cemetery, which made Monsieur Aubergeois hesitate at first, for he had a horror of spectacles of that sort. However, a dense row of cypresses hid the sight of the crosses and tombs. The cypresses in question had been planted on the edge of a vegetable garden and against the wall separating the garden from the road that skirted the cemetery.

Monsieur Aubergeois bought the vegetable garden—with the cypresses, naturally. He paid dearly for it, but he did not regret it. In his concern for hygiene and his love of nature, he was able, while breathing fresh air, to see the panorama of the town and country, all the way to the infinity of the sky. In the foreground was the black curtain of the evergreen cypresses, which reminded him of beautiful Provence and his the lugubrious cemetery from him, without him having to fear that he would ever see it, since the trees were now his.

Meanwhile, Monsieur Aubergeois made friends with the curé and the Maire. They acquired the habit of playing cards and dining together on Thursdays and Sundays, and that was pleasant for all three of them, for they had a similar liking for conversation, playing whit and good food.

Now, the deputy Maire was a pharmacist named Régulus Fleury. He had a passionate fondness for good dinners and the game of whist, which he only knew imperfectly. He was, moreover, self-satisfied, touchy and vindictive. He made great efforts to be invited by Monsieur Aubergeois, but the latter was obstinate in never doing so, for he thought the deputy Maire, rightly or wrongly, to be vulgar in his manner and imbecilic in his speech.

Régulus Fleury, finding his efforts vain, felt wronged in his passions and wounded in his self-esteem. He began to hate the three friends, most especially Monsieur Aubergeois, with all his might. And that hatred, which could not be satisfied in any manner, grew in the pharmacist's soul into a frenzy over the six years when things remained the same. At the end of that lapse of time, in September 1892, the Maire fell ill and died.

That was a cruel blow for Monsieur Aubergeois. He accompanied his friend's funeral procession as far as the cemetery, and that field of rest inspired an insurmountable horror in him.

The pharmacist Régulus Fleury was then appointed Maire, and, without hindrance, was able to yield to his evil instincts and slake his rancor. The curé was moved and a day came, the thirtieth of November, when Monsieur Aubergeois, alone and sad, consoled solely by his beautiful garden and the slight of the vast countryside, full of the charm of autumn, learned from the mouth of Régulus Fleury himself, who had come expressly to tell him, that the town of Médar-le-Vieux had the most urgent need, in order to enlarge the road by the cemetery, of a one-meter-twenty strip of land taken from the edge of his vegetable garden. Now, the cypresses that permitted Monsieur Aubergeois to enjoy life were one-meter-five from the present wall. It was therefore necessary to fell them—in exchange, Monsieur Fleury explained amiably, for just compensation.

Monsieur Aubergeois was struck as if by a thunderbolt. He became angry, threatened, begged. He offered to pay all the expenses for the work, if the town would consent only to enlarge the road that no one used by eighty centimeters, in order that he could keep his trees. He even went so far as to offer considerable sums to the town, if it would abandon its pretentions.

It was all in vain. The pitiless Régulus contented himself with making the remark that the interests of a single person must yield before the interests of all; that no individual had the right to impose his will on the collective, even by the power of money; and that, finally, that Aubergeois' final offer to him of a sum of thirty thousand francs constituted an attempted corruption that he, Régulus Fleury, in his capacity as Maire, could not forget.

"Monsieur," said Monsieur Aubergeois, then, "you are committing at this moment a crime against my person: the person of an old man who has never done any harm. That cemetery will kill me, but...."—he paused momentarily, then continued in a profound tone: "I know the human soul, and I shall be able to avenge myself. Now, get out!"

Régulus Fleury went, a trifle anxious, but resolute. Monsieur Aubergeois went to bed and fell ill.

Meanwhile, the work, rapidly undertaken, was completed, and the road was suitably enlarged, with the suppression of the cypresses. Then Monsieur Aubergeois had the crosses and tombstones constantly before his eyes, including the tomb of his friend, which he could recognize from afar. He did not have the courage to leave his house; he had grown old and weak.

The terror that gradually overwhelmed his soul was redoubled by an unhealthy curiosity that kept him awake at night "to see the dead." His health declined, and also his morale. Having made his will, in a moment of lucidity, he died seventy-one days after his cypresses had been stolen from him. Some people opined that he had been killed by the fear of death.

Monsieur Aubergeois' will was opened. He left more than half his fortune—the income from a house situated in Paris and producing about thirty thousand francs a year—to the poor of the town of Médar-le-Vieux "Where he had been so happy," as he put it.

There was universal delight.

"I misjudged him when he spoke of vengeance," Régulus Fleury said to himself. "He was a good man." And the legacy was accepted.

Monsieur Aubergeois' obsequies were enthusiastic and solemn. The funeral procession was followed by the municipality, the gendarmes and the firemen, who were followed by the entire population of the town, especially the eight poor people of the locality, who were clad in mourning at the town's expense, with affliction on their faces and joy in their hearts, at the enchanting perspective of sharing, between the eight of them, thirty thousand francs a year.

Monsieur Aubergeois was honored with a splendid sepulcher. That evening, in his honor, everyone got drunk. And all went well.

But not for long.

The rumor of that prodigious generosity spread, with prodigious rapidity, and all the beggars in the region arrived, in order to claim their share of the beneficent thirty thousand francs. Animated by that natural ambition, they had themselves inscribed on the official charity roll, and at the end of a year's residence—during which time they lived on plunder and theft—they attained the objective of their desire. Also registered were all the casual workers of the town and countryside, who preferred to earn money by doing nothing than dying of hunger by working.

Entire families arrived from everywhere, clad in rags and haggard, their eyes fixed on Médar-le-Vieux as on a propitious haven, where one could eat and sleep without paying. Naturally, the mores of these people were not absolutely pure, nor their hygiene entirely salutary. They imported various contagions, and propagated them with great success among the population that was still working, which was gradually corrupted. Gradually, those people came together and they too, left to their own devices, abandoned all human sentiment.

They put their old parents, formerly honored at the hearth, out into the street, explaining to them with serenity that the hospice was there, ready and waiting. Parents shoved their offspring unceremoniously into the gutter, for the orphanage. The young made the acquaintance of debauchery and practiced it to excess. The number of births increased, but also that of deaths, and to a greater extent, and among the new-borns, physical defects multiplied. Brawling, theft and poaching wore out the gendarmerie, whose strength was doubled.

And the indigents kept on arriving. One might have thought that they were coming from all parts of France, so numerous and various were they. Bretons wrote collective letters to the Maire to ask him whether it was true that the poor could live for free in his town. Savoyards and Italians came hundreds of kilometers on foot in order to reach Médar-le-Vieux, the land of Cockayne,

The day came, however, when the poor already in residence decided that there were quite enough of them to share Monsieur Aubergeois' heritage, and exercised a tight surveillance in order to repel any further intrusion of wretched strangers. The new arrivals, driven back into the countryside by furious battles, then began to pillage the nearby farms, attack isolated houses or die on the roads.

After a while, the indigents established in the town thought that they were sufficiently powerful to increase their demands. They wanted to be shown accounts. Supported by their electoral power, they began to put pressure on the decisions of the municipal authority. In their opinion, the rents in "their" Parisian house were not high enough. The ground floor accommodated a concert hall, and a few indigents were delegated to visit it. They found that the artistes were too highly-paid for what they were doing and demanded that the derisory wages of those unfortunates should be further reduced.

Meanwhile, the town council, weary of constant and pitiless struggle, resigned *en masse*. Régulus Fleury, undermined by an intolerable existence, caught the mange and ceased to be Maire, and even a pharmacist. Ruined, he disappeared from the region. Various scandals erupted, and finally, a great battle was sustained against debauchery by those inhabitants who still remained immune to it. With the aid of the gendarmes they succeeded in driving their adversaries to the north of the town, into a quarter named La Bourbière.[16] A new and vast gendarmerie barracks constructed in that place served as a dike against that population. Thus, the locale was partially returned to civilized life.

I recently visited Médar-le-Vieux and undertook a descent into La Bourbière. The inhabitants of the place offered, in all verity, unparalleled charms, but on which it is better not to insist. Nowhere else have I seen poverty of that sort: slovenly; cynical; comfortable, in a manner of speaking; aggressive and self-satisfied; reeking of drunkenness, dirt, vice, and the joy of being in the world.

And I saw, in the cemetery, whose gate is a marvel of wrought iron, Monsieur Aubergeois' tomb. It is a huge monument. Demolished and covered in filth, and among the awkwardly-scrawled anathemas and insults, the white marble slab, broken and stained, still allows the following words to be read:

---

16. The Quagmire.

TO OUR BENEFACTOR
The Grateful Town

GORDON'S AUNT
TRIUMPHS AND DIES

I was at home, quite tranquil in doing nothing, when my friend Gordon arrived. I had not seen him for eight months, because he had been traveling in the country of his birth, the United States of America.

I was glad to see him. Gordon is a good fellow. He had numerous and various adventures all over the world, wherever his life took him. There were frightful ones, singular ones and comical ones. But nowhere was Gordon's strength of mind ever defeated for an instant, and he was always able to rise to the occasion and maintain his "aplomb against fate." I will add that he looks at people and things from his own angle, and that, finally, he is endowed with an extraordinary narrative flair, which he exercises—when he consents to do so in French— with such personality, from the viewpoint of syntax, and such a fortunate choice of expression, that I know nothing superior for entertainment.[17]

So, Gordon arrived. He shook my hand forcefully and silently, and sad down, looking sad. His faithful umbrella, which never leaves him, was between his legs. He lit a cigar and sighed.

"Is something wrong, my friend?"

"No," said Gordon, "but with affliction in my heart. My last remaining aunt just died, a month ago, in Wisconsin, and I'm

---

17. The specific grammatical errors that Gordon makes in speaking French do not translate into English, so a translation is only able to hint indirectly at the character of his verbal eccentricity.

abandoned, weak and isolated, with no more relatives in the vast terrestrial solitude...."

"You're not so weak," I thought I ought to tell him, in consideration of his athletic bearing and his appearance of robust health, "and as for isolation, you have sincere friends."

"Yes," he said, "You—and I'm very glad, and I thank you. But a friend isn't an aunt, is he? And my sentiment's in the weakness of no longer having anyone of the name of Gordon in the picture...for old Aunt Bettina was the last one, apart from me...."

"And of what did the poor respectable spinster die? For she wasn't married, was she?"

"No, certainly not. She remained a maiden, and perished in the prime of life, at fifty-two. And it was for the Gordon honor that it terminated so unfortunately. And I, who excited her in that fatal race, regret it and feel pain, although glory is more comfortable than vital existence, and my sublime aunt Bettina has cast a triumph impossible to efface on the name of Gordon."

"A triumph? A race? What do you mean?"

"Well, you don't know, here, what true sport is. In America, we know. You know it by fashion. We know it by soul. There are people in your country who are beginning. That's good. And I'm happy to see the eminent men that you're inculcating patiently in that sort of thing. It will make the French people, whom I love, great and strong, instead of going to the café, except for a game of billiards. And I like your schoolboys, who are being directed toward football and cricket. But we, in America, have always done that, haven't we? And have you seen the glory that the wife of one of our great financiers obtained by running against a locomotive in Savannah and overtaking it? There was delirium about that throughout North America. Very good.

"And then, races were invented with regular rules. Ladies were running against locomotives, and also against one another. They were crazy about winning. These ladies were wearing pretty outfits expressly designed, each with its colors, like jockeys. And the locomotives were colored too, blue, or even pink. And the carriages were also colored, and the...engine driver, and the stoker. It was jolly and poetic to see. There were prizes, and the husbands or fiancés of the young women who were running the race were in the carriages, for the excitement or to lay bets.

"Then, in Wisconsin, people wanted to be in on the latest craze, didn't they? A race of that sort was arranged near Madison, the capital. And there was a furious effervescence in the whole region. And the ladies were mad keen to win it. And there was a reward of ten thousand dollars, the admirable champion's sash, golden laurels, and a banquet, and a universal triumph for the lady who won.

Well, in Wisconsin is the seed-bed of all the Gordons. And it's there, in Madison itself, that Miss Bettina Gordon, my aunt, lived in tranquility, virtuous and free, with whisky on Sunday and the service for the consolation and soothing of pains. And then, when there was talk of holding the race, and the ladies were going into training, my aunt, with whom I was staying, became preoccupied and morose. And I knew that my aunt had been an athlete in her younger days, and I knew how it pained her having nothing to do.

"And one Sunday, before the day of the run, my Aunt Bettina, on coming back from the divine service, toward whisky time, said to me: 'My nephew Gordon, know that your Aunt Bettina has decided to run the race against the locomotive. Your Aunt Bettina has been an empress of sport in these parts, and can't suffer this solemnity to take place without acting thus. She can't suffer that opprobrium be upon the glorious name of Gordon, by the defection of the only woman who is a Gordon. She can't suffer that the wretched Miss Clarke, who took your aunt's seat at divine service last month, and who sniggered, is saying everywhere that she, Miss Clarke, will win the prize, and that old biddies can't keep up any more. This Clarke is twenty-three, my nephew Gordon, and your aunt is much older, but your aunt will be running for the honor of the Gordons and this despicable Clarke to win the money. Have faith in your Aunt Bettina, my nephew Gordon.'

"And I had faith in my Aunt Bettina, but I was anxious, for this Miss Clarke was tall and nimble. My aunt entered, of course. And she trained flat out in preparation. And there were heats for elimination. And my Aunt Bettina came out victorious, with four others, good for the great final combat. But I was anxious, for Miss Clarke also came out victorious from the elimination heats, and had the air of being bang in form, and was saying everywhere that she was sure to win, and sniggering at my aunt. But my Aunt Bettina said nothing, and pinched her lips, and was resolved. Me, I was anxious.

"Now, came the day of the impassioning race. The whole country was there to see it. Large amounts of money had been bet, especially on Miss Clarke. But the old men were betting on my aunt, remembering her strength when young, and in support of her valor, and because they wanted to humiliate the young. And me, I put a thousand dollars on my aunt, and I said: 'That's a thousand dollars I'm going to lose, but it's for the honor of the Gordons.' And my aunt's colors were apple-green, and the colors of the ditestable Miss Clarke were yellow. And the locomotive faded into the background, there was so much interest in the competing ladies, my aunt and Miss Clarke—for the other three ladies were far less strong. And I tell you that it was on the ladies that there was interest in these races, for the locomotives are deliberately driven rather slowly, so that a good runner can overtake them. That's to make the race interesting and give pleasure to the ladies.

"So, the day comes and everything is set. My aunt shakes my hand and says to me: 'My nephew Gordon, I tell you this: I've bet my fortune and my house on myself, If I lose, there'll be nothing for it but for you, my nephew, to take your Aunt Bettina elsewhere and prevent her from perishing of starvation. But have confidence: your Aunt Bettina is running for the honor of the Gordons.'

"And I got into the automobile in order to follow the route at close range, alongside. And I saw, not far away, a stupid young fellow, Miss Clarke's fiancé, who was sniggering. I said nothing.

"And the impassioning race started. That Miss Clarke took the lead. But I saw my aunt full of resolution, and I had some hope. The locomotive was also going, but soon, that Miss Clarke in the lead and my aunt not far behind, went past it. The interest was very great. Everyone was shouting like thunder and waving handkerchiefs. I saw that my aunt was gradually making up ground. The finish was a long way off and Miss Clarke was making very strenuous efforts, but my aunt was also getting down to work. Then I forgot everything else except that poor aunt whom I loved and who was running with so much courage. And I was standing up in the automobile on seeing her apple-green costume and waving my umbrella and I shouted: 'Courage, Aunt! Stick at it, Aunt! For the honor of the Gordons, Aunt Bettina!'

"And I wept like a fool, seeing that she was running hard, that sublime aunt. And that Miss Clarke was also excited by the young fellow who was her fiancé and was running like the wind, but she was running for the money and the love of a man, while my aunt was running for nothing at all except pure glory and the honor of the Gordons, which was in her heart, and she had to triumph.

"Now the finish wasn't far away, and there were efforts so terrible that I no longer dared even to shout encouragement to my aunt. But she, the intrepid and superhuman woman, her feet were hardly touching the ground, and the power of youth was in her musculature, for she was going as fast as a swallow... and there was the finish, and my aunt went past...and that Miss Clarke was humbled, twenty yards behind.

"Me, I arrived next to my aunt, utterly delirious. All the people were howling, and it was utterly glorious. But my Aunt Bettina was standing there, motionless, deep red all over. She opened her mouth. 'For the honor of the Gordons,' she said to me, in a strangled voice. And you know what she did? She dropped dead, all stiff.

"Me, I started to tear out my hair, and sobbing in despair. But that ditestable Miss Clarke arrived, with her yellow jersey and her dirty face covered in sweat, and saw my aunt dead, who had been picked up. And without repentance at having caused her to run so violently, that woman, truly disgusting, said she had won and wanted the prize because the first home had perished. And the stupid churl who was her fiancé said the same. Then I, in a fury, punched him in the mouth, and kept on punching, blacking an eye, breaking a tooth and cracking a rib. And I felt better. And everyone recognized that the prize was my poor aunt's, and mine, who was her heir. And there was much glory for the Gordon name....

"Now, I ask you whether my Aunt Bettina isn't worthy to measure against the most ancient, and the warrior of Marathon. And perhaps, you see, it was better than dying in her bed—and the honor of the Gordons, thanks to her, has risen to the skies."

CARNIVAL

Yes, Monsieur, it's the veritable truth. And the episode cost me twenty francs, an almost new frock-coat, a pair of trousers, a pair of boots and a box of cigars, not to mention the fatigue and the emotion, and without bringing me anything but an ambiguous invitation to a soirée to which I certainly won't go…if I have any choice in the matter.…

It was last carnival, on the eve of Lent. I was going home at about half past two in the morning. I'd spent the evening with friends in cafés, as one does, of course. And I was a little chilly, because the weather was damp. So, to calm myself down, I decided to go home on foot. Do you know where I live? Way out on the far side of the Trocadero. It was quite a long way, but I thought that the walk would do me good and I needed time to reflect, because I felt sad, thinking that I was wasting my time in a life so short, going on the spree like that on every occasion, and even without an excuse, instead of toiling for glory and fortune.…

And I swore to be wiser in future, and was full of good resolutions, when a shrill voice nearby said: "For the love of God.…"

I jumped. "What is it?" I said, unable to distinguish anyone.

"For the love of God," the shrill voice repeated, like a creaky hinge.

And I saw, emerging from under a bench, a kind of horribly ragged individual, in a damp and muddy state that made him hard to see and disgusting. By the light of a street-lamp, I saw that he was wearing a pink cardboard mask, with a huge deformed nose, and a huge black beard. Under a hood, pulled down, in the pink cardboard, the eyes were like two black holes. He was very thin and bent double, with his hands in his pockets, and the ripped tails hanging from his coat were flapping at every breath of wind like an old flag.

"Well, I said, "what do you want?"

"Let's go home," he said, pushing me.

"What, my home?"

"Let's go, my dear chap," he said, shoving me harder. "I'm frozen."

I was scared. I shouted "Help!" and "Murder!" He grabbed my be the throat as if with pincers, made me shut up by almost strangling me, and shoved me forward with thrusts of his knee, which was as hard as a piece of wood.

"It's this way, eh? It's this way, eh?" he repeated, driving me forward, and I felt his fingers, which were gloved, digging into my neck.

There was no one about. The night was as soft and dark as crêpe, and I was afraid of being killed, there, all alone, strangled by that creature with the gloved hands, with his rags and his big pink cardboard nose. I didn't put up any more resistance. He relaxed his grip slightly, contenting himself with keeping me in front of him by holding on to my ear.

"At the double," he said. "I'm frozen."

And we both started trotting along the deserted avenue, with him holding on to me with one hand and holding his jaw and nose with the other, as if he were afraid of losing them. And as we ran, we were making a sound like castanets, with the result that I was utterly dazed and wondered whether my joints had been wrapped in tin-plate, to disguise me as a Spaniard for the occasion of the carnival. It made no sense, but I felt ill and my teeth were chattering.

Finally, we arrived, and the other, without letting me go, came into the house with me.

"Light the fire," he commanded.

I lit the gas stove.

In the meantime, he calmly took off the rags that covered him, as well as his hood and his false nose. Underneath, so far as I could see, there was nothing but a skeleton of flesh and bone—or, rather, nothing but bone, with no flesh at all. He stretched himself, cracked his joints and his fingers, and calmly went to take the lovely curtain from my window in order to wrap himself up in it. Then he came back to the stove, put both feet on the mantel, and sighed with satisfaction.

"That's good, the warmth," he said. "Give me a cigar, old chap. I have a mortal chill. But for you, I'd have been done for. I've only just avoided pleurisy. It's truly disgusting."

I was a trifle emotional, of course, but I didn't want to show it. "What's disgusting?" I asked, putting on an air of assurance.

"The confetti," he replied. "And the rain, and the people one meets, and also the bench I was under, and all the rest—everything. Everything disgusts me."

"But why were you rooting around under the bench?" I said. "And why were you being showered with confetti, when...."

"When I could have been tranquil in my vault, reading or asleep, eh? That's true. But what do you expect? One's never able to be content with one's good fortune.... Anyway, it'll teach me a lesson...."

"So," I said, "you came out."

"Yes, believe me. I'll be honest, and tell you the whole story. I live over there in Père-Lachaise, obviously. And I beg you to believe that we're a somewhat choice and amiable society. We get together every night. We dance, we smoke, we play knucklebones, we recite monologues. There are ladies, you know, and men who can make admirable conversation. There are some who make us die with laughter. I won't tell you their names—they wouldn't like it. But if you could hear them talking about their times, and putting right the things that the books get wrong... what an education! Anyway, we were chatting about the carnival the other night, and everyone was giving his description of it, of his memories, and the old ones were saying that it mustn't be like that any more, and the newcomers were saying that it's still amusing, all the same....

"Then we got curious, and five or six of us decided to go and spend the evening outside, on the day of the festival, to see it at close range. Usually, we never go out—we're content to climb the wall, or on to the monuments, and look at Paris like that, from afar, while chatting under the stars...but for once, we wanted to see for ourselves how things were going. I confess that, for my own count, I had a great desire to do that, and I was the most determined to attempt the adventure—a very excusable fantasy among folk as stay-at-home as we are.

"There were five of us who wanted to come: old Moreau, Louis de Larive—you know, the family that has such a fine monument in the first side-path to the right—Thompson, an American who doesn't speak a word of French, Madame Sophie and me. But we needed masks, you see, and clothes, and money...for me, clothes especially, for my shroud was in tatters and for a man of thirty-four...."

"You died at thirty-four?" I said. "That's very young."

"You don't say," he interrupted, impatiently. "I was actually sixty-seven, which is quite honorable, but we start counting from the day when we come to reside in the old cemetery. So, I'm thirty-four, and, for a man of my age, a few clothes are necessary. It's not worth the trouble of looking at my rags scornfully—they're all I could find in the shop of the damnable old second-hand dealer that we...that we ...*visited* yesterday evening. What do you expect? We only had that means, and the man needed distraction....

"So, this evening, at nine o'clock, we sorted ourselves out as best we could and left. At the last moment, old Moreau decided not to come, on the pretext that he had a toothache, but that wasn't true, and it was only because his wife is as jealous as anything and had forbidden him to go out. Then we climbed over the wall and started down the hill toward Paris, but we'd scarcely gone fifty meters when Madame Sophie said that she had a stomach ache and wanted to go back, and Louis de Larive offered to accompany her, and they both went back.

"If you ask me, that was arranged in advance. They wanted a little time together on their own and they'd only put on a show of wanting to come…he has feelings for her, and she wanted him to give her a sheet of lead from his coffin to line her jaw, which is falling apart. Up there, in the old cemetery, there's no means of seeing one another intimately, because everyone knows everyone's business and there's more gossip there than in a provincial village, and the Larive family keeps an eye on its offspring.…

"So, that left two of us, Thompson and me, and we took a cab to go down to the boulevards—but good God, what a crowd, and what behavior! I hadn't expected it to have changed so much since my time, and I shan't be coming back. And the confetti! In an instant, someone had lowered the widow of our fiacre and thrown it all over us. My orbits were full of it, and it blinded me, and Thompson was sneezing for a quarter of an hour because he's swallowed a bit, and he lost the first phalanx of his left thumb giving a slap to some dirty swine who pulled his false nose.…

"And there were people, Monsieur who were picking up a mixture of sand, sticky paper and horse manure from the ground over which they were walking, and flinging it in the faces of their neighbors. And there were poor little children in the crowd who'd been dressed up as negro kings or soldiers, and were beaten for doing that, and hard, for they were weeping, as everyone could see.

"But our driver couldn't go any further. He told us to get down, and there we were in the middle of the crowd, and soon, we began to get excited, Thompson and me, among all those people. We were shoved toward a café, and on the terrace, Thompson had quite a lot to drink, and got drunk. He bought some confetti and he started throwing it too, and I did the same, and we did what everyone else was doing, naturally. I shouted, I shook people's carriages as mine had been shaken, and I tickled women…but then some ruffian dressed as a shepherd stuck his hand in my pocket to rob me. I jabbed my elbow into his ribs—

and believe me, I have sharp elbows. He shouted that I'd stabbed him.

"It wasn't true, but the crowd gathered, the ruffian disappeared and someone shouted that I'd murdered a woman. Police arrived, and I ran away, Monsieur, because in my day, when one saw the police arriving and one hadn't done anything, it was better to make oneself scarce. And while I was battling my way through the middle of the crowd I saw Thompson, in the distance, who had climbed on to some sort of ridiculous Roman chariot, and had lost his left arm, and he was singing in English, gesticulating, and kissing a fat woman who was beside him, without giving any thought to coming to my aid. He was drunk, and I don't know what's become of him....

"I don't know how I was able to get myself out of it. Someone in the crowd had stolen all my money...all the second-hand dealer's money....and I'd lost a rib somewhere near the Madeleine, and I got lost myself in this damned Paris that's been completely rebuilt.

"I stopped, tired of walking without knowing my way, and hid under the bench to wait for the first gentleman who passed by, in order to explain my plight to him, as a man of honor, ask for a few clothes in order to go home decently, and a few sous to pay for a cab, in order to get there before daybreak....

"A few clothes—yes, that frock-coat will suffice, and those trousers, and that pair of boots. Damn it! Your feet are shorter than mine...but they're all right for width. Is my hood dry? I need to go. Give me a louis for my cab-fare. I'll let you have it back as soon as possible. I'll take the box of cigars—they're very good. I'll also take the curtain. And thanks very much. À bientôt. Come and see us one of these days. You only have to hide up a tree until the wardens have made their evening rounds, and then come down.... Do come—you'll find that we're good company. And anyway, you'll have to come sooner or later... although I don't know your situation in the world, you'll permit me....

"Anyway, I hope...and thanks, my dear chap. À bientôt...."

And he left.

THE YOUNG MAN
WITH THE VIPERS

It happened in the studio of the painter Réginal Givre,[18] who was the victim of it. It wasn't him who told me about it—the poor fellow can no longer tell anyone about anything, as you'll understand shortly. I heard the whole story all the same, and I'm revealing it in order that Réginal Givre's friends will know the reason for the sudden and disadvantageous change that has been recently manifest in his personality, and in order that they can intervene if necessary.

It was a few days before the deadline for the submission of paintings to the Salon; in the hearts of artists who hadn't yet completed their masterpieces there was a sentiment neighboring on delirium, and they were spending every minute in frantic toil.

Réginal had almost finished, and on that last evening, the eve of the great day, he was in his studio at about half past ten. Sinister and bizarre shadows filled the vast room, for the only lighting consisted of a large reflector-lamp with a scarlet globe, which was projecting all of its light toward a canvas resting on an easel. Réginal's studio is vast and sumptuous, and appeared even more so in that bloody gloom. A ponderous warmth was

18. This story is adapted from "Réginald Givre et Soi-même" [Reginald Givre and himself], one of the dramatic pieces in Boutet's earlier collection *Les Victimes grimacent* (1900). *Givre* is hoar-frost or any similar white patina; the name was presumably selected as a wry echo of the surname of Dorian Gray.

emerging from a large stove that was glowing ruddily in the background. The ebony clock, standing against a wall, was patiently counting the seconds.

A large antique mirror beside the easel was tilting its oval face on a tripod. Réginal Givre, a pale and handsome painter with black hair, was dressed that evening in a grandiose red velvet simar. Sitting on a swiveling sandalwood chair he was persisting, in spite of a slight distress caused by the three glasses of whisky and soda he had drunk, in perfecting his painting.

I had seen that painting in progress. It represented Réginal himself, somewhat embellished and rendered interesting by various unusual decorations. He had a golden viper around his temples, another around his neck and a third around his right arm. The hand of that arm, raised in a definitive gesture, was holding a large and singular flower whose stem was the undulating body of a serpent and from whose corolla, reminiscent that of a lily, emanated a red forked tongue, and a violet perfume, by which the entire upper part of the paining was bathed, as in a crepuscular mist. Réginal, on the canvas, had his eyes half-closed and an expression of being detached from things of this world. He was very pleased with the work, which, in his estimation, was symbolic, and which he called *The Young Man with the Vipers*. Personally, I didn't like it, and because of that, he had told me that I had no understanding of artistic matters.

At any rate, that evening, Réginal, satisfied with himself and the whole world, in the solitude of his studio, was talking to himself, while caressing his image with the tip of his brush.

"Whisky and soda," he said, "is a really good thing. It's necessary not to abuse it—obviously—but when one takes it in moderation, it's a fount of inspiration." He drank a healthy draught and added a few touches, and then went on: "That violet mist makes my pale face seem suitably romantic.… I look very handsome, there.… I really am very handsome…very seductive. No better than in reality, though. I…I'm counting on a success…on a great success…from every point of view. My future is assured…it's very fine, my future. What I need now is the Légion d'honneur…and afterwards…a good marriage…celebrity…art…great Art…the founder of a school…a young master.…

"Oh, enough!" someone interjected abruptly in an irritated tone. It was none other than his own portrait.

Réginal jumped. "What's enough? What do you mean, enough? Do you have the intention of preventing me from talking in my own home now?"

"I have no intention of doing anything at all," the portrait replied. "I merely think that it's more idiotic and pretentious than is permissible, when I'm in pain.…"

"That's too much," said Réginal. "You're in pain, in this comfortable and…sumptuous studio? For, all things considered, my studio is sumptuous. With me, your father, your friend…with all the amiable people who come to see you, to admire you.…"

"First of all," observed the portrait, "it's not me they're admiring—it's you, as a painter and as a model. Secondly, your amiable people are just a load of boors that you call your friends, and profligate whores that you make into your mistresses as soon as you can, without any regard for my modesty. If you think I'm made of wood, you're mistaken.…"

"I know that," Réginal sniggered. "You're made of oil-pigments."

"And you're made of whatever composes an imbecile!" cried the portrait, angrily. "And I've finally had enough. It's disgusting living here. It's even more disgusting to think that I'll soon be going to exhibit myself to the examination of entire populations with the grotesque appearance that you've chosen to give me.…"

"What? No art criticism!" Réginal interjected. "Anyway, if I exhibit you, it's for our glory."

"It's for your glory, you mean—and it's truly shameful that no one kicks you out of exhibitions, because you paint like a pig. Oh, no! Enough! Don't drink any more! I've a lot to say this evening, and you're already drunk.…"

"I'm not drunk," Réginal observed, majestically, albeit with a slightly thick tongue. "I'm not drunk. I haven't touched a drop. And as for what you want to tell me…well, I don't want to hear it. You're annoying me."

And he emptied his glass.

"Miserable drunkard," groaned the portrait. "It's truly revolting for me to think that I depict such a dirty individual."

"What?" said Réginal.

"For sure. When I think that I could have depicted someone respectable—a magistrate, a bishop, a general…."

"Phooey! Soul of a grocer!"

"The souls of grocers are worth as much as any other," said the portrait. "That's not what it's about. Listen to me…."

"No," said Réginal, pouring himself a large glass of whisky, to which he only added a few drops of soda.

"Yes," said the portrait. "You're going to listen to me, or else, when the minister comes to visit the exhibition and is brought to stand in front of me—for that's been the goal of your efforts these last three months; I know what you desire, my lad—when the minister is standing in front of me, I'll give him a slap in the face with my lily, and bang goes your decoration!"

"You won't do that," said Réginal, calmly.

"Yes I will," the portrait affirmed.

"No," said Réginal, "because, by that time you'll be varnished, and the lily too, and you wouldn't be able to move in public anyway!"

"I won't allow myself to be varnished," said the portrait. "I'll pull faces…."

"Damn! Damn!" said Réginal to himself. There was a pause. He went on, very softly: "What do you want, then? Be polite."

"I intend to be polite," said the portrait. "This is what I propose. It'll annoy me to be exhibited. It'll annoy you if I'm not. Well, take my place on the canvas during the exhibition; I'll take care of things for you in the world in the meantime."

"I don't want to," aid Régnial. "You'd destroy my reputation with your grocer's soul, and also, it's too important a time for me to allow myself to be replaced." After two minutes of reflection, he added: "Furthermore, you're an imbecile."

In that case, I'm not going to the exhibition," declared the other, bluntly.

"Yes," said Réginal, who had finished the whisky and was finding it difficult to pronounce his words, "you will go...because...otherwise...I'll stick you in the loft—with the rats. You're my conscience, eh? Well, you'll go to the loft...my conscience...to the loft!"

He writhed.

"You'd lose by it," said the portrait. "Listen—I'll make you an offer...."

"Go on," said Réginal, collapsing in his armchair.

"Well, here it is: we'll wager my liberty against my exhibition. If you lose, you'll take my place. If you win, well, you can exhibit me. I'll let myself be varnished, meekly. I'll be good. I'll be a great success...."

"He's back to that. He wants me to take his place!" Réginal exclaimed, joyfully. "He's an utter idiot. I...I agree!" he shouted at the portrait.

"Good," said the latter. "Fetch the dice...."

"I have everything to gain," Réginal said to himself, drunkenly, as he searched for the dice. "Everything...to gain.... He's an idiot.... He'll never be able...to take my place. I'm me.... I'll never be able...to be him... If I lose...well, I'll take him up to the loft...with the rats.... He'll have to let himself...be varnished.... If I win...that'll be even better. Where are they, damn it!"

"To your right," said the portrait, quite calmly, while Réginal was turning everything upside down. "To your right, in the Chinese vase."

Réginal fell upon the Chinese vase and knocked it to the floor. He followed the dice on all fours, and finally got to his feet, with difficulty, clutching them.

"Right," he said, indecisively. "How are you going to play?"

"You'll play for me," said the portrait, "with your left hand."

"Good," said Réginal. "Good—that'll work. I'll begin. For me: four…and three…four and three make…? Seven! That's seven for me! To you: in my left hand;; Bang! Five.and two…. Five and two…. Five and two…?"

"That makes eight," said the portrait. "I've won. Pay up!"

"Ha ha ha!" exclaimed Réginal, who was no longer able to see very clearly. "Ha ha ha! You were lucky. You're going up to the loft, if you don't behave. Yes!"

"Let's go," said the portrait, calmly. "I'm coming down. Come and take my place."

"Come down…come down…old chap," said Réginal. "Come down…but…. But…what's happening? I can feel the painting… the oils…. And here I am…all flat…colored…. What's happening to me? Help! Help! Anyone! And that wretch standing in front of me, sniggering, in *my* studio, on *my* armchair, among *my* works, smoking *my* cigars…. It's ignoble! Oh la la! Oh la la! He's reading my letters. He's rummaging in my papers! He'll destroy my reputation with his grocer's soul. He'll introduce himself into the intimacy of people I know. He'll be me, every-where, forever…. My God! My God! Why did I have to be stupid enough to agree to that! I must be an imbecile!"

Meanwhile, the other Réginal, standing in the studio, stretched his arms. "Ah!" he said. "That's a good day's work. I'm tried. Let's go to bed."

He headed for the door, and once there, turning back toward the frame in which, painted in oils, flat and non-existent, Réginal Givre was raging dementedly, he said: "And tomorrow… varnish…or the loft!"

LUCIE'S PERSISTENCE

This happened in February 1901. The night was glacial and rainy, and I was hurrying home. I was amazed to find at my door, waiting for me on the pavement, a fellow named Canal. I knew him well, having been to college with him, but, given his mores and character, he was the last man I would have thought capable of stationing himself, in the rain, at three o'clock in the morning, at the door of a friend who might not be coming home at all. I ought to add that we had quarreled a couple of months earlier.

"Why," I said, "what are you doing here?"

"Waiting for you," he replied, a trifle nervously. "I...I wanted to ask you to come with me...."

"Go where with you?"

"Home...I'm worn out. I've been...exhausted for ten days. I need sleep. I have to...."

He raised his eyes and looked me in the face. I'd never seen him so pale, and he was agitated by a sort of tremor—or rather trepidation, like a steam-boat under pressure.

"But you don't need me to go to sleep," I said, by no means seduced by the prospect of not sleeping in my own bed, which was already waiting for me, I thought. "You have only to go home and go to bed. What's stopping you?"

"Well...well...." He swallowed his saliva and his voice choked. "At home, I'm scared...."

At this point, certain items of information regarding the natural history of Canal are necessary. He was born in a respectable prefecture, to similarly respectable parents, who worked successfully in the notariat. Their only son had always given them pleasure, being of a robust and well-mannered temperament. After a reasonable adolescence and glorious studies, he had made a brilliant entry into the École Centrale, and begun to prepare himself a brilliant career as an engineer.

He was in his second year when destiny led him to encounter in the street a twin soul named Lucie, who was nineteen years old, a typist, and romantic. She was virtuous too, and her seduction cost Canal no less than four months of effort, but he loved her during that time, and was able to express his sentiments, even though the study of mathematics absorbed the better part of his faculties. The twin soul had ended up loving him too, for good and all, and had yielded.

They had moved in together, on the fourth floor of a tranquil house, she letting go of her family and typing, and he pursuing with his studies with only slightly less ardor: a course full of sagacity, which Lucie encouraged with all her might, while keeping house as best she could, in order get by on her beloved's allowance without going into debt. The latter allowed himself to be adored, and found it natural.

Things had gone on in that fashion for the duration of Canal's studies, and for some time after their glorious consecration: diplomas, certificates and qualifications of all sorts, for he was a capable young man. In the meantime, his love for Lucie was somewhat eroded, in spite of or because of the fact that he had nothing for which to reproach her.

Meanwhile, Canal's parents reasoned as follows: Now our son is completely grown up. He's a handsome fellow, intelligent and well-educated. With the six thousand francs of income that we'll give him and all his diplomas, he ought to be able to marry three thousand francs and expectations. Then he'll be able to launch himself in industry as a manufacturer and become a considerable man, which will be advantageous for everyone. Mademoiselle Bodin will fit the bill very well.

Young Lucie, too, was following a reasoning, which was

incompatible with the preceding one from the practical point of view: When he met me, I was honest; he knows that. Since then, I've been faithful to him. I'm his wife before God and he's going to marry me before his fellow men now that he's an engineer and can live on his own income. I'm very happy because he loves me, and I'll love him for as long as I live. Should I not have consummated my marriage?

Canal, personally, was not reasoning at all, but he was unenthusiastic in contemplating the imminent day when the notariat and Lucie would come into conflict.

That day came, as every expected day comes, whether it be feared or desired, whether it brings dolor or joy. Canal *père* found out that Canal *fils* had a gilt-edged, and therefore dangerous, liaison, and recalled him to the prefecture in no time. There were a few family discussions, in which the highest questions of social morality were addressed, as well as the duties of children to their parents, and, by way of conclusion, an explanation of the essential perversity of vicious schemers who take possession of the hopes of family—all of it very moving.

The hope of the family began by standing up quite well to the familial objurgations and depreciations, but as he had a naturally egotistical heart, having never suffered, and organized his life according to what he believed to be the practical modern method, he convinced himself rapidly enough that the best thing for him to do was to please his family, and let go of the schemer in order to marry Demoiselle Bodin, already picked out, the daughter of the office's principal client.

That decision made, young Canal did not hesitate; he wrote Lucie a letter in which he "prepared the break," according to his own expression. He followed the letter three days later and continued to "prepare the break" in person, with all the usual considerations.

He prepared it so well that, after a formal explanation, Lucie—who clung to her plans and proved to be impulsive by nature, and denuded of philosophy—went to throw herself in the Seine, not wishing, as she explained in a pathetic letter, to become a ruined girl, nor to survive abandonment by the only man in the world she was capable of loving forever, and whom another woman was about to take from her, although she was his spouse before God.

She was found two days later, snagged on a pontoon, and brought back dead to the small apartment where she had lived with her husband before God—and for him there were painful hours, for he suddenly woke up from his ignorance of life and his ingenuous egotism. A few of his friends, of whom I was one, thinking that he had not acted well, took responsibility for communicating that fact to him, without indulgence, and he returned to the prefecture in a state of some distress.

The scarcely-concealed joy of his parents threw him into great perplexity, with intervals of satisfied indifference that followed bouts of the most cruel remorse. However, in view of his well-mannered character, he accomplished his duties as a fiancé scrupulously, and he was, all things considered, well on the way to forgetfulness.

He returned to Paris, having affairs to put in order and needing to obtain estimates for the construction of a factory. Doubtless, he plunged himself into work, and perhaps he retained a certain resentment regarding our observations, for he did not come to see any of his friends. Ten days went by, as I subsequently learned—and it was then that I found him, one night, waiting for me outside my door, in order to ask me to go home with him, because he was afraid.

"Afraid of what?" I asked, somewhat taken aback, because he was in a state of horrible anguish and I would not have thought him capable of such emotion.

"I'm afraid," he replied, distractedly. "Listen: I need to tell you everything. Since my return—which is to say, since the event, since I left straight away—I haven't be able to sleep at home...or stay there by night."

"Why, what's the matter?"

"This is it: when I came back, ten days ago, I had some difficulty going back into the apartment...you understand?"

"Yes, I understand."

"You told me that I'd acted badly, but I assure you that I had no intention of doing so. It was so new for me…I didn't know. My father always told me that when a student had finished his studies he left his mistress and got married…."

"That depends on the woman, and…."

"Yes, but I didn't know. Since…well, anyway, I went back home; it was ten o'clock in the evening and I had a candle. I put my valise in my study, which is on the right. The bedroom…her room…is at the end of the corridor, at the back. I went toward the door to go in. And then…then I fled along the corridor, down the stairs and into the street, running as fast as I could, to find people and light…and I could scarcely stop myself crying out, I was so afraid."

"Of what?"

"Of…of what was behind that door. *It* was waiting for me, I tell you.…

"And since then, every night.…

"In the daytime, I'm not scared, and I don't even understand how I could have been the night before, and I make the resolution to vanquish it. I work, I make preparations for my marriage, carry out my business calmly and make a firm resolution to go into my bedroom that night…and every night, I'm more scared than the previous one, and I flee, to wait for daylight in cafes, in all-night establishments, anywhere that there's people and light.…

"Every evening. And I would never have supposed, before, that I was capable of suffering like this.…"

He stopped, out of breath.

"Why don't you go back to the province?" I said. "You can tell your father everything and settle your nerves before getting married."

"No," he said. "I'm not ill and I shan't say anything to my father. I couldn't. I don't know how I can tell him. You know me well, you see; you know that I'm of sound mind…but is it me or a madman that's telling you this? This evening.…"

"Well, what about this evening?"

"Well, I'd made a resolution to finish it. I went up to my apartment at about ten, and it seemed to me that I was better and that I'd be able to go into the bedroom.... In the corridor, with the candle, I wasn't afraid, and I mocked myself.... Well...."

He gripped my arm with all his strength.

"Well...the door opened in front of me. Understand this: it wasn't me who had opened it—it opened without me touching it. It opened of its own accord, you understand! And...*it*'s waiting for me behind the door...I know it! I thought that I was going to die without being able to get away. And you have to come with me in order for me to be able to go back in, because I'm now a ruined man if I can't succeed in vanquishing *it*. I've been worn out with fatigue, I tell you, for ten days, but I have to get over this if I want to become a man again. Understand this: it's my entire life! You have to come with me so that I can go back in. I need to sleep at home tonight, or I'll never sleep again. Will you come?"

"Yes," I said, "I will. I'll go into the bedroom with you, you can lie down, and I'll spend the night next door, in your study, on the camp-bed. You need to get out of this. After all, although you've been unjust to her...that's no reason for.... As you told me, you didn't know. Let's go."

We soon arrived at his apartment. Canal didn't say anything more, but when we were in the corridor leading to the bedroom I saw that he was on the point of fainting. The door didn't open of its own accord and nothing remarkable happened. We went in. I opened the windows and the cupboard briefly; I shook the curtains and devoted myself to various reassuring exercises. I even cracked a joke, and Canal seemed much better. He lay down, and when I saw that he was quite calm and ready for sleep, with his permission, I went to establish myself in the study. I read for a while, then, everything being in order, I went to sleep.

The doorbell woke me up with a start. It was shortly after dawn. Workmen, accompanied by policemen, were bringing back Canal's badly battered corpse, which they'd picked up in the street.

He must have thrown himself out of the window to escape *the thing*, whatever it was, that was waiting for him behind the door, and had revealed itself after I had left the room.

THE MAN WHO
TOLD THE TRUTH

Melchior was born of respectable parents of average stupidity, who were sufficiently honest liars, like everyone else. His brothers and sisters exhibited no abnormal vices. Nothing could have allowed foresight of the extraordinary and fatal vocation that took possession of him as soon as he ceased to be a little soft package, red-tinted and unconscious.

That vocation, which was more like a very special form of mental illness, by which no human being had ever been afflicted before, consisted of a frenetic and immoderate love of the truth.

While he was still almost in swaddling-clothes, Melchior could not imagine that anyone might deceive him, and he would never have given the slightest thought to concealing his impressions. To his relationship with his nurse he brought the most perfect good faith, and required it in return. To a lady who desired to kiss him and whose face he did not like, he replied: "No, you're too ugly," with the same innocent sincerity as when he demanded the fulfillment of an impossible promise that had been made to him to get rid of his insistence.

His disappointments led to terrible crises. He did not want to admit that anyone could make commitments with no intention of keeping them. At eighteen months of age, he almost died of indignation because of the moon he did not have, although his father had promised it to him, one evening when it had been reflected in the garden pond and had howled to have it. His filial affection never recovered from that blow.

As can be imagined, such mores occasioned much unpleasantness and rendered interaction difficult. Instead of diminishing, as is usual with education, his vice was progressively augmented, and the child became so unbearable that his parents packed him off to school as soon as they could.

Melchior began to make the acquaintance of life, and did not find it in accordance with his dream. Having a lively intelligence, in spite of his monomania, he was able to recognize that all the favor of his teachers went to liars, whereas his unreasonable frankness made him the object of all punishments and the enemy of all his comrades—who, with good reason, called him a dirty rat and beat him with their fists when he denounced them for some common fault while owning up to it himself.

The printing-press also caused him cruel disillusionments. He had total faith in everything he read, and accepted any implausible story with confidence. It was impossible for him to admit fiction. What was written ought to be rue; if it was not true, it should not have been written. Such was his reasoning and the fables of La Fontaine became for him a dangerous poison, for he was always looking for talking animals, and was believed to be an idiot.

He grew up without correcting himself. In spite of experience and education, he only contrived with great difficulty to get it into his head that one could not always be sincere, and that lying is necessary to life. His suffering was great when he finally understood that the truth, for humankind, is not always an object of scrupulous and irreproachable respect. At the same time, he developed increasingly, for that dangerous product, a grim and absolute passion. One could obtain anything from him by hiding nothing. The most brutal cynicism was welcome to him, for he saw it naively as a proof of veracity.

His comrades knew that well, and they made him do all their work, simply by saying: "We're lazy, do our homework; in the meantime we'll be playing forbidden games. Afterwards, we won't beat you any less at recreation."

"I'll do it," said Melchior, "to reward you for having told the truth." And he applied himself to it with courage and devotion, working for everyone while the little wretches impaled beetles, blew up frogs by blowing into them through a hollow quill, or let off fireworks under the benches. The less vicious played cards or force-fed silkworms.

Thus Melchior grew up, and when that abnormal being became an adult, he left school, beginning to find the burden of that constant sincerity very heavy. He was unhappy too, for he did not hide it from himself that it would be very difficult for him to practice it rigorously in society, and that thought was unbearable, because he loved the Truth more than anything in the world.

At about that time, and because, to his bitter regret, he had already been forced to one or two semi-deceptions, his lucky star—or, rather, the baleful destiny that oppressed his fate—permitted him to render a considerable service to an Angel of the Lord, like the one featured in the Bible. And the grateful angel granted him a wish, promising to fulfill it.

Melchior did not hesitate. "I wish," he said to the angel, "always to tell the truth, and that everyone should tell it to me."

The angel started in astonishment. "My poor boy," he said, "I asked you for a wish that would give you pleasure and might make you happy."

"I wish," said Melchior, "to be a person who never deceives, and is never deceived. Only that can make me happy."

"Let it be as you desire," said the angel. "I promised. But you'd have done better not to render me the service."

The angel returned to Heaven, and Melchior entered into life.

His relationships with his fellows were disastrous, thanks to his terrible gift, which made him into a kind of pitiless calamity, deadly to social conventions. After having been, for a very brief period, considered an object of savage and singular curiosity, he soon acquired and established reputation as an odious boor and uncouth imbecile, toward whom everyone was obliged to be brutal and uncivil, as he was toward everyone.

Without mentioning the suits for slander and countless

brawls, he fought, in the early days, an average of one duel every four days. The majority of the duels, fought with pistols, were without danger, but a few encounters with the épée did him harm. Once a void had formed around him, however, he no longer had any but rare collisions with unknowns in the wake of fortuitous instances of frankness.

Then he suffered from the state of isolation in which he lived, and the sentiments of horror that he inspired in other humans, whoever they might be, as soon as his deadly property became manifest.

He fell in love in his twenty-fifth year.

She was a pretty young woman, good and intelligent. Although he already had a bad reputation, and in spite of his unpleasant sincerity, she loved him too. They became engaged, and he was happy. Unfortunately, he could not keep quiet.

"Do you love me?" he asked, one day.

"Yes," she said. And he shivered with joy, because he knew that it was true, as was everything she said to him.

"Do you love me more than anything else in the world?" he asked then—for he dreamed, like every man, of absolute love.

She hesitated, and blushed. "No," she said. "I love my mother more."

"Ah!" said Melchior, whose mood darkened—and he worked courageously to make himself loved more.

He succeeded, and on one expansive day, he repeated his question. "Do you love me more than anything else in the world?"

"Yes," she said, without hesitation.

He was happy, but he did not have the strength to moderate himself. "Will you love me forever?" he asked, with the muted consciousness of doing something stupid.

"Forever," she replied, immediately.

He took her hand in a transport of joy, but already, turning her head away, she was stammering: "That is to say...forever.... I don't know...." She cried, with passion: "But I love you now! If you left me, I'd die!"

"Alas," he said, sadly, "I don't know either whether I'll love you forever. We don't love one another enough. What point is there in going on with something that must come to an end...?"

He went away and never came back. In accordance with what she had told him, she died, for she loved him more than anything in the world, at that moment.

The story became known, and Melchior—whom, naturally, no one understood—became a kind of ferocious beast in the eyes of many people. The most indulgent believed him to be mad. He was unworried by that because, prey to grief and remorse, he almost regretted the angel's gift—but it was too late.

Nevertheless, he tried to devote himself to some kind of endeavor, among those that his intelligence and education rendered possible to him, but in vain. Whatever the goal of his studies might be, he could not pursue them. The sciences were sealed off at the first hypothesis. He was unable to believe that two and two make four. History stopped at the first date, and geography at the first rigorous description. Finance, commerce and the bar were not for him. To philosophy he did not give the slightest thought, nor to statistics. A vague literary essay was flat and insipid; he threw it in the fire and did not try again. Some unknown aberration made him think, momentarily, of politics, and he stood for a seat in Parliament.

His first public meeting was remarkable.

"Electors," he said, from the platform, "I offer myself to you in order that you might elect me as your representative. I ought to tell you that your interests do not interest me, and that I find you rather disgusting. I consider you to be a vile herd, ripe for being made fools of by words that serve no other purpose. All that my committee has promised you in my name, I will not do. If I desire to be elected, it's solely to make money, to have influence and to be able to speculate...."

He was obliged to interrupt himself; various projectiles, amid clamors of hatred, rained down upon him. The electors charged him, furiously. He fled via the roof of the hall in order not to be murdered. It required twenty-seven stretchers to take away the corpses that public opinion justly inscribed to the account of the malefactor.

That attempt was the last he made to live the life of his fellows. He shut himself away with his misanthropy and had evil thoughts, because he knew that he had never done any harm deliberately and thought himself the object of an unjust hatred. He was isolated, morose and disgusted with everything. He fell ill and did not seek any treatment. It got worse.

"I'm going to die," he said to himself, one morning.

Those words, pronounced by his infallible mouth, terrified him. He called a doctor.

"What is it?" he asked, after being examined.

"I don't know," said the physician.

"I'm going to die," said Melchior.

"Yes, in a few minutes," the physician replied. He stopped, astonished by his own brutality and the confidence of his diagnosis. He wanted to redeem himself with hopeful words, but only repeated: "You're...going to die."

"That's the Truth," Melchior replied, with hatred in his voice.

And he did it.

GABRIELLE
AND HER FAUN

Gabrielle's father was unknown and her mother was a laundress. As the latter destined her daughter for great things—a dressmaker in the Rue de la Paix, or perhaps a pupil at the Conservatoire—she did not torment her at all, save for a half-hearted and perpetually-deferred threat to make her take piano lessons. In the meantime, she spoiled her as much as she could and let her do whatever she wanted. Gabrielle, who was called Gaby, was one of those fortunate individuals who pleased everyone, and whom everyone strove to please. She was, moreover, a good little girl who spent her childhood either wandering the streets or sitting under the big ironing table in her mother's shop, listening, with a desire to educate herself, to the dirty talk of the washerwomen, which she only understood incompletely, but much more than was believed.

Her mother sent her to school regularly, and she went willingly, when the weather was not too fine. The teacher was an old lady with a few qualifications; Gabrielle was her favorite, to the extent that she kept her close during class in order to give her lumps of chewing-gum and tell her long marvelous stories. In these tales, which the old lady made up according to the inspiration of the moment, at hazard, the heroes and events of real history were mingled pell-mell with fairy tales, Biblical traditions and mythological legends, one story leading to another—to the greater delight of Gabrielle, who had imagination. She reveled delightedly in the superhuman adventures, the hybrid monsters, half-human and half-beast, and the fabulous heroes who had such sublime adventures.

And young Gaby spent considerable number of hours lost in an enchanted world in which she was a queen, among magical palaces, with marvelous amours....

Thus she lived, satisfied; but she learned soon enough that reality is not the sister of dream, and her practical debut in the knowledge of things forbidden to little maidens lacked grandeur.

That occurred one evening in July in a large abandoned waste-ground full of long grass and bushes, where she had taken refuge before going home for dinner to her mother's stifling shop. A scapegrace of her own age, who had curly hair and she knew well, joined her by sliding, as she had done, between two dislocated planks in the fence, and having drawn near to her, in a sly and awkward manner, with no other preamble but vague sniggers, asked her if she knew what the difference was between men and women.

"Women have long hair and no beard," Gabrielle replied, with a naivety that was not exempt from dissimulation.

"That's not all," the boy replied. "The beard can be shaved, and women...." He stopped, in spite of his natural impudence. He blushed slightly, hesitated, and made a decision. "The difference is there," he said, with a gesture.

"Oh!" said Gabrielle, recoiling, shocked but curious, and added: "That's not true!"

"It's true," said the boy, whose ears were red and whose voice was even hoarser than usual. "Would you like me to show you? You can show me too."

"You're dirty," said Gaby. "I'm going to tell Maman."

A vain threat. She stayed, still telling herself that she was going to go. The conversation continued, punctuated by embarrassed silences and anxious shivers...and Gaby ended up wanting to observe the difference, and to show it, provided that no dirty words were spoken. None were, and the exchange took place....

Gaby lifted up her dress; two faces, reddened to the ears, looked up at the same time; embarrassed eyes met.

"You're disgusting!" Gaby exclaimed, suddenly bursting into sobs.

And she fled at a run.

Gabrielle conserved of that visual initiation a memory of shame and troubled joy. She maintained in appearance an irreducible hatred for the curly-haired scapegrace, and a grateful affection for the waste ground that had drawn her into her first adventure, inglorious as it was.

After a while, waste ground and abandoned gardens became forests in miniature, where little wild beasts lived freely in the midst of the profound tumult of the city. Between the bushes and the clumps of grass, under dead leaves, the brown and yellow earth was visible. Birds nested in the branches, whose leaves obstructed the view from the adjacent houses in summer. The wind howled during winter nights and the rains of spring streamed down the slopes, hollowing out torrents, which went to drown the wild rats in their holes, in the midst of the rejuvenated grass.

Gabrielle was soon familiar with all the enclosures in her neighborhood, of which there were many. She knew those in which the most tranquility, and the least troubled solitude, reigned. She introduced herself into them easily, by climbing some low fence or sliding between dislocated planks. She chose the largest, the most uncultivated and, especially, the ones least frequented by the urchins of the neighborhood.

She spent long hours there, on fine days, dreaming her childish dreams of happiness and sumptuousness. Something new was now mixed into them, and the memory of the scapegrace with the curly hair gave her ideas to complete her imaginary adventures. Mythological stories were alloyed with the novels whose deadly attractions she was beginning to savor, fabricating for her a world that was quite unreal but which gradually took on more importance for her, and which caused her increasing desolation in seeing how different the constituents of everyday life were: the shop, with its common and dirty washerwomen; the obscene jokes or sentimental stupidities of street urchins or petty employees; the libidinous pursuits of old gentlemen hunting in the streets; and even the exaggerated tenderness of her mother, who was no longer able to refuse her anything and let her do as she wished.

Gaby reached her sixteenth year thus. She had long dresses and more coquetry, and her mother spoke to her insistently about the Conservatoire. She shook her head and smiled; she wanted to be happy, but not to take any trouble over it. Then too, her dreamy little girl's mind was still the same, and she liked her liberty too much to consent to a harder school than that of the old lady with the qualifications, who had just died.

She was slightly melancholy, however, for she was very desirous of amour, but none of those surrounding her seemed worthy of her. The idea of surrendering herself to the curly-haired scapegrace, who pursued her obstinately, or any of his peers, horrified her...and she wondered when the one for whom she was saving herself would come.

Gabrielle was sad that morning, and took refuge in the most profound of her waste grounds, the one that was so big that she was not sure of knowing all its turnings, and which had been abandoned for so long that the concierge on the far side of the road, who was at least eighty, said that it had always been thus, and that the dilapidated old walls, the immense wild field and the great gnarled trees had never had a master.

Gabrielle had turned into the deserted side-street, and opened the big worm-eaten door, for which she had contrived, with one of those cajoleries that always succeeded, to be entrusted with a key, for there was no means of climbing in. She closed the heavy batten with the sensual feeling of entering into solitude, and the verdant expanse was hers. The May dew was still softening the soil, but the sun, the divine archer, was launching his golden arrows between the fresh leaves and making the dewdrops suspended in the grass scintillate as Gaby rapturously moistened her shoes therein.

She followed the effaced pathways where new verdure was trembling, and eventually reached her favorite spot: an old arbor sheltered from the wind and rain by a roof and partitions of elder branches interwoven with climbing plants. In that covert there was the enervating heat of a hothouse, and the leaves filtered a green shade patched here and there with pale rays of sunlight. Aromas emerged from the earth and the trees....

Gabrielle felt herself invaded by a voluptuous laziness, and her thoughts drifted, delighting in the mythological dreams she had been taught. She evoked, in accordance with what she knew of them, the fabulous times when the gods and mortals had talked to one another and loved one another, in which all the things of the earth had been animated by a mysterious soul, when the sylvans, satyrs and fauns haunted the profound woods with their ambiguous forms, their amorous games, their lascivious laughing pursuits....

She thought that she was a nymph forgotten by time, and her dream, outside life and outside time, cradled her softly in the eternal emotion of spring, sunlight and amorous desire.

Suddenly, in the happy unconsciousness into which she had plunged, she heard the sound of a slight rustling of branches, and a head appeared between the leaves. Gaby shuddered, but did not move. The branches parted further, a face appeared, and Gaby recognized the form of her dream.

The being parted the branches with his bare shoulders and arms, and leaned forward to consider her, his face attentive and bearded. He seemed to be young. A crown of ivy around the temples mingled the short curls with dark and shiny leaves, which did not conceal the little backwardly-curved horns. He bore some resemblance to the urchin who had once shown her the difference, but Gabrielle did not perceive any; she thought, without astonishment, that the adventure had finally arrived, proving the extent to which it was her that had reckoned with everyone else in the world....

She remained motionless. Feigning sleep, she was half-recumbent, and her dress was raised over her bent knee, allowing the other round and slender leg to be seen, molded in its bright stocking. Emotion swelled her young breasts, and the slack neckline yawned slightly over the moist skin.

The faun's eyes were shining like the morning dew; desire dilated his broad nostrils. He laughed soundlessly, showing his white teeth, and advanced.

Gabrielle observed him, between half-closed eyelashes. He seemed a trifle breathless; short hair curled on his muscular chest and the little hooves terminating his rigid and hairy legs placed themselves soundlessly in the soft grass.

He leaned over Gabrielle and gently picked up the hem of her dress, which he lifted up slightly. She could not help making a slight movement, but he stopped immediately—ready, it seemed, to flee. Then she remained motionless, and he resumed, lifting the pleats of the supple fabric. He fixed his ardent and joyful eyes on the pretty legs, which he gradually uncovered all the way to the top.

Gaby gathered all her strength in order not to budge. That gaze, lingering upon her, searching avidly, in the imperceptible gap in the cloth, for the scarcely-revealed flesh, stimulated her to the point of crying out, but she was too afraid that the apparition might vanish....

And she felt a small, strong, slightly tremulous hand groping around her waist to undo the buttons of her girdle, which then pulled away the light fabric under the lifted dress....

With the obliging desire to assist the operation, with no further thought of her modesty—had anyone had any, in mythological days?—she raised herself up slightly...and sensed that she was nude from the waist to the knees. The cool caress of the air made her shiver. Her corsage was undone, and her breasts, beneath a small avid hand, erected their virginal tips....

Another hand made her shudder profoundly in an instinctive and intimate revolt...but already, the warm and hairy body had descended upon her; she saw the laughing red face right up against her face, the kiss of bearded lips opened her lips and she felt a tearing pain that convulsed her fibers and made her clench her teeth in order not to scream. Then that went more smoothly, and she surrendered herself gladly to all that was demanded of her by the mythological lasciviousness of the man with goat's feet.

Thus occurred the amorous initiation of Gabrielle, an imaginative and sensual little girl who had dreamed dreams that were not of her time....

The joys of that morning were never renewed for her. At noon, drunk with love, she quit her mysterious lover, saying to him "until tomorrow"—but it was forever. When she came back the next day, there was an army of workmen—malevolent gnomes, she thought—ravaging the great poetic terrain, demolishing the old walls and clearing the profound wild thickets. To the questions of the distressed Gabrielle they replied with jokes and lewd comments. The former owner had died and his heir wanted to have houses constructed to rent out.

Gabrielle searched fruitlessly for the being who had taken her on that May morning. She never saw him again, for the creatures of his species shun the tumult of workplaces, and their fabulous appearance cannot manifest itself in cobbled streets or the meager little gardens of modern houses.

Gabrielle was in despair, but, with time, as she was a good little girl and it was necessary to live, and to live happily in relative luxury and idleness, she became a courtesan.

She obtained a dazzling success in that art, which gave her glory and money, but never made her forget her first and fabulous lover, who remained the best.

ABOUT THE TRANSLATOR

BRIAN STABLEFORD has translated more than a hundred volumes of French prose into English. His principal interests are the French Romantic Movement and its Decadent/Symbolist aftermath, with particular reference to the evolution of the *conte cruel*, and the evolution of the *roman scientifique* from its origins in the eighteen-century *conte philosophique* to the aftermath of the Great War of 1914-18.